S

PANDEMIC

Patrick Daley

authorHOUSE™

1663 Liberty Drive, Suite 200
Bloomington, Indiana 47403
(800) 839-8640
www.AuthorHouse.com

First published by AuthorHouse 11/18/05

ISBN: 1-4259-0062-3 (sc)
ISBN: 1-4259-0056-9 (dj)

Printed in the United States of America
Bloomington, Indiana

This book is printed on acid-free paper.

DEDICATION

Pandemic is dedicated to my paternal grandparents Michael and Margaret Dailey two of the 500,000 American victims of the 1918 Flu Pandemic. They lost their lives to the Flu in early 1919 both at the age of thirty two years old leaving four orphaned children.

ACKNOWLEDGEMENTS

Many thanks to my family and friends
who reviewed Pandemic for me

Mary Caruana
Jim Byrne
Ruth Daley
Sean Daley
Stephen Garrick
Jennifer Gibbs
Susan Gibbs
Sue Quinn
John Weir

Thank you also to my editor Christine Phillips
for a fantastic job of editing

THE OVAL OFFICE

"Mr. President, I would like to amend the agenda for this morning's meeting, with your approval, of course."

"You have it, Mr. Roche, assuming your amendment is critical and involves the national security of the country."

Bob Roche was National Security Advisor to President Doyle, a lifelong friend of Sean Owen Doyle's, and one of the first to endorse Doyle for President two years earlier."Mr. President, we are receiving reports from the Department of Homeland Security that certain terrorist cells, possible breakaway units of an al-Qaida group, have been very active in Southeast Asia. The British also report through their informants that a particular cell in Malaysia is about to launch a full-scale terrorist attack against the U.S. and the European Union."

"Bob, do we have any specific information as to what type of attack this group may be planning?" the President asked.

"No sir, we do not, but there has been worldwide chatter coming out of locations known to harbor this particular group of terrorists. The FBI believes this could be the worst attack since 9/11, and with more widespread devastation, including many more deaths than we experienced in 2001."

Sean Owen Doyle had been elected one year before in a landslide victory, capturing sixty-eight percent of the popular vote. He had run on a platform of restoring the economy back to where it was when the Republican Party took over the White House, and to finally provide affordable health care to all citizens. His approval rating after one year in office was eighty-seven percent; his popularity with the voters was compared to that of former President John F. Kennedy after two years in office.

A United States Congressman, a former Vietnam veteran and a prisoner of war who had escaped from a Vietnamese prison camp, Sean Doyle had the Democratic Party beaming with enthusiasm when he first announced his run for the Presidency. Doyle was a real, live American hero with fifteen years in Congress chairing key committees, making him the perfect choice of the Democrat Party.

"Bob," President Doyle asked, "when does the FBI expect this incident to occur and do they know yet where it might happen?"

Bob Roche shifted his weight in his chair as the other members of the President's inner circle recognized Bob's nervousness about what he may—or worse—may not know about this report.

"Mr. President, our Homeland Security people, including the FBI and the CIA, are unaware of how or where this attack may take place. The Director of Homeland Security would like to authorize our moving immediately to level Orange; the threat of terrorism is imminent, even though we are not sure what form it may take."

The President turned to his staff and asked, "Does anyone here disagree with the move to level Orange?"

"Mr. President," interjected the White House Counsel George White, "it would be better to announce only if we had more detailed information. What are we going to say to the media and to the general public when asked why we are going to threat level Orange? They will ask such questions."

President Doyle turned to Bob Roche and said, "Bob, this is your territory. What do we say to the media?"

"Sir, we just say that the terror alert has been raised because of the chatter heard around the globe and that this is why the system had been devised. We are going to Orange so that we will be at a state of readiness for any event that may involve weapons of mass destruction."

"Okay, Bob. Have the Secretary of Homeland Security hold a press conference and make the announcement. In the meantime, I want a detailed report from the FBI, and please keep me informed no matter what time of day or night. Understood?"

"Yes, Mr. President. Consider it done."

"Okay, staff, let's get on with the rest of the agenda," urged President Doyle. "Mr. Sitarek, what do you have for us on the Health Care initiative?"

Ken Sitarek was White House Chief of Staff and probably the brightest appointee in the President's inner circle.

"Well, Mr. President, it is not good news. Senator Atkins is threatening a filibuster if he doesn't garner more concessions and even some of his own party are fearful that he may be successful."

"So what does he want, Ken?" asked the President."Primarily the prescription plan that has been put forth by our side of the aisle.

Atkins believes that it is too restrictive for the lower income bracket and too liberal for senior citizens. God knows the seniors have been taking it on the chin for how many years now, expected to pay rising prices for their prescriptions and with only minute increases in their Social Security benefits."

The President pondered the statement for only a few seconds and in his usual decisive way he said, "Okay, Ken. Let's get the senator in here to have a little sit down and see if we can work it out. Invite Senator Clinton, also. She's been pushing health care reform for years and I happen to know that Atkins likes her despite her political persuasion."

"Yes, sir, Mr. President. I will get right on it. How about next Monday or Tuesday?"

"Ken, you check my schedule and work around that. Now what else do we have?"

After another twenty minutes of minor issues that needed President Doyle's input, the meeting adjourned and the Chief Executive was informed by his secretary, Aggie, that the Ambassador from Malaysia had arrived for his 9:15 meeting.

On that note, Secretary of State Arnold Roberts walked through the door to the Oval Office and with him was the new Ambassador of Malaysia, Mr. Abdullah Husain Mahamood. President Doyle rose to greet his visitor.

"Ambassador Mahamood, welcome to the White House. To what do I owe this unexpected pleasure of your company?" "Mr. President, I have been asked by our Prime Minister to give you a message and he believes that urgency is of dire importance. I am sorry for any inconvenience, sir."

"No, no, don't even think that, Mr. Ambassador. You are not inconveniencing us at all. If your Prime Minister feels that this is urgent, then please, let's sit down and hear what he has to say."

"President Doyle, you know how diligently our country has supported your continued war on terrorism. We have arrested over two hundred suspects so far this year and we are certain that quite a few of them will go to trial and be convicted as charged."

"Yes, Mr. Ambassador, and the United States is very grateful for the help Malaysia has given us. You are a faithful and loyal ally and we value that support."

"Thank you, Mr. President. Now let me tell you what has happened in the past few days back home. Our security agency believes through informants that are usually very reliable that there is a new terrorist group, formerly part of al-Qaida, that has set up numerous cells in Malaysia. We have not been able to uncover these locations as of yet, but we have intercepted many communications that lead us to believe that there will be an attack of some type and very soon. We also have information that tells us that the attack will most likely be here in the United States, as well as over in Great Britain."

The President leaned forward in his chair and said, "Mr. Ambassador, we, too, have had heard much chatter over the past few days, and similarly, we also believe something is imminent. This, however, is new information to us. As we speak, our Secretary of Homeland Security is scheduling a news conference to announce that we are going to raise our terror alert level to Orange. I want to thank you for your information and ask that you allow our FBI to contact your Director of Security to work together on uncovering these cells of yours."

"I will relay your request to my Prime Minister and report back as soon as possible."

Patrick Daley

President Doyle stood to indicate that the meeting was ended and said, "Mr. Ambassador, thank you again for your prompt delivery of this information. Please let us know of any further developments. I will look forward to hearing from you soon."

Ambassador Mahamood extended his hand and with a short bow, excused himself with the promise of calling very soon.

Once the door to the Oval Office had closed, the President turned to his Secretary of State and said, "Well, Arnie, what do you make of that? Is this bin Laden or is it really a new group we're dealing with here?"

Arnold Roberts was a big man, over six-foot-five, and he towered over the President, who at five-foot-ten had to crane his neck to look at Arnie.

"Mr. President, I'm sure that this is a new group. We have heard additional information that leads us to believe that the Malaysian cells are not the only ones operating. They all seem to be tied into the same group, and all formerly al-Qaida. The frustrating piece of the puzzle right now is that none of our intelligence tells us exactly what they are up to. We're just waiting for the big bang. I don't think we are going to get any more notice than we did when the World Trade Center Towers were attacked."

President Doyle, as he so often did, stroked his chin and with a pensive look on his face said, "Jesus, Arnie, do you realize what you're saying here?"

"Yes, Mr. President, I do, and it scares the hell out of me."

"Arnie, get together with Roche and tell him I want every available resource on this situation. I do not want another 9/11. Although the country was very strong back then and dealt with it as well as it possibly could, our resolve is running thin. We do not want another blood bath like the one in 2001."

"Yes, Mr. President. I'll keep you up to date. "Good day, sir."

As Arnie Roberts left the Oval Office, Sean Doyle looked out into the Rose Garden and wondered, *what can these maniacs be up to this time? Let's hope to God that this is just another one of those scares where we go to Orange and in a few weeks, we are back to Yellow, and more or less back to normal.* But then he thought, *what the hell is normal anymore?*

CDC, ATLANTA

"Dr. Doyle, the President is on your private line." "Thanks, Mrs. Burns. Hold all my calls, please."

John Doyle picked up the phone and said, "Good morning, Mr. President. To what do I owe this pleasure today?"

"Listen, John, I've told you a dozen times you don't have to call me Mr. President; Sean will be just fine."

"Aw, Sean, you know that it's just proper protocol, but if you insist, then I'll only do it in public. Now what's up?"

The President said, "John, I would like you to take a trip with me up to Pennsylvania."

"Is this business or pleasure?"

The President replied, "Business, and long overdue if you ask me. Governor Miranda has asked that I come up and dedicate the new monument that they have constructed in Philadelphia to memorialize the victims of the Spanish Flu of 1918-1919. Since our grandparents both died during the pandemic, Governor Miranda feels we have a strong connection, and of course, he's absolutely right. As the Director of the Center for Disease Control, it makes perfect sense that you should accompany me to the dedication."

"Well, Sean, it sure makes sense to me. It's about time something has been done to honor the victims of the Spanish flu. Do you realize that it killed close to thirty million people worldwide? Many people are unaware that we were never able to develop a vaccine at the time, or that the flu disappeared as quickly as it appeared. If it ever comes back, my job is going to be a nightmare. It will take at least six months before we can develop a vaccine, even with today's technology. The death toll would be disastrous."

"Well, John, hopefully we have seen the last of that flu. Listen, how does your calendar look for the first week of October?"

"I have a symposium on Monday and Tuesday, but the rest of that week is open."

"That's good, John. Governor Miranda would prefer the end of the week, so why don't we say Thursday or Friday? I'll have Aggie check with his office and get back to you with the exact date."

"Okay, Sean. By the way, I guess I have to dress up for this shindig."

"A blue suit and nice tie will be fine, John. Talk to you soon."

"Thank you, Sean. See you in October."

"Goodbye, John."

"Goodbye, Sean."

*   *   *

John Doyle was the son of President Sean Doyle's uncle, Joe. Sean's father and John's father were two of four brothers who were orphaned when their parents, Michael and Margaret, succumbed at the age of thirty-two to the Spanish flu in 1919. The four boys, ages two, four, six, and eight, were raised by their maternal grandmother, Sarah O'Bannon. John's father, Joe, left home as a young man and moved to New York City and raised his children a few years later in northern New Jersey. It was there that John grew up and after graduating from high school, was accepted on a scholarship to Princeton University.

There, John majored in biology, graduated magna cum laude, and went on to John Hopkins to receive first his master's degree in epidemiology, and then his doctorate. John had done his thesis on halting the spread of communicable diseases that had never had a cure or vaccine developed. He selected the infamous Spanish flu as his primary subject and was known as the top expert in the country on this particular subject. Upon receiving his doctorate, John was offered a position at the Center for Disease Control in Atlanta as a research assistant. Within two years, he was promoted to Director of Research. After ten years, John was named Director of Epidemiology and was now Director of the Center.

Thirty years of research, hundreds of publications, and front-line confrontations with crisis after crisis, including diseases such as SARS, mad cow, and the Ebola virus, had qualified John Doyle worldwide as the expert to consult.

President Doyle's invitation to join him in Philadelphia was exciting to John. Finally, those millions of victims of the worst flu outbreak in history would at last be remembered properly. The disease had primarily attacked the young, vibrant, and healthy citizens in their twenties and thirties; it left senior citizens and young children almost untouched. John's grandparents, Michael and Maggie, as well as one of his great uncles, John, had succumbed to the flu; another great uncle, Matt, had disappeared while working as a merchant marine. He had left the army at the end of World War I and had taken a position as a radio operator on an ocean freighter, but his family never heard from him again. Suspicion over the years since was that he might have contracted the flu and died at sea. The family always hoped and prayed that he would someday return.

This family history had driven John Doyle to research the Spanish flu, and his fascination with the disease never waned. Now he would attend a dedication to the victims. Of the approximately thirty-to-forty million estimated killed worldwide, the deaths in the United States had totaled nearly five hundred thousand. The worldwide death toll, though, could never be accurately counted, as there were so many countries affected that did not keep records.

Accessing the palm pilot software on his personal computer, John went to his date book, and blocked out Thursday and Friday of the first week of October, 2006.

SOMEWHERE IN MALAYSIA

"Kemal, we have information that the American pigs may be on to our plans."

"What leads you to that conclusion, Sulanni?"

"Our source in the Ambassador's office has reported that there was a meeting at the White House between the American Satan, Doyle, and the Ambassador. He also reports that they discussed heavy chatter. Does that mean we have a leak somewhere?"

"I do not believe the stupid Americans have any idea what we have planned for them. I am not worried one bit. Our plan is solid and we will institute it very soon. Our Holy War will inflict more deaths than they could possibly imagine. Our victory of 9/11 will be small compared to the coming battle. How are our cells in Scandinavia responding to this report from the embassy?"

"They do not seem worried, Kemal. The plan is in place and ready to implement. Their anticipation of success has all of our brothers anxious to see the results."

"Fear not, Sulanni. The results of our plan will be something the entire world would not even think possible. Better yet, they will not have any suspicion that it was an attack by us. Our cells are in place and much better organized than our former leader was. Bin Laden was stupid to think that the Americans would not come after him, sitting over there in the mountains like he was invincible. Our success will prove that we are the best at killing the American pigs. Allah will honor *us* with a place at his side when we leave this earth."

"When will the attack begin, Kemal?"

"Sulanni, you know that is only known by the top leadership and the soldiers who will carry it out. I can only tell you that it will be soon, very soon. Be patient, my brother, and you will witness the wrath of Allah on the infidels. Make certain that we have any further information from our source in the Ambassador's office checked thoroughly and if you find any credibility regarding what we've heard, contact all of the cells here in Malaysia, as well as Scandinavia and Casablanca."

"Yes, my brother, I will make it my number one priority. I cannot wait to bear witness to this monumental attack."

10 DOWNING STREET

Prime Minister O'Keefe began his briefing at No.10 Downing Street by asking the Director of British Intelligence, Martin Harrington, to bring the Cabinet up to date on recent developments. Everybody at the table turned their attention to Mr. Harrington, who rose to make his presentation.

"Ladies and gentlemen, good morning. I have asked Prime Minister O'Keefe to allow me to brief you, and I do apologize for such short notice, but we do believe that time is of the essence.

"For the past week our intelligence listening posts have reported a very unusual and large amount of chatter. As you all know, the terrorism cells across the world are monitored on a full-time basis. It appears that this increase in chatter could signal movement on the part of these cells. Most of what we are hearing is vague, generating from three areas of the globe. Those areas include Malaysia, where we know there are possibly two hundred cells. Scandinavia is a second source of activity, but we have not yet determined exactly where. The third area is in or around Morocco, possibly Casablanca," Harrington said, glancing down at his agenda.

"We have compared notes with our friends in the States," he continued, "and they also confirm the increased computer chatter.

The Americans suspect that something may be imminent and President Doyle has asked his Director of Homeland Security to increase their level of readiness to Orange.

"There is a press conference scheduled for 4:00 p.m. Eastern Standard Time in the States, which will be ten o'clock London time. Our intelligence, together with what we have received from the Ambassador of Malaysia, suggests that we might also go to a higher level of readiness." Prime Minister O'Keefe asked, "Martin, do we have anything more specific than just chatter and supposed locations of sources?"

"Mr. Prime Minister, what we have heard is that these cells are all saying the same thing: that whatever they are planning will make 9/11 pale in comparison. Other than that, we have very little information that would tell us what they are up to. Whomever is planning this event has maintained the utmost secrecy and we have been unable to find any leaks whatsoever."

The Minister of Defense, James Stanford, asked, "Mr. Harrington, what, if any, connection does Malaysia have with a locality such as Scandinavia? Have we had any intelligence in the past that would indicate a terrorist cell in any of the Scandinavian countries?"

"Minister Stanford, we had garnered reports a few years ago that a cell might be operating in Sweden, but that was found to be inaccurate. Since that time, we have not had any information until now that might suggest a Scandinavian connection. We have monitored cells in Morocco before, but we are unsure what the connection may be to Malaysia. There is one possibility, however, and that is that there may be a breakaway group that split from al-Qaida soon after Operation Enduring Freedom, the Afghanistan War. They've recruited hundreds of fanatical Muslim extremists, forming cells throughout the world, with over one hundred confirmed to be located in Malaysia."

"Martin, do you have any gut feeling about this, about what they may be up to?"

"Mr. Prime Minister, I wish I did, but unfortunately we are at a loss as to what they may be planning. I do, however, recommend that we go to a high state of readiness, because whatever is planned is imminent."

"Thank you, Martin. I will take it up with the leaders in Parliament and let you know tomorrow at the latest."

"Thank you, sir. As per usual, my office will continue to update you as events develop."

Prime Minister O'Keefe stood and said, "Ladies and gentlemen, thank you for coming. We will meet again soon, I am certain."

THE WHITE HOUSE

President Doyle left the Oval Office at five minutes past six o'clock and headed for the private Presidential quarters. The press conference held by the Director of Homeland Security was conducted fairly routinely. The government had gone to level Orange so many times in the past, that the representatives of the press almost took this as a routine step whenever intelligence indicated a threat that may or may not happen. After a few questions that did not produce any solid information, the press seemed to lose interest and the conference was over in less than ten minutes.

As the President walked to his private quarters, he wondered, *have our citizens, as well as the media, become complacent about terrorism? It is difficult to convince people that they must be on guard every day, but since no major incident has occurred since 9/11, that false sense of security has once again crept up on the entire population.* The fight against terrorism had been taken overseas, with hundreds of suspected cells broken up and thousands of arrests made by allies of the United States. As he approached the family quarters Sean Doyle thought, *the lives of our citizens are so filled with personal matters, it is easy for them to conduct themselves under that old cliché "out of sight, out of mind."*

"Well, Mr. President, it's about time you showed up for dinner."

Sean Doyle embraced his wife, Maggie, and said, "And how was your day, First Lady?"

"It was marvelous, Sean, until I saw that press conference this afternoon. What in the world is going on now? Is this just another scare tactic or are the locals looking for more overtime for their emergency responders?"

"Oh, come on, Maggie! You know better than that."

"I know, Sean. Sorry for the poor attempt at humor, but you know as well as I do that the general public doesn't seem to take these alerts that seriously anymore."

"Yes, luv, you're absolutely right; I was just thinking the same thing on the way from the office. It's a shame, because this time we believe an attack is imminent, but we don't have a clue what they are up to."

"Oh my God, Sean!" Maggie exclaimed. "I had no idea it was that serious! The media didn't seem to react as though this was a big threat! They simply acted like they have the last five times we've gone to Orange."

"Yes, Maggie, that's the gist of it. Our country, I am afraid, has fallen into complacency, but when we don't have any concrete information to share, it is difficult to shake anyone up. Do you have the Manhattans ready yet, Maggie?"

"Of course I do, Mr. President. They are chilling as we speak. Why don't we go in and sit and enjoy a little relaxation time. Marcus has already put out some shrimp cocktail with your favorite sauce and lots of lemon for me. He says dinner will be served at seven, unless you want it earlier."

The President stretched and loosened his tie while he turned his head from side to side, stretching his neck to relieve the tension of the last ten hours.

"Here is your Manhattan, my dear, and your shrimp. Is there anything else I can get you?"

"No, Maggie, just tell me about your day."

"Actually, it was a pretty good day for me. I spoke to Kevin on the phone at lunch time and he was planning his annual trip to New York City with the boys for the Sabres game against the Rangers. Barb and the kids are staying in Buffalo, of course. This tradition of 'boys only' continues. By the way, he said, 'Make sure you say hello to Dad.' You know, Sean, he really misses being able to talk to you on a regular basis. You should call him from the office when you have a minute."

"Yeah, Maggie, you're right. Being President should not stand in the way of calling our kids on a regular basis like I did when I was in Congress. I'll call him tomorrow."

"That will be fine, but don't wait until Friday because the gang is flying out on Northeast Airlines for New York and then going to the hockey game on Saturday. You can be sure they will all be partying at John Barleycorn's on Friday, although I don't think they stay out as late as they did when they were younger."

The President laughed and said, "That's for sure! Things sure do change when you are married with children. Those single, riotous days for Kevin and his friends are in the past. Not only that, but now he has the Secret Service following him around and I know he hates that, but it comes with the territory."

Maggie Doyle leaned forward, looked her husband squarely in the eyes, and said, "Sean, are you going to tell me what the hell is going on with this level Orange thing or am I not allowed to know the details?"

"No, no luv, that's not the case. The truth is that we don't know what the hell is going on and it scares me to death. All we know at this point is that there is an unusual amount of chatter around the world, primarily coming out of Malaysia where we know there are terrorist cells mostly comprised of Muslims who broke away from al- Qaida after we kicked bin Laden's ass. The only information we have is that they are planning something imminently, claiming that the result will be so devastating, that it will make the attack on 9/11 pale in comparison. The major problem is that our intelligence guys have not been able to determine what it is exactly that they've planned."

"Do you think it will be another attack like they did on 9/11? Will the White House again be a target?"

"Maggie, now don't go worrying about that possibility. The steps that have been taken by the airlines have almost completely eliminated the likelihood of a hijacking and subsequent attack like we experienced in 2001."

Maggie got up off the eighteenth century divan and started pacing up and down. "But Sean, what could they be up to then? We know their weapon of choice is almost always some type of explosive. Look at the history of terrorism, and especially in the United States. Every incident has been overwhelmingly a bomb or other explosive devices."

The President nodded, and set his drink down on the table. "Yes, Maggie, I know the history. But I just have a gut feeling that it won't be that type of terrorism this time. We have information that it could be a radiological dispersal device, which comes under the heading of explosives, but I believe the terrorists think they can wreak more havoc with some type of biological agent. We cannot let that happen or we could have chaos."

"Sean, when do you think we might have a handle on what they are up to?"

"I wish I knew Maggie, I wish I knew. I just hope that it's soon."

"Tell you what, Mr. President. Dinner is in fifteen minutes. Why don't you give Kevin a quick call and tell him to have a good time in New York?"

"Sounds like a marvelous idea, Maggie."

"My God, Sean, I just thought of something. If this threat is imminent, should Kevin be going to New York City?"

"Maggie, please don't get yourself all upset now. Look at you; you're starting to get goose bumps all over your arms. Kevin will be fine, and so will his friends. Hand me the phone, please."

The White House operator put the President's call through immediately and Kevin answered on the second ring.

"Hey, Kev, it's your father calling."

"Hi, Dad. What's up?"

"I just wanted to call and tell you and the guys to have a super time in the Big Apple this weekend."

"Thanks, Dad. You know we will and hey, guess what? We even talked Brendan into coming with us."

Brendan Doyle was the President's oldest son, a year and half older than Kevin. Close in age, they often did things together, but it was highly unusual for Brendan to take a weekend off and fly to New York.

"Kev, that is monumental," the President said. "How many of you are going?"

"Six of us, the usual cast of characters, plus this damn Secret Service guy who follows us everywhere."

"Sorry about that, Kev, but you know the rules. You and your brother and Barb and the kids are protected under the law, and I know it can be a pain in the ass, but it makes me feel better just knowing you guys are watched.""Yeah, Dad, I understand, but it does get to be old. Hey, what about this level Orange thing? Are we going to be attacked by some crazy terrorists or is the media just overreacting again?"

"No, Kev, it's not an overreaction, but we must be prepared for anything."

"I guess by that statement," Kevin surmised, "you really can't tell me. Just keep them out of New York City for the weekend."

"I'll try to do that," the President answered. "Listen, Marcus is about to serve us dinner. Tell Brendan to have a good time, and you too. Call me when you get back from the Big Apple."

"Okay, Dad, thanks for calling. Talk to you soon." "Good night, Kev."

Maggie turned to the President and said, "Did I hear right? Is Brendan going with Kevin to New York for the game?"

"Yes, luv, he is. Isn't that a nice surprise? Brendan never takes any time off from his teaching. Must have cleared his schedule for the weekend."

Maggie looked even more stressed than before as she said, "Oh yeah, Sean, that's just what I needed. Now I have to worry about both of them until they get back home."

"Maggie, you always remind me that it's a woman's job to do the worrying."

With the tinkle of a small bell, Marcus, the White House chef, entered the room and said, "Mr. President, First Lady, dinner is served."

The President rose from his seat and said, "Marcus, I can't wait. What do you have for us tonight?"

"Mr. President, it is one of your favorites: my special meat loaf recipe."

"Marcus, what a perfect end to a not-so-perfect day. Let's go get that meat loaf, Maggie. I can taste it already."

*   *   *

Margaret "Maggie" Doyle, code-named "Claddagh" by the Secret Service, had met Sean Doyle two years after her husband had passed away from cancer. Sean had lost his wife years before and when he and Maggie began to date, it was obvious they had much in common, and that their lives would always be compatible. The former Margaret Hamilton, whose ancestors had come from Scotland, was a beautiful lady from the inside out. Not only was she stunning to look at on the campaign trail, but her personality endeared her to the American public because she was so down to earth. All Americans, rich or poor, were able to relate to Maggie. There had not been a first lady this popular since Jackie Kennedy. Maggie told it like it was and very seldom made a mistake; she was Sean's number one asset.

They had been married twenty years when Sean was elected to office and her relationship with Sean's sons, Kevin and Brendan, flourished from the beginning. Teenagers when their mother died, their father's remarriage was a difficult transition for them. Their maternal grandmother, Jane Corbin, always told them, "Your mother is an angel and she has sent Maggie for your father as the perfect replacement. You should be happy that your mother is taking care of things from above."

LAGUARDIA AIRPORT, NEW YORK CITY

"We apologize for the extreme delay of Northeast Airlines flight 897, arriving from Tampa, Florida. The aircraft is now on the ground and will be deplaning at Gate 23. Thank you for your patience."

Jack English heard the Northeast Airlines announcement and wondered how many flights had been delayed today because of the Nor'easter currently churning up the east coast of the United States. Jack was the supervising agent for the TSA, the Transportation Security Administration, at LaGuardia. This Federal security agency had been formed at the request of the President after the 9/11 tragedy at the World Trade Center and the Pentagon.

Over the past few years, the TSA had traveled a rough road. Initially, the organization had been praised for its diligence in searching baggage and putting passengers through extensive scanning, and the nation's citizens felt a little safer when traveling by air. Two years into its existence, however, the TSA experienced severe criticism when items were found aboard aircraft, items that should not have been there. Actual box cutters, such as those used by the 9/11 hijackers, were discovered in baggage that had supposedly been searched by the TSA personnel. Investigation after investigation had taken place and security overall had been tightened, and Jack was confident that they were back on track.

LaGuardia Airport in New York City was one of the busiest hubs in the nation and Northeast Airlines, one of the major carriers flying in and out of there daily, was a formidable presence. Just as the hubs in Pittsburgh and Charlotte, LaGuardia was a connection point for thousands of Northeast Airlines travelers.

Jack English had just finished his lunch of linguine and clam sauce and was on his way back to his office when his pager beeped. The caller was Tony Camilleri, the TSA manager in charge of the terminal servicing Northeast Airlines. Jack dialed the number and upon hearing the familiar hello he said, "Tony, what's up?"

"Hi, Jack. Sorry to bother you, but I think you should come over and take a look at something we found in an overhead compartment on one of the Northeast Airlines flights that arrived about half an hour ago."

Tony Camilleri was a former Marine who had seen combat in the first Persian Gulf War and then again in the liberation of Iraq. Upon retiring from the Marines in 2003, Tony went to work the following month for the TSA. Jack said, "Tony, what exactly do you have over there?"

"I would rather you come over and see for yourself, Jack. It just looks suspicious."

"All right, Tony. I'll be right there."

As Jack entered the passenger scanning area, Tony was waiting for him.

"Hey, boss. Sorry to drag you over here during lunch."

"Don't worry about it, Tony. I'd finished and was on my way back to the office. Where is this something you wanted me to look at?"

"Down at gate 23, where Northeast Airlines flight 897 just arrived."

Tony led Jack to the gate and through the security checkpoint, where they were met by a Northeast Airlines representative. Tony turned back to his superior and said, "Jack, this is Bob Putrillo, the steward on flight 897. Bob, this is Jack English, my supervisor at TSA."

"Nice to meet you, sir," Bob said, as he extended his hand.

"Same here," Jack said. "What do we have here, Bob?"

"If you will, follow me, Mr. English, onto the plane. We left it exactly as we found it so you could check it out yourself."

Bob led the way onto the Boeing 757 and down the aisle to row 18, where he raised the overhead compartment. Jack leaned in and observed a small overnight bag with a black Nike emblem on the side. It was only large enough for maybe a change of clothes, toiletries, and possibly a hardcover book if squeezed in tightly.

Jack turned to Tony and said, "Have you viewed the contents yet?"

"Yes I have, Jack. Help yourself."

Jack reached into the compartment, lifted the bag out, and slowly unzipped the center pocket. It revealed a man's sweat suit, size large, with the same Nike logo emblazoned on the shirt. Underneath the sweat suit was a King James Bible. Next to the Bible was a man's shaving kit. Jack removed the sweat suit and Bible and then the kit, which he proceeded to unzip. As soon as he saw the contents, he shouted, "Son of a bitch! How the fuck did this get on board?"

At Jack's yell, the timid Mr. Putrillo jumped back and gasped. "Mr. English, you will have to ask your TSA people that. It is their job to scan and search and make sure this kind of stuff doesn't make it on our aircraft."

"I know, Mr. Putrillo! You don't have to tell me that it's our responsibility, and I'm not blaming your airline. I'm just totally pissed off that this was allowed to get through!" Jack growled.

He threw all of the contents back into the overnight bag and handed it to Tony. "Mr. Putrillo, please have your supervisor send me a report on this incident as soon as possible."

"Sure, Mr. English. It's being prepared as we speak," Putrillo replied.

"Thank you, Mr. Putrillo. Tony, let's get back to the office and see what we can find out about this."

"Sure thing, boss. Should I call the FBI?"

"We can decide that when we get back to my office."

*   *   *

Ten minutes later, Jack English and Tony Camilleri sat at Jack's conference table and inspected the contents of the bag. The usual toiletries were there: toothbrush, toothpaste, deodorant, hairbrush, shampoo, mouthwash, shaving cream, and the items that should not have been there at all. They should have been scanned by the TSA agents at Tampa International Airport. At the bottom of the bag were two packages of razor blades and a new razor. The similarity of all the items in the bag was that everything in the bag was brand new, never used. It appeared that whoever left the bag had purchased the contents before boarding the flight, as they were all unused and the blades were still in the original package.

"God damn it, Tony! Someone is going to get his ass reamed out for this one or maybe even fired from TSA! How could agents miss something like this after all the shit that has come down over the past two years? As far as the FBI, don't mention anything about this to anyone until TSA completes its own investigation. Understand?"

"Jack, I'm an ex-Marine. I do what I'm told when I'm told to do it, and I don't ever go around the chain of command."

"Thanks, Tony. I knew I could count on you to keep your mouth shut. Now, put this thing in storage after we check it out completely for fingerprints. Before you do that, however, see if you can trace any of the contents, including the Bible and the sweat suit."

"You got it, boss. Consider it done."

Tony left Jack's office, and a feeling of relief swept over Jack as he leaned back in his chair. As always, when Jack was stressed, he pulled at his left earlobe. *Damn*, he thought. *We are so lucky that this stuff was not used. I wonder if it was simply an innocent passenger that the TSA missed, or an actual terrorist who either chickened out at the last minute or was scared off for some reason? Better still, were there any other accomplices on the plane with him if the passenger was a bona fide terrorist?*

LONGYEARBEYEN, NORWAY

The weather in Norway in the month of October is always unpredictable, but one thing both natives and visitors can be certain of is that the nights are longer and the days much shorter. The northernmost part of the country is cold and on some of the islands, the ground never completely thaws. The permafrost level is right below the layer of earth that thaws in the spring. If one were to dig down into the earth, to the permafrost level, anything buried there is just as if it were frozen in time. This is a natural phenomenon, especially as compared to preservation created by cryogenics, except there is no modern technology needed, especially in the town of Longyearbeyen, Norway.

Located on an island off the Norway mainland and six hundred miles from the North Pole, it was a very cold, dark night on October 3 in Longyearbeyen. At St. Gustaf's Cemetery, a visitor made his way up the knoll to the gravesite where he was to meet his contact. Stepping out from behind a tall mausoleum, a man of medium height and with long blond hair, wearing a Russian-style, fur winter hat with earmuffs not quite big enough to cover his blond locks yelled, "State your name and business!"

The visitor slowly approached the blond man and quietly said, "I am Sulanni, messenger from Kemal, and I come in the name of

Allah. If you are who I have come to meet with, I would ask that you kindly keep your fucking voice down."

"You are on my soil now, Mr. Sulanni, so don't think you can tell me what to do or say, or you might end up in one of these graves."

Sulanni took a step back and said, "Are you threatening me?"

"That was not a threat, Mr. Sulanni; that was a promise. Now let's get down to business. I have more important things to attend to than spending the night in an icy cemetery with a fucking terrorist."

"If you think that you are exempt from any blame for what we are about to do to the world, then you are sadly mistaken."

"Sulanni, I don't care what you or your Muslim friends do. I just want my compensation and then I am out of this frozen tundra and off to warmer climates."

"Before I 'compensate you' as you call it, let me see the original gravesites and confirm that they are restored back to their original condition."

"Right this way, Mr. Sulanni," the blond man said, and led Sulanni over to a row of very old graves with only rough stones at the head of each grave and the date November 1918. None of the graves had names on them, but each looked like it had been there for almost a hundred years and had never been disturbed.

Sulanni examined each of the graves and was very impressed. "You have done an excellent job, sir. In this attaché case is the balance of the American dollars you had requested. You will find $500,000 in small bills."

The blond man reached for the case and set it down on top of one of the graves, kneeling to open it. As the case snapped open, the man could see that there was, in fact, a lot of money. Once counted, it would most likely be the half million that he was owed by Sulanni and his friends. He looked up to thank Sulanni and found himself staring into a silencer attached to a 357 magnum. Before he could open his mouth to protest, Sulanni had pulled back on the trigger and the blond man's head was splattered over the grave.

Sulanni reached for the briefcase and simultaneously let out a slow whistle. Presently, four men appeared from behind a mausoleum. Sulanni said, "Okay, my brothers. Get this mess cleaned up. I do not want any sign of this animal anywhere in this cemetery."

*   *   *

Arriving back on the mainland of Norway, Sulanni placed a call to Malaysia. After the second ring, the phone was answered.

"Praise Allah."

"Praise Allah," Sulanni repeated. "The mission in Norway is complete and I am on my way to Casablanca."

"Go in peace, my friend. Death to the infidels will soon be upon us."

Sulanni said, "Thank you, Kemal. I will contact you soon. Praise Allah."

Sulanni clicked the off button on his cell phone and prepared to board his flight to North Africa. Approaching the pre-boarding checkpoint, there was an extremely long line; the reason was immediately apparent to Sulanni. Two men who appeared to be of Middle Eastern descent or of the Muslim faith were being detained and searched rigorously by the Norwegian authorities. The men had their shoes, socks, and belts off, and their shirts were unbuttoned. Their carry-on suitcases were opened and the contents were spread out to be viewed by everyone in line. Sulanni cursed under his breath. *These infidels will pay some day for this. How is it that no one else is being subjected to this type of inspection and searching? Every person of Arabic descent is subject to suspicion. Some day this will end and Allah will rule.*

After waiting in line for nearly twenty minutes, Sulanni stepped up to the checkpoint and put his bag on the conveyor belt, along with his tray of coins, keys, money clip, and of course, his Rolex watch.

His coat was next, and then he was waved through. No alarms, and nothing but cordiality to Sulanni.

"Have a nice trip, sir. Enjoy your day."

Sulanni smiled at the inspector as he thought, *if you only knew that this face, which looks German or Irish, is really that of a devout Muslim whose mother was from Afghanistan and who is one of the top operatives of the Malaysian terrorist cell. The infidels are such overconfident fools,* Sulanni thought, as he boarded his flight and smiled at the flight attendant.

"Mr. Frost, what would you like to drink? I will bring it right to you."

As Sulanni, a.k.a. Donald Frost, settled into his first class seat, he looked up and said, "Pepsi, please."

PHILADELPHIA

The trip from Atlanta aboard Air Force One was smooth and the pilot made record time to Philadelphia. President Doyle leaned across the table and said "John, I should fly with you more often. That was one fast flight. You bring me good luck. I hate long flights, even though we have the comforts of home aboard."

John Doyle replied, "Mr. President, you just think it was a short flight because you were so damn busy while onboard. Do you always have so many interruptions and things to attend to even when you're in the air?"

"Yeah, John, it seems that way. Sorry we didn't get to spend much quality time, but I promise we will on the way back later today. So glad you were able to accompany me on this trip. You should be doing this dedication. You know more about this old flu than anyone in the country and throughout the world."

"Sean, it's not my duty to do dedications. Remember Mr. President, you are the leader of the free world; they don't even know who I am."

The President smiled at his cousin and said, "John, I guess you're right. I'm just so happy that this is finally going to happen. It has been too many years since all of these people lost their lives."

Air Force One taxied to the gate and the red carpet was rolled out on the tarmac. As the door swung back, President Doyle turned to John and motioned for him to accompany him down the stairs. John stepped forward and a Secret Service agent moved aside for John to follow the President. At the bottom of the gangway, the governor of Pennsylvania was waiting to greet both men. "Mr. President, welcome to the City of Brotherly Love."

"Thank you, Governor Miranda. I've been looking forward to this trip for months. Have you met Dr. John Doyle of the Center for Disease Control?"

"No, I have not, Mr. President. Mr. Doyle, I have heard a lot about you and your research. Welcome to Philadelphia."

"Governor, it is a pleasure to meet you," John replied, as he looked at the massive gathering there to greet the President.

"Governor," President Doyle said, "you have outdone yourself to get this many people out on a weekday. Where did they all come from?"

"Mr. President, I had nothing to do with this demonstration of affection. They love you no matter where you go. They just want a glimpse of their President." Upon hearing this, Sean Doyle looked back at his Secret Service people and gave them a nod of his head, as if to say, *I am going over to the fence now, so watch carefully.* The Secret Service detachment covering the President and Mrs. Doyle knew better than to tell the President he could not do something or go somewhere. President Doyle was walking along the fence shaking hands before the agents could even get there.

John Doyle had never seen this response up close before. Of course, he had viewed it on television and always suspected these turnouts of the public were probably arranged by some political operative. It seemed that today was definitely spontaneous and John, for one, was quite impressed. He walked along behind the President and thought, *this guy could get re-elected over and over again. Too bad there is a limit on serving more than two terms in office.*

After ten minutes of shaking hands and kissing babies and talking to his admirers, the President and John were ushered into the Presidential limousine, which turned and headed for Independence Hall. The twenty minute drive brought them to one of the most famous sites in the United States. Here was where the Constitution was written and signed by the founding fathers of the nation. "Here," Sean said to John, "is hallowed ground. This is where democracy began its history as we know it today."

As they made their way to the dedication stage that had been set up, John could not believe his eyes. There had to be about 250,000 people in attendance. He could see the crowd stretched for blocks on end and all to get a look at President Doyle. John thought, *the majority of them have probably never heard of the Spanish flu and don't have a clue about the devastation that it caused throughout the globe.*

"My fellow countrymen and women, we are here today to honor the over 500,000 citizens of our great land who lost their lives, though not to a foreign enemy in a war distant from our shores, but to a different deadly killer. They were young and vibrant, mostly in their twenties and thirties, and millions of other nationals from countries all over the world lost their lives as well.

"Ladies and gentlemen, we are here to honor our fellow citizens who lost their lives to a silent, but deadly enemy: the infamous Spanish flu.

"Right here in Philadelphia, the birthplace of the Constitution that gave us so many rights and freedoms, we lost thirteen thousand citizens. A young generation lost some of its most promising men and women to this horrible disease. My own grandmother and grandfather were taken by the Spanish flu only three months apart. They were both thirty-two-years-old, and left four boys orphaned, ages two, four, six, and eight. This story was repeated over and over again throughout our great nation.

"I am honored today to unveil this memorial to all of our citizens who lost their lives to this enemy, and what better place than in the City of Brotherly Love."

Sean leaned forward and pulled on the braided cord, which dropped the curtain covering the memorial. The monument was twelve feet high and twenty feet wide. Constructed of smooth, black granite and etched with gold inlay, the dedication read: "In memory of our brave Americans, whose lives were taken by the Spanish Flu of 1918-1919." The monument sat directly across from the entrance to Independence Hall, on the grassy mall not far from the building housing the Liberty Bell.

The crowd went wild, screaming, applauding, and then chanting, "Four more years! Four more years!"

Sean waved and acknowledged the masses and followed the Secret Service agents off the stage, followed by John Doyle. As they walked to Market Street, where the Presidential limousine was waiting, John thought, *this guy could run for king of the world and get elected.*

NYC WEEKEND

"Welcome aboard Northeast Airlines flight 294 to New York City. Our captain has asked that everyone please make sure your seatbelts are fastened and all electronic devices are turned off until we are in the air and the captain authorizes you to turn them back on. Our flight this afternoon will take about fifty-eight minutes. The temperature in New York is a balmy seventy degrees and the skies are overcast. After takeoff, we will be around to serve you a beverage. Meanwhile, sit back, relax, and enjoy the flight."

Kevin Doyle leaned across the aisle to his friend, Gonzo, and said, "Hey, dude! The action begins right here, right now, and whether the Sabres beat the Rangers or not, we are going to have a ball!"

"Yeah, Kev-man, you got that right. It would be a little easier, however, if the Feds weren't following us everywhere we go."

"They're following me, not the rest of you; just me and Skippy."

"Well, we happen to be with you. It was a lot easier before your old man became the leader of the free world." "Gonzo, stop complaining! You love every minute of it and you know it! Besides, you're an old man now with two kids. You can't fool around anymore; your wife would cut you off forever."

"How could I not behave myself with your Secret Service goons hanging around?"

The intercom clicked and the flight attendant announced, "The captain has turned off the seatbelt sign, so you are free to leave your seat if necessary."

Kevin Doyle had just reached down to unfasten his seatbelt, when he saw two more of his group coming up the aisle from the rear of the aircraft. His friend, Hyper, approached and said, "Hey, dude! Your bodyguard is eyeing up that cute little blond chick back in row 26."

Kevin turned to get a better look and said, "You know, Hyper, you have a vivid imagination. You think everyone is on the prowl like you, don't you?"

Andy Cooper, alias "Hyper," said, "You better believe it, dude. It's true."

All of Kevin's friends had nicknames. It was part of growing up in the old neighborhood. If you didn't have a nickname, then you weren't part of the group. They had been together since early high school, some since grammar school. The old gang had known each other and had stayed close for over twenty-five years. There were about sixteen of them. They partied together, played baseball together, attended sporting events together, took vacations with their families together, and some traveled together to the annual game between the Buffalo Sabres and the New York Rangers hockey teams. On this trip, there were six of them: Kevin and his brother, Brendan, a.k.a. Kev-man and Skippy; Tom Conley, a.k.a. Gonzo; and Andy Cooper, a.k.a. Hyper. The last of the six-pack were Jack Rooney, a.k.a. Pumpkin, and Matt Mahoney, a.k.a. Booger.

The trip to New York was always a "let your hair down" event for the group. They partied all weekend and then flew home to recuperate before going back to their individual jobs. Most times, the Sabres lost the hockey game, but it didn't really matter to the gang. They were in the Big Apple to have fun and act like kids again. Who cared whether the home team won or lost?

As usual, there was a heated discussion between Gonzo and Hyper about what the point spread on the game was and how many goals would be scored, when the intercom clicked and the flight attendant announced, "We are on our final approach. Please take your seats and fasten your seatbelts."

Hyper looked at Kevin and Brendan and said, "Man, that was the fastest flight I can remember! How fast do you suppose this dude is going?"

Kevin laughed and said, "Hyper, just take your seat. It's almost time to party."

As the group of friends headed for the terminal after deplaning, Agent Jackson of the U.S. Secret Service had to nearly jog to keep up with them. His responsibility was to keep the Doyle brothers in his sight. The rest were not his concern. He managed to catch up with Brendan and said, "Could you remind your brother that I need to be part of the group? You know, sort of 'blend in.' So don't be leaving me in your wake."

Brendan looked at the agent and chuckled. "You know, Jackson, you really don't fit in. You look older than us, and I guess you could pass for an older brother if you weren't African-American, but not for part of the group."

"Come on, Bren, that isn't true. I'm only five years older than you guys, and I don't look any older than you. I definitely could be part of the group, so who's to know? Let's just make sure that you guys don't get away from me. You don't want to see me doing guard duty outside the White House, do you?"

"Come on, Jackson, I was only joshing with you. Don't worry; we'll keep you in the group. Just don't go back telling my father how hard we party."

"Bren, I don't think you have to worry about that. I'm sure your Dad already knows about you guys."

They approached the baggage area and everyone kept on walking right past it. Agent Jackson yelled, "Hey, everyone! Hold it up! Isn't everybody getting their luggage?"

They all turned and said in unison, "Hey, Jackson! We have our luggage in our hands!"

Red-haired Pumpkin said, "No one checks luggage for a two-night stay! All we bring is a carry-on!" All six of the men turned and headed for the door.

Agent Jackson yelled, "Wait a minute 'til I get *my* bag!"

With a few shrugs, the group held up at the revolving door. Gonzo turned to Kevin and said, "This dude is going to slow down our entire weekend. I think we should lose him if we want to enjoy the next two days."

"Come on, Tom, you know we can't do that," Brendan said.

"Yeah, Tom, big brother is right. We need to behave a little more responsibly than that. After all, we are representing the free world."

"Do I note a little sarcasm there?" Booger chimed in.

Kevin's Irish temper began to turn his face a light blush color. "Okay guys, enough. Let's just have a good time this weekend and forget about our buddy over there looking for his bag."

Just then, Agent Jackson appeared and they all headed for the curb where Hyper had flagged down a taxi-van to take them to the Roosevelt Hotel in downtown Manhattan.

The trip from Newark Airport was about thirty minutes. As they drove up to the front of the hotel, there were flashing lights and commotion. Vehicles were lined up at the sidewalk, and some drivers had exited their cars to see what was going on.

Kevin said, "Jackson, what do you suppose is going on at the entrance?"

Agent Jackson leaned out the window and then immediately sat back down. "It looks like someone is being put into an ambulance. There's an NYPD patrol car there, too. Guess we can get out here and walk the rest of the way."

Jackson handed a wad of bills to the driver and asked for a receipt. By the time the seven travelers reached the front entrance, the ambulance and the police car had driven away, lights on, but no sirens.

As they checked in at the front desk, Pumpkin questioned the desk clerk.

"Excuse me, but was someone hurt? Did someone have a heart attack? We just saw an ambulance leave the hotel."

With a heavy, middle-European accent, possibly Hungarian, the clerk replied, "That was the third one today, all the same. They have some kind of pneumonia-like sickness. The first one passed out in the elevator. The second one was found in his room almost unconscious, and the one you saw leave called for the house doctor. The doctor ordered him the ambulance."

Pumpkin turned to the group and said, "Did you hear that, guys? I hope we aren't walking into some TB ward." "Okay, Pump. Don't go getting everyone bent out of shape," Kevin admonished him. "This is a big hotel. That doesn't mean everyone here is going to get some kind of cold or flu."

Gonzo picked up his bag and said, "I don't know what the rest of you are going to do, but I'm throwing this in my room and heading for the Oak Bar. Last one there is an asshole!"

Brendan said, "Tom, you have a way with words! See you there, asshole!"

*　　　　*　　　　*

Four hours later, after drinks at the Oak Bar and then dinner at Morgan's Steakhouse, the group enjoyed a drink on their friend Artie, from back home. Their favorite bartender from Buffalo now ran the bar at Morgan's. After promising to see Artie the next time they were in town, the group headed for John Barleycorn's Pub for a night of drinking and mischief. Agent Jackson thought to himself, *this is going to be one long weekend, I'm afraid.*

Sunday morning it was Bloody Mary's all around for breakfast. The Sabres had defeated the Rangers on Saturday night in what began as a tight game that was tied 3 to 3 at the end of the second period. The Sabres came on in the third period, however, to score two power play goals and then with thirty-two seconds left in the game, got an empty net goal to win the game 6 to 3. That was enough cause to celebrate right into the early morning hours and now the group was paying dearly for their escapade. After an enormous breakfast, the type a football player could eat, the hungover group dug in to soak up the remnants of the night before, and then it was off to LaGuardia for their Northeast Airlines flight back to Buffalo.

On the way to the airport, Gonzo began coughing uncontrollably and Booger said, "Gee, Tom, are you going to make it?"

"I don't know," he wheezed. "My chest feels like it's going to explode. I can't breathe very well either. If I could just stop the coughing . . ." Tom's voice trailed off.

Kevin sat back in his seat and thought, *I wonder if we picked something up in that damn hotel? I don't feel so good myself. Probably just sympathy pains for old Gonzo.*

SAN FRANCISCO INTERNATIONAL

"San Fran Control, this is JAL2195. We are about fifteen minutes out from your mainland."

"JAL2195, this is San Fran. Descend to 23,000 and maintain air speed."

"Roger. We are descending to 23,000 and maintaining present air speed."

The jumbo jet, a Boeing 747, began its descent and the pilot picked up the intercom mike.

"Ladies and gentlemen, this is your captain speaking. Please return to your seats. The seatbelt sign will be turned on in a few minutes. We are approaching the California coast and should be on the ground in about twenty-five minutes. We hope you have had a pleasant flight from Malaysia and enjoy your stay in the United States of America."

As with many overseas flights, prior to landing the flight attendant often sprays a pleasant-smelling deodorizer to freshen the cabin air. That procedure was performed on flight JAL2195, and the passengers welcomed the smell of fresh flowers. It had been a long flight, with a stop in Honolulu, and the jumbo jet had become stuffy and stale.

The big airliner made its approach over San Francisco Bay and with very little fog, the skyline was ablaze with lights twinkling as far as the eye could see. The views of Telegraph Hill and the Golden Gate Bridge were spectacular. The landing was very soft; not a passenger on board felt one bump. Another perfect landing of a jumbo jet had taken place. The 747 taxied to the gate at the international terminal and was deplaned in less than fifteen minutes.

Once the jumbo jet was empty, the maintenance crew entered the cabin to vacuum and clean the rest rooms in preparation for the next flight. The flight crew picked up their bags, said good night to the maintenance team, and left the aircraft. One of the cleaners entered the galley area to pick up the used canisters of deodorizer spray, and replaced them with brand new cans. The empty cans were thrown into the black plastic bags with the rest of the refuse from the flight and then thrown out the cabin door, into the dumpster below.

WHITE HOUSE SITUATION ROOM

Bob Roche, National Security Advisor to the President, always worked weekends. There had not been a forty-hour week for Bob as long as he could remember. He longed for the day that this would not be the case. All of the missed important occasions that took place for his wife and two boys were a strain on any marriage. For Bob, the ultimate workaholic, a seventy-to-eighty hour week was not unusual, leaving Karen, his wife, to attend the school functions and the sporting events. He planned on making it up to her one of these days, but that day never seemed to materialize.

The ringing of the telephone brought Bob out of his daydreaming, a habit that had become more and more common. "Situation Room, Bob Roche here."

"Mr. Roche, the British Prime Minister is on the line and he says he needs to speak to the President."

Bob got out of his chair. He was a much better thinker standing than sitting. "Did you tell him that the President is at Camp David?"

47

"Yes sir, I did, but he said he needs to speak to whomever is in charge of security. I told him you would be the best one to speak to."

"Thank you, Ms. Woods. Please put him on the line." "Yes, sir. Right away, sir."

Bob heard a click and immediately the connection was made. The Prime Minister's voice sounded anxious. "Mr. Roche, this is Prime Minister O'Keefe and I am calling from 10 Downing. I have Marty Harrington, our Director of Intelligence, with me. I believe you two know each other."

"Yes, sir, Mr. Prime Minister. Marty and I are well acquainted."

"Hello, Bob," came the voice from No.10 Downing.

"Hi, Marty. I guess this must be urgent if you're involved. What can I do for you, Mr. Prime Minister?" "Mr. Roche, I tried to get a hold of President Doyle, but I understand he is away for the weekend."

"Yes, sir, that is correct, but he is due back this evening," Bob answered.

"Very well, Mr. Roche. We need to get this message to him. I'll let Marty here fill you in, and I assume you will contact the President as soon as it is convenient."

"Yes, Mr. Prime Minister, I will do that ASAP." "Thank you, Mr. Roche. I'll be attending to other matters now. Please continue with Marty."

Bob heard a click and knew he was alone on the line with Marty Harrington. "Okay, Marty. What do you have for me?"

"Bob, you know we have had a lot of reports lately of chatter across the globe from suspected terror cells." "Yes, Marty, we've had the same information and a lot of it coming from Malaysia."

"That's correct, Bob, and what I have to pass on to you is directly from one of those cells. We intercepted a conversation originating in Malaysia to a cell phone somewhere in Scandinavia, but we're not sure where, as it is increasingly difficult to trace these damn cell phone numbers.

"In any event, the cell in Malaysia has been identified and agents converged on the safe house just one hour ago. Unfortunately, there must have been a tip-off, because when our people arrived with the Malaysian federals, the house was empty, completely cleaned out. The conversation, however, told us that an attack on the United States is imminent and it will be in the form of some type of bio-terrorism. We don't have a lot of intelligence on the possible agent or how it will be introduced, but we do know that it has something to do with the airline industry. "You Yanks had the worst incident back on 9/11. Since it involved aircraft, I am sure you really don't want to hear this, but we are positive an attack is imminent. We just don't know where or when."

Bob sat back down in his chair and let out an audible sigh.

"Bob, what do you think? I'm anxious to hear if you have any information that will help in this report," Marty asked.

"Marty, I wish I could tell you differently, but at this point we don't have a clue as to what they are up to. We have heard similar chatter and to date, we are at a loss when it comes to pinpointing what the threat may be. This is the most concrete information we have heard. Are you sure, absolutely positive, that your information is valid, Marty?"

"Bob, you know me well enough that I would never call you unless we were certain. Trust me on this one, my good friend."

"Marty, thank Prime Minister O'Keefe for me and thank you for the call. I will contact the President immediately after we hang up here and inform him. It sounds like we made a good decision to go to level Orange on the threat scale. The locals are already complaining about how they are going to pay for overtime and worse yet, we cannot tell them exactly what we're expecting."

"Bob, I'm sure you will handle it. Give my best to Karen and the kids. Let me know if there is anything we can do from this side of the pond."

"Thanks, Marty. I'm sure we will be talking often in the near future."

Bob Roche hung up the phone and thought about what he had to do next. He picked the receiver back up and hit the speed dial button for Camp David. The phone was answered by George White, counsel to the President.

"George, Bob here. I need to talk to the President ASAP. We have a problem and he needs to be informed."

"Sure, Bob, hang on a minute and I'll get him on the line." About thirty seconds elapsed and Bob Roche thought, *just enough time for George to get the President and give him the message that I'm on the phone with important information.*

"Good evening, Bob. What are you doing working on a Sunday? Like that is not a common thing for you."

"Mr. President, we have received a call from Prime Minister O'Keefe and Marty Harrington, his Chief of Intelligence. They have confirmed that we have an imminent threat from the terrorist cells we've been monitoring and that it will come in the form of bio-terrorism."

There was a brief silence before the President said, "Bob, do we have anything more concrete than the 'imminent threat'? Do we have any idea how it may come about?"

"No, sir, I'm afraid we don't, except that somehow the airlines will be involved. There is no further information on how they come into the picture, but the British Intelligence Agency is very seldom wrong in its assessment."

"All right, Bob, we'll head back to Washington tonight. Call a National Security meeting for eight o'clock this evening."

"Yes, sir. See you when you get back."

ALEXANDRIA, VIRGINIA

Bob Roche drove up to his two-story colonial at exactly 4:00 p.m. He had contacted everyone for the National Security Council meeting and had then placed a call to Karen telling her that he would be home for dinner. The bad news was that he would have to be back at the White House by seven-thirty for an eight o'clock meeting. *At least,* he thought, *my wife will be happy to have a few quality hours to enjoy Sunday dinner with her husband.*

As he entered the foyer, there she was waiting with his favorite cocktail. Bob looked at it and had second thoughts about drinking it, knowing he would have to be sharp later, but then thought, *well, I do have four hours before the meeting.*

"Hi, honey. That looks perfect." He walked over to retrieve the martini and kissed his wife before taking it from her hand.

"Robert, it is so nice to have you home, if for only a few hours. But what is dragging you back out to the White House?"

"Honey, you know I can't discuss what the meeting is about. Suffice it to say that we are at an Orange level state of readiness and while we are, there will probably be many meetings and nights like this."

"Oh Bob, you sound so serious and mysterious. Let's sit down and enjoy our drink. The roast will be ready in an hour and the boys are due back from the Redskins game by five-thirty at the latest."

Bob entered the family room and sat down in his favorite Lazy Boy, where he spent most of his Sunday afternoons watching football. He flipped through the channels on the cable television until he came to CNN. The trailer across the bottom of the screen revealed "Breaking News."

Bob turned up the volume just as Dan Quigley was saying, "We have just heard from Dr. Simpson at St. Vincent's Hospital here in New York City that there are now six cases of this unknown flu-like virus. The first three victims were all brought into the hospital on Friday and one is now in critical condition. The only commonality of the three patients is that they were all registered at the Roosevelt Hotel in downtown Manhattan. The newest patients have nothing in common except that they all have the same symptoms; to prevent further infection, the area of the hospital where all six are being treated has been quarantined. The medical personnel are wearing gowns and masks reminiscent of the SARS scare back in 2003. We do not have much information about this strange virus, but we will be at the press conference at eight-thirty this evening and hope to have more information for you at that time. This is Dan Quigley at St. Vincent's Hospital in Manhattan."

Bob wondered what this was all about and made a mental note to catch the press conference later. He then flipped the channel to the station that had covered the Redskins loss to the Cowboys. The fans were streaming out of the stadium. His sons would be home soon.

After dinner, Bob said his goodbye's to his family and patted his golden retriever on the head and said, "Be a good boy, Clark. See you all later."

On the way into the city, Bob tuned to the Public Information radio station and heard another broadcast on the virus about which Dan Quigley had reported. Two of the patients were now critical and one was on life support. *What the hell is going on?* Bob thought. *Could this be a prelude to worse things to come? Is it possible that this has anything to do with the bio-terrorism threat?*

NATIONAL SECURITY COUNCIL

President Doyle approached the door to the White House Situation Room at precisely eight o'clock that evening. As he entered, the entire assemblage rose from their chairs. "Please, please, ladies and gentlemen, take your seats. No need to stand." He then turned to Bob Roche and said, "Okay, Bob, would you proceed and fill the council in on what we know so far?"

Bob Roche rose, as he always did when giving a presentation. He quickly went over his conversation with the Prime Minister and Marty Harrington and the fact that it had been determined that any attack would come in the form of bio-terrorism. Questions flew around the room. Everyone wanted to be heard first. "Hold on, folks. One at a time, please."

Ken Sitarek was first to speak. "Bob, what do we have that is concrete, if anything? And do we have any information on how the airline industry could be involved?" "No, Ken, we don't, but the FBI has contacted and advised all of the major airlines to take extreme precautions. The last thing we need is a repeat of 9/11." "But Bob," Ken countered, "you've just said that the threat is bio. Why would the airlines be involved?"

"Not sure what the connection is, other than possibly transporting the biological agent aboard the aircraft, but with security as tight as it has been since 9/11, I can't believe that would be possible."

"Bob, over the past three years, I have come to believe that absolutely anything is possible when it comes to terrorism," George White chimed in.

"Yes, I agree, George. We need a break on this one, and so far nothing has materialized."

Henry Volner, Director of the CIA, raised his hand and Bob Roche recognized him. "Bob, I'm not sure if there is any connection to this threat, but did anyone happen to see the CNN report this afternoon from St. Vincent's Hospital in Manhattan?" A few of the members at the table nodded that they did see the coverage.

Bob Roche said, "Henry, I did see that and wondered at the time what we might be dealing with there. The first three patients were taken to the hospital from the same Manhattan hotel, the Roosevelt, which seemed to be the only thing they had in common."

The President said, "Bob, what is this all about? I haven't seen a television all weekend. What are we talking about here?"

"Well, Mr. President, Dan Quigley reported today about a strange flu-like virus that three people staying at the Roosevelt had contracted. There are now six in the hospital with similar symptoms; two of them are in critical condition and one is on life support."

Looking like he was in shock, the President said, "Jesus, that's the same hotel my boys stayed at this weekend. Do we know any more about this virus, Bob?"

"No, sir, but there is a news conference scheduled right about now, that CNN will be covering live."

"Ken," the President said, "turn those monitors on and let's see what they have to say."

Ken Sitarek picked up the remote control and clicked at four television flat-screen monitors positioned strategically around the Situation Room. The press conference was just beginning. A distinguished looking gentleman with graying hair, and a moustache and goatee to match, and dressed in a white lab coat, was at the podium about to speak.

"Good evening. I am Dr. George Simpson, Chief of Staff here at St. Vincent's Hospital. We are here to report that earlier this weekend, we received three patients over a period of six hours who were brought to the hospital from a hotel in downtown Manhattan. All three men were suffering from extremely high fevers, including one who had a temperature of 105 degrees. Each also had serious respiratory problems. Severe, uncontrollable coughing and overall body aches and fatigue were other symptoms.

"Throughout the weekend, an additional three patients were admitted. All exhibited the same high fever and the coughing. We have prescribed antibiotics, but to no avail. The first patient admitted on Friday is now on life support, due to severe respiratory distress. The patient's lungs are in danger of collapsing. We presently have three patients in our intensive care unit, including the one patient on life support. I will now take questions."

"Dr. Simpson, Dan Quigley from CNN here. Are you classifying this as an influenza virus and if so, have you identified exactly what type of flu it is?"

"Mr. Quigley, we have performed extensive testing in our lab on samples taken from all six patients. What we do know is that they are all suffering from the same strain. What that strain is we do not have information on at this time. I can tell you, however, that it definitely is not SARS, the respiratory disease that we experienced back in 2003 in China and Toronto, Canada."

"Dr. Simpson, a follow-up question. Are we to assume that the antibiotics are not working and if not, can you tell us why?"

"Your assumption is correct, Mr. Quigley. We have not made any progress in arresting this virus with the antibiotics administered so far. We must understand, though, that it is still early. We need to give some of these drugs time to act."

The press conference continued for another five minutes and Ken Sitarek muted the sound on the monitors as President Doyle asked, "Does anyone here believe that this may be the start of a biological incident?"

Henry Volner was first to speak. "Mr. President, I believe that it is too early to make that assumption. After all, it appears to be confined to one hospital in New York. It could be something like Legionnaires' disease. When that hit during the mid-1970's, it was confined to a hotel where the victims had stayed. Maybe this is something similar."

"Well, Henry, let's hope that's all it is. If this thing spreads and turns out to be a bio-terrorism threat, we need to combat it very quickly. Bob, keep on top of this and let me know if anything, and I mean anything, develops. I need to excuse myself and go up and call my sons. I hope to God they are healthy. Good night, everyone."

"Good night, Mr. President."

UNITED ARAB EMIRATES

After checking into his suite at the Crown Plaza Hotel in Dubai, Sulanni dialed the phone number he had memorized months before.

"Hello, how may I help you?" the voice on the other end asked.

"I would like to visit your warehouse, sir. My name is Sulanni."

The voice responded, "And how do I know that you are Mr. Sulanni?"

Sulanni replied, "St. Gustaf's illness."

"Very well, Mr. Sulanni. Be in front of the hotel in fifteen minutes. I will have my driver pick you up." "Thank you, sir. I will be wearing a blue and gold Notre Dame University golf shirt."

"We are looking forward to seeing you, Mr. Sulanni." The line went dead and Sulanni changed out of his suit and put on a pair of khaki Dockers and the golf shirt.

Exactly fifteen minutes later, a black Mercedes drove up to the front entrance of the Crown Plaza. The window on the passenger side slid down. A very attractive woman of about thirty years of age, with olive skin and long, shiny, auburn hair said, "Mr. Sulanni, please get in."

Sulanni opened the door of the Mercedes and got into the front passenger seat. "Thank you for picking me up. And you are?"

"I am Dr. Farah Zayed."

"Oh yes, Dr. Zayed. I should have recognized you. I have heard many positive things about you and your research."

Dr. Zayed said, "Should I take that as a compliment?" "Definitely, doctor," Sulanni replied.

Less than ten minutes later they arrived at a large warehouse on Al Rasheed Boulevard, and Dr. Zayed drove to the rear entrance. Above the door was a sign in Arabic that read *Best of Dubai Imports and Exports.*

"Mr. Sulanni, welcome to the Best of Dubai."

They both got out of the Mercedes and walked to the entrance. Once inside, Sulanni could see crates and boxes of various sizes piled almost to the full height of the forty-foot ceiling. *The warehouse must be at least 20,000 square feet,* he thought.

"Right this way, Mr. Sulanni," Dr. Zayed directed. He followed the doctor into what appeared to be a shipping office and through to a back room with shelving along three walls. Dr. Zayed walked to the shelving on the right and reached underneath the third shelf and the entire wall moved out to reveal a concrete staircase.

"Please enter, Mr. Sulanni. Watch your step as you descend."

Sulanni hesitated, and then slowly walked down the stairway and at the bottom, found a dimly lit hallway to the left. At the end of the hall there was a door made of solid oak. Dr. Zayed reached the bottom of the stairway and said, "Follow me, sir."

Sulanni followed the doctor to the door and then through the doorway to another room, the dimensions of which were approximately ten feet by ten feet. At the other side of the room was a second door, which Dr. Zayed opened to reveal a very large, brilliantly lit room with high-density overhead lights and stainless steel tables down the center. It was obviously some type of laboratory, as there were microscopes on every table and Petri dishes everywhere.

At the far end of the room, two large stainless steel doors took up half of the wall. These appeared to be walk-in coolers, the sort one might see in a restaurant or in the warehouse of a grocery store for dairy product and meat storage.

Just as he was about to ask Dr. Zayed about the coolers, her superior walked into the room and said, "Ah, Mr. Sulanni. Welcome to our little operation. I am Muhammad Sutwa. We spoke on the telephone."

Sulanni reached out to shake hands and said, "It is an honor to meet you, Mr. Sutwa. Kemal sends his greetings and best wishes. Praise Allah."

"Thank you, sir. I have enormous respect for our leader. We will prevail and bring the infidels to their knees. Our plans are running as smoothly as we could have possibly expected. Being here in Dubai right under their noses is a brilliant coup. The stupid Americans don't even think that we would operate out of the country of one of their closest allies."

"That is so true, Mr. Sutwa. Tell me: are the deliveries on time and when can we expect the next shipments?"

"We are shipping as we speak from here in Dubai to our location in Casablanca, and then the teams of brave men and women have been given their orders and their weapons to carry out our mission. Your operation in Norway allowed us to collect enough of the samples that we needed to produce a weapons grade arsenal of the potent killer; this is what we are now shipping. I understand that you have named it after St. Gustaf, from the cemetery where we retrieved the frozen samples."

"That is correct, Mr. Sutwa. We are already beginning to see the effects of our campaign beginning in New York City. It will not be long before it will be throughout the United States. The stupid American pigs deserve everything we will do to them. They do not deserve to live another day."

After taking a tour of the facility, Sulanni thanked his host and bade farewell.

"I am flying back to Casablanca in the morning to finalize our shipment schedule and then back to Malaysia to watch the campaign unfold on CNN. Dan Quigley is a tremendous asset to us. We could not have a better PR person. He reports the breaking news and that is exactly the way we want it."

Sutwa said, "Farewell, my friend. May Allah go with you."

"Thank you, Mr. Sutwa. Praise Allah."

"Dr. Zayed, thank you also. Allah will reward you a hundred thousand times over. Praise Allah."

"Praise Allah. Be safe," Dr. Zayed replied.

MONDAY MORNING

It had been a short night for Bob, with very little sleep; he was back at the White House at 6:30 a.m. He was reading through some of the chatter that had been intercepted overnight when his phone rang.

"Bob Roche here."

"Bob, this is Henry Volner. Have you heard the news just announced on CNN?"

"No, Henry, I don't have my television on. What is it?"

"Bob, San Francisco General Hospital held a press conference last night to announce that they have ten patients with a flu-like virus that sounds exactly like the one we discussed last night. Doesn't it seem strange to you that we have reports of this on both coasts simultaneously?"

"I suppose you could say that Henry, but let's get more information on this before we come to any conclusions. I'm going to recommend that we have the President direct that samples be sent to the Center for Disease Control to see if they can come up with anything. I don't even want to think that this is the biological attack that we've been expecting."

"Okay, Bob. Keep in touch."

"Will do, Henry."

*   *   *

Bob waited one hour until the President was at his desk, and then headed to the Oval Office.

"Mr. President," Aggie announced, "Bob Roche is here to see you."

"Send him right in, please."

Bob entered the Oval Office and said, "Good morning, Mr. President."

"Thanks, Bob, but I don't know how good it is. The look on your face certainly doesn't tell me that it is even close to good."

"Mr. President, I just learned from Henry Volner that CNN has reported on a news conference held last evening at San Francisco General, where hospital officials have announced that they have ten patients with a similar, if not the same, virus that St. Vincent's Hospital has."

"I'm afraid, Bob, that it's worse than that," the President replied. "I saw on CNN that New York City has reported twenty new cases since last night. They have also reported three fatalities, one of them the fellow that arrived there on Friday with the fever of 105 degrees."

"Mr. President, we need to get a better handle on this, especially if it turns out to be the biological attack we've been anticipating."

"Yes, Bob, you're right. Turn CNN back on and let's see if there are any updates."

The television came to life and Dan Quigley was on the screen once more, mid-report.

" . . . this strange ailment seems to be showing up more quickly than the SARS virus did back in 2003. We now have ten reported cases in San Francisco, twenty-six in New York City, with three deaths, and we have this just in: there are eighteen cases between Marin County, San Jose, and Oakland. Philadelphia, Cleveland, Toronto, and Baltimore have a total of thirty cases. This is happening very fast and authorities do not have any commonality to determine how these patients contracted this virus. This is Dan Quigley, reporting from CNN, Atlanta."

The President reached for his phone and his secretary immediately came on the line. "Aggie, get me Dr. Doyle at the CDC in Atlanta."

"Yes, sir, Mr. President. Hold one minute, please." "Bob, it sounds like we're going to need John's expertise on this before it gets out of hand." The phone rang and President Doyle pushed the speaker phone button. "John, are you there?"

"Yes, Mr. President, I'm here. Why the speaker phone?"

"John, I have Bob Roche here with me, my National Security Advisor, and I want him to hear this conversation."

"Okay, Mr. President, what can I do?"

"John, I need you to get on top of the flu-like virus that is rapidly appearing across the country. I also need to tell you that we have been expecting a terrorist threat and possible bio-terrorism attack for the past week. We are concerned that this flu-like virus may well be that attack and we need to identify it before it gets completely out of hand on us."

John Doyle sighed and then said, "Sean, I have already received samples from St. Vincent's Hospital and San Francisco General air-freighted samples to me overnight. We are in the midst of testing right now, but it is unlike anything we have seen in the past. This is serious, Sean. We may be looking at an epidemic of enormous proportions. For a virus to travel that quickly and across the country in just a few days is unlike anything we have experienced. Not only do we need to identify it, but we need to know how it was spread initially."

"John, I could not agree with you more. Please let us know as soon as you have anything positive to tell us." "Yes, sir, Mr. President, I'll do my best to get this done expeditiously."

"Thank you, John. Good luck."

"Good luck to all of us, Mr. President."

BUFFALO, NEW YORK

Erie County Medical Center, also known as ECMC, was once the county hospital, county-funded and county- operated. It had recently been privatized and was well known for its Burn Treatment Center, its Head Trauma Center, and also for its Cardiac Care Center, where over fifteen hundred bypass surgeries were performed each year. ECMC served the Buffalo area and surrounding suburbs throughout the county, as well as patients from Southern Ontario, Canada, across the Niagara River from downtown Buffalo.

ECMC was also the Health Department's designated treatment hospital, as outlined in its Emergency Response Plan, in the event of an outbreak of any contagious illnesses. The Health Department believed it was better to bring all victims to one hospital to keep the spread of infection to one area. ECMC was written into the Health Department's plan right after the SARS virus occurred. Today, it was one of the many hospitals across the country to have admitted victims of the mysterious flu-like virus that was attacking citizens from coast to coast.

Dr. Jim Byrne, President of ECMC, was sitting in his office with Agent Jim Jackson, contemplating the phone call he had to make. "Agent Jackson, have you notified your superiors about the situation?"

"Yes, sir, I have, but they are leaving it up to you to contact the President."

Agent Jackson handed over a slip of paper indicating the telephone number for the White House. Dr. Byrne punched in the number and waited. On the second ring, a woman answered the phone.

"This is the White House. How may I help you?"

"This is Dr. Jim Byrne at the Erie County Medical Center in Buffalo, New York. I have Secret Service Agent Jim Jackson here with me. I need to speak to the President immediately on a very urgent matter."

"Thank you, Dr. Byrne. Hold on, please." Two minutes went by and finally the telephone clicked.

"This is President Doyle. Are you there, Dr. Byrne?" "Yes, sir, I am. Thank you for taking my call. Your Secret Service Agent, Mr. Jim Jackson, insisted that I make this call. Sir, I will be brief. We have admitted your son, Kevin, and three of his friends to our facility with the flu-like virus that is spreading across the country."

The silence that ensued made Dr. Byrne wonder if he had been disconnected. Then suddenly the voice began. "Dr. Byrne, what is the condition of my son?"

"Mr. President, he is presently holding his own, so to speak. He came in with a fever of 104 degrees, but it is now down to 101. He has some congestion, but not as bad as his friend. One of the young men is in very bad condition. I would say he only has a forty percent chance of survival. We now have ten confirmed cases presenting with flu-like virus symptoms in Erie County. Nothing we try does much with this virus. It is a very strong strain and it is either going to wear itself out, or we will have many fatalities." Dr. Byrne paused before adding, "I'm sorry, sir. I didn't mean to imply anything."

"No, don't fret, Dr. Byrne. I understand. Kevin is a tough character. I am confident he will survive this horrible ordeal. I will clear my calendar and fly up there tomorrow. Thank you for calling, Dr. Byrne."

Sean Doyle hung up the telephone and massaged his temples, feeling a severe headache coming on. *I hope my cousin John comes up with something real soon. I cannot bear the thought of losing my son.*

The intercom brought Sean out of his thoughts. "Yes, Aggie, what is it?"

"Mr. President, it's time for your news conference. Sherry Katz is waiting for you."

"Tell her I'll be right along, Aggie."

Sherry Katz was Sean Doyle's Press Secretary. She was tough and handled the press better than anyone, often reminding Sean of the actress that played her role on *The West Wing* for so many years. He could never remember her name--Janey something, or maybe it was something Janey. *Oh, one of these days I'll remember it.* Before he left the Oval Office, Sean called Maggie's cell phone to tell her about Kevin. He said they would get to Buffalo as soon as possible.

Maggie said, "Sean, I warned you about the boys going to New York City! Now look at what's happened! I am so scared, Sean. What are we going to do?"

"Maggie, with the grace of God, Kevin will be fine. Please try to be calm. We have to be very strong for Kevin when we get there tomorrow."

"I'm sorry, Sean. I didn't mean to take it out on you. I am just so stressed over this."

Sean said, "Luv, I will see you as soon as possible. I am on my way to a press conference right now. Will call you later. Love you . . ."

"Love you too, Sean."

*   *   *

"Ladies and gentlemen, the President of the United States."

Sean walked into the White House Press Room and up to the podium.

"Good afternoon, everyone. I will make a brief statement and then we can begin the questions. Last weekend, on Friday, October 7, three patients were admitted to St. Vincent's Hospital in New York City with an unknown virus. Since that time there have been over two hundred victims of this malady; we can now confirm there have been twelve deaths.

"The Center for Disease Control is working around the clock to come up with some answers. Testing, as you all know, takes time, and any information I could give you now would be inconclusive. The best thing we can do as a nation until such time as this virus is identified is to stay away from large gatherings where you could be exposed to a potential virus. This is a time of tragedy, yet we need to stay focused and we need to pray that our staff at the CDC will be able to identify what we have here and eradicate it. Questions?"

"Mr. President, Kim Carney from the Washington Post. Is it true that none of the antibiotics used so far has worked to combat this virus?"

"That is true, Kim. I have been advised by our Surgeon General that the standard drugs--penicillin, ampicillin, and Cipro--have not been able to stem this virus. What has worked is strict bed rest for some of the victims. Once the disease enters the lungs, it becomes very difficult for the patient and most of the deaths have been from suffocation. The lungs fill with fluid and the patient is unable to breathe."

"Mr. President, Dan Quigley from CNN. We have been at the Orange Alert Status for almost two weeks now. Some people in Washington, including Senator Atkins, are speculating that the illness that is attacking so rapidly could be some type of biological agent released by terrorists. Do you believe, sir, that this is possible?"
"Dan, we do not have any information at the present time that would lead us to believe that this is terrorist connected. We believe we are dealing with an unknown virus, just as we did a few years ago when SARS hit around the globe."

"But Mr. President, are you ruling out the possibility of a terrorist connection?"

"No, Dan, I did not say that. At this time, I am not ruling out anything. Believe me, as soon as we know, you will know. Next question, please."

The press conference continued for another ten minutes, during which time the President promised to keep the media as well-informed as possible.

FBI AT LAGUARDIA

Ted Graham, the Director of the Federal Bureau of Investigation, had ordered his teams of agents to check with all airlines across the country to determine whether any had a connection to the virus. The team covering LaGuardia Airport in New York City had methodically visited each airline throughout the terminals, questioning as many employees as possible, hoping to uncover just one thing that did not seem proper. Agents waited in the Northeast Airlines lounge, prepared to question an incoming crew they believed had also flown into New York the previous day, before the first virus patients had come down with the still unknown illness.

Shortly after today's flight landed, the crew entered the lounge and Special Agent Terry Crowley stood and approached them.

"Good afternoon, folks. Are you the crew from Northeast Airlines 897?"

"Yes, sir, we are. I'm Bob Putrillo, and this is Nancy Short and Maddie Westbrook."

"Nice to meet you all. I'm Agent Crowley." He held out his I.D. for the three crew members to see. "I'd like to ask you a few questions, and then you can be on your way."

Bob said, "Go ahead and ask. I can't promise we'll have answers, but we can try. What is it you're looking for?"

Agent Crowley said, "We want to know if any of you experienced anything strange or different in the past few weeks with any of your flights?"

Both women shook their heads no, but Bob said, "Wait a minute. There was a security violation about two weeks ago."

"What kind of violation, Bob?"

Bob looked at the agent, tilted his head to the side, and said, "Don't you guys work together?"

Perplexed, not knowing where Bob was going with the question, Agent Crowley asked, "What 'guys?'"

"Well, the FBI and the TSA guys, of course."

"Bob, why don't you go ahead and tell us what happened."

Bob said, "About two weeks ago, we flew into LaGuardia here, and after the passengers were gone, we did a final check of the aircraft. Upon inspection, we found a carry-on bag in the overhead near row 18 with a razor and lots of razor blades in it, a clear violation that the TSA scanners did not catch."

"Did all three of you see this bag?" Agent Crowley asked.

Bob answered for the two women. "No, Maddie wasn't on that flight. She took Sandy's place. Sandy was the one who actually found the bag."

"And where is Sandy now?" Crowley asked.

"She was buried two days ago. She was a victim of this horrible virus thing that's going around," Bob answered.

"Thank you, folks. I'll follow through with TSA. If I need anything else, I'll be in touch. I'm sorry about your friend," Agent Crowley said, before he closed the door and left the Northeast Airlines lounge.

Agent Crowley called his partner en route to the TSA office; Roger Naylor answered on the second ring. "Hey, meet me over at the TSA office in ten or quicker."

"Okay, man. See you there."

Five minutes later, both agents arrived simultaneously at the Transportation Security Administration office.

"Terry, what's going on? What are we doing here?" Roger asked.

"Going to pay our Mr. English a special visit and find out why he never reported a security violation to Homeland Security," Terry replied.

Just then, Jack English emerged from his office. "Well, men, to what do I owe this unexpected pleasure? Has the FBI put me on its Ten Most Wanted?"

"No, Jack, nothing like that. Just a few routine questions," Terry answered.

"Nothing is just routine with you guys. Spit it out. What are you looking for?"

Terry Crowley never liked Jack English, with his smart-alecky attitude and cocky approach to his job. "Let's start with this: why did you not report a security violation to the Department of Homeland Security regarding Northeast Airlines flight 897?"

"I don't know what you're talking about," Jack sneered.

"I doubt that, Jack. Get us the overnight bag so we can inspect it. It still has the razor blades and razor in it, doesn't it, or have you disposed of the evidence, too?" "Now wait a minute, Terry. I would never do anything like that. It could jeopardize my position with TSA."

"I hate to tell you, Jack, but you already have. Now get the bag."

Jack reached for his telephone and called Tony Camilleri, who answered on the first ring. "Tony, this is Jack. Get that Nike bag from the Northeast Airlines flight out of storage and bring it to my office."

"So, Jack," Terry continued, "you gonna tell us why you held this evidence for so long without notifying Homeland Security?"

"I was doing my own internal investigation first." "You know, Jack, that isn't proper procedure. I could have your ass for this."

Jack snarled at Terry, "And you'd just love to do that, wouldn't you?"

The door swung open. Tony Camilleri walked in and placed the bag on Jack English's desk. He turned and looked at the two agents sitting there. "Well, if it ain't the Fibbies. What you guys have, a day off?"

Crowley ignored the comment and picked up the bag which he unzipped and dumped out on Jack's desk. *Looks very innocent, all of the normal stuff a guy would take on a weekend trip to the City,* he thought. *Probably some guy who was running late and never gave it a thought to check the razor and blades. Innocent or not, he should never have made it through the scanner. Someone was asleep on the job.*

"Roger, write Mr. English here a receipt for his Nike bag. We're taking it with us."

Jack stood up. "Come on, Terry. You can't take that with you."

"I sure as damn well can, English. We'll let you know if we find anything. You need to get your house in order, here. Your people are sleeping on the job if this got through. Here's your receipt. See you later."

Terry and Roger walked out, leaving Jack English with the paper receipt. Jack was furious; an onlooker might have observed wisps of smoke coming from his ears. He turned to Camillieri and said, "Tony, those fuckin' Feds are going to hang us on this one."

*　　　*　　　*

Once back in the terminal, Agent Crowley said, "Roger, get this bag down to Quantico ASAP and have them check it out for us. It's probably nothing, but better to be safe than sorry."

MEET THE PEOPLE

"Cue camera number one!" the set director's voice announces. "Bring the lights down just a little! Everyone! On my mark, five, four, three, two, one, and . . . you're on."

"Good morning, and welcome to *Meet the People*. I'm Tim Clark and our guests this morning are Senator Atkins, Chairman of the Health Care Committee, and Congressman Knowles of Atlanta, who serves on the House Armed Services Committee. We would like to get their opinions on the current health crisis facing the nation."

Tim turned to the senator. "Senator Atkins, welcome to *Meet the People.*"

With his famous, charming smile, Senator Atkins replied, "Thank you, Tim, for having me. It's always a pleasure."

"Senator, as you know we have a health crisis in the country right now and as Chairman of the Health Care Committee, what is your take on this unknown virus?"

"Tim, I'm not so sure that it is a virus, even though the medical community is telling us that. It appears to me that we may be looking at a bio-terrorism situation here and I don't see anyone in the White House addressing that issue."

"Are you saying, Senator, that the administration is ignoring the possibility that this flu-like virus could possibly be biological?"

"What I'm saying, Tim, is that no one seems to have a clue and we have people dying all over the country. I believe the total amount of fatalities as of today is near thirty and climbing; I also know that this virus has appeared in Britain as well. Now, don't you think it's strange that the two countries that Middle Eastern terrorists hate the most are the only two that are suffering with this disease?"

"Senator," Tim interjected, "let me take you back to an interview that you did last April. In that interview, you said and I quote, 'There has only been one bio-terrorism event in this country: when some whacko put botulism in a salad bar. Although it is a possibility we will see a bio-terrorism event again, I do not believe it is a probability.' Senator, have you changed your position on bio-terrorism?"

"Tim, I did say that back then, but regarding what we are faced with today--and with no answers—I'm saying that this is a possibility that should be explored."

"Thank you, Senator, for coming in this morning." "Thank you, Tim."

"Our next guest is Congressman Knowles from Atlanta, senior member of the Armed Services Committee. Welcome, Congressman Knowles, to *Meet the People*."

"Thank you, Tim. Nice to be here."

"Congressman, you just heard Senator Atkins allude that the current crisis we are going through could be terrorist related. What are your thoughts on this?"

"Tim, on my committee we consider any type of weapon of mass destruction as a potential threat to our nation, including biological agents. As far as whether this current situation falls into that category, I would prefer not to speculate, but rather to wait for the report from our CDC in Atlanta. Once they have identified what this thing is, then we will know whether it is just another SARS-type scare or whether we have a real terrorist threat on our hands."

"Congressman, they are already referring to the virus as an epidemic. Do you believe that this outbreak, if you will, is reaching epidemic proportions?"

"Absolutely, Tim. We have a full-blown crisis here and it isn't letting up. There are more cases reported every day and the death toll is rising." The seriousness of the situation could be seen in the Congressman's eyes as he added, "We definitely have an epidemic on our hands."

"Folks, you heard it from both houses right here. We have an epidemic on our hands, and there is a strong possibility that it is the result of an act of bio-terrorism. The Congressmen would rather wait until the Center for Disease Control announces its results before going so far as to say that this is an act of terrorism. This is Tim Clark. Thank you for tuning in. See you next time on *Meet the People*."

ERIE COUNTY MEDICAL CENTER

Air Force One landed at Buffalo Niagara International Airport on Sunday morning while Tim Clark was doing his show. President Doyle had watched the entire show while in flight. He was always amazed at how quickly people could jump to conclusions, and often simply because they might not be privy to exactly what was being done about a situation. Senator Atkins had no idea how diligently Bob Roche and his people were following this crisis. If there was a terrorist connection, Bob would certainly find it, and it would not be kept from the American public.

President Sean Doyle stepped off the aircraft with his wife, Maggie, and proceeded to the private terminal area. There they were met by an Air Force Colonel who helped them board one of the choppers that the President had at his service. The flight from the airport to Erie County Medical Center was only five minutes. The Center had its own helipad, and flying was faster and more efficient than taking a limousine down the Kensington Expressway.

As they climbed in altitude, Sean looked down at all of the familiar landmarks he had known growing up in Erie County. To the right was the University of Buffalo, where he had gone to college. Far out to his left was the town of Orchard Park, where the Buffalo Bills played at Ralph Wilson Stadium. Sean was proud of his hometown, with all it had been through financially over too many years. It still seemed to survive. Buffalo had also produced two other Presidents besides him: Grover Cleveland and Millard Fillmore. Not too many cities could make that claim.

Before Sean could even think about asking how much further, the chopper began its descent. They were landing at Erie County Medical Center. As the First Lady and the President stepped off the helicopter, they were met by their daughter-in-law, Barb, who burst into tears at the sight of her in-laws.

"Oh, Maggie! What am I going to do?" Barb wailed. "He's so sick and people are dying right and left! I'm falling apart!"

Maggie held her, and Barb could not stop sobbing. The President put his arm around her and said, "Barb, we are going to get through this and so is Kevin. He is one tough guy and if anyone can beat this, he can. Now let's go in and see him. You don't want him to see you crying, do you?"

"Mr. President, it's so tough. The kids don't understand what's going on. They see all this crap on the television and they keep asking, 'When is Daddy coming home?' Kevin's friend, Tom, is on life support and they don't have much hope for him. Kevin doesn't know that; he's in and out of it most of the time so he doesn't know too much anyway."

Maggie had tears in her eyes as she reached for Barb's hand. She thought, *what is poor Tom's mother going through at this moment?* Then she said, "Barb, let's go on in. We must all be strong for Kevin."

The Secret Service guided the Doyles into a limousine for the short drive around the rear of the facility where they took a private elevator to the seventh floor. Dr. Byrne met them at the elevator and introduced himself to the President and First Lady.

"Mr. President, I'm afraid you and the First Lady will not be able to go in until we cover you both in gowns and masks."

"Of course, Dr. Byrne. We understand. Show us the way. We want to see our son."

Maggie and Sean were directed to put on two gowns, one backward and the other frontward. They then donned green booties, such as are worn in surgery. Next, they put on surgical caps and latex gloves and finally, a mask that covered everything but their eyes. Dr. Byrne then led them into Kevin's room where his brother, Brendan, was sitting like a mummy at his bedside.

When he saw his parents enter, Brendan jumped up and greeted them with a hug. The President could sense that Brendan had probably been here day and night; seeing only Brendan's eyes told Sean that he had done a lot of crying. The President looked over at the bed and saw his youngest son, who looked almost twenty pounds lighter than the last time he had seen him. His gray pallor did not look human. He was hooked up to a heart monitor, IV's, and had an oxygen tube in his nose. He was sleeping and his breathing was very labored.

Maggie put her arm around Sean's shoulder, pulled him aside and whispered, "My God, Sean, he looks terrible. I just want to hug him and make him feel better; I feel so helpless. What are we going to do?"

Sean pulled her to him and said, "Maggie, the best thing we can do for Kevin is to pray to God that he will spare our son and give him back to us."

At that moment, Barb entered the room and motioned for the Doyles to come out into the hall. Once there, Barb fell apart, weeping uncontrollably. The President attempted to console her and asked if he could get her a soft drink.

"Mr. President," she sobbed, "I just got word that Tom Conley—Gonzo--passed away about twenty minutes ago."

Brendan howled, "Oh my God, no! Kevin will be devastated! He was the best man in Gonzo's wedding! How are we going to tell him?"

"Brendan," the President calmly said, "we are not going to tell Kevin anything until he is recovered and can deal with it."

Maggie put her arms around Barb and held her until she stopped crying. She thought to herself, *why is God doing this to us? This is tearing families apart across the country, even across the world.*

ONE WEEK LATER

The First Family spent two nights at the Erie County Medical Center, but the vigil did not produce any change in Kevin's condition. He was alert for only a few moments at a time and twice realized that his parents were there, but was too weak to carry on a conversation. President Doyle needed to get back to Washington, but the First Lady was determined to stay until Kevin was at least rid of his fever and conscious. Before leaving to return to the White House, the President accompanied the First Lady to the funeral for Tom Conley. After paying their respects to Tom's widow and children and his mother, the limousine took Sean back to the Buffalo Niagara International Airport and Air Force One. As the jumbo jet lifted off, President Sean Doyle wondered if he would ever see his son alive again.

*   *   *

A National Security Council meeting had been scheduled at 10:00 a.m. that morning. John Doyle, the Director of the Center for Disease Control, was to give a briefing on their progress in identifying the virus. London now had thirty-nine confirmed cases, and the death toll in the United States stood at 157, mostly young people in the prime of their lives. Only three children under the age of eighteen had died, and only four senior citizens. The majority of the deaths were in the twenty-to-forty-year-old age range. Kevin Doyle's category.

The President, back from Buffalo, entered the Situation Room to find John Doyle setting up his PowerPoint presentation. After a brief handshake and a "Good morning," John returned to arranging his materials. Bob Roche began the meeting, introducing those whom John Doyle had not met, before turning to John. "We are set to continue any time you're ready, John."

"Thank you, Bob. First, let me say that I do not yet have a definitive answer for you regarding what we are facing, but CDC scientists are very close. I have gathered my most accurate hypothesis to present to you today, but it will be at least a few more days before we can confirm my suspicions."

John clicked to his first slide. "What you are looking at on this slide is bacillus influenzae bacteria, better known as 'the flu.' Back in 1918, the world experienced the worst influenza pandemic in history. Although it was eventually named the Spanish flu, it actually began at Fort Riley, Kansas; the first victim was a soldier who grew up on a farm there. U.S. servicemen who were shipped to the front lines during World War I carried the virus overseas. The Spanish flu spread throughout Europe and the rest of the world over a two year period. Estimates of between thirty and forty million people were victims of this deadly disease. Twenty-five percent of the population in our country was affected and over 500,000 U.S. citizens lost their lives. I might add that the President and I can count our grandparents as two of those victims; both succumbed at the age of thirty-two."

Dr. Doyle advanced the following frame. "In this next slide, you see the demographics of the Spanish flu. The fatalities were predominately in the twenty-to-forty-year-old age group. Most victims were in good health and vibrant prior to contracting the flu. Within six months of the onset, the world had a full-blown influenza pandemic. More deaths were recorded then than during all wars of the previous one hundred years," John revealed.

"In the next slide you will see that identifying the flu was very difficult. At the time, many medical experts argued that the disease was so deadly that it had to be something other than influenza. Some suggested some other type of bacteria or possibly a new microbe. Others questioned, 'Is it even a virus?' In the end, the analysis confirmed that it was indeed influenza, but a strain that had never been seen before. The medical community performed lengthy research and attempted to use all medications available at that time, but doctors were unable to develop any vaccine capable of combating the disease."

"In this slide," John continued, "you see the symptoms and the progression of the disease. Most victims of the 1918-1919 pandemic began with an overall dizziness, fatigue, and body aches, followed by high fevers ranging to upwards of 104 degrees. A sore throat followed, with an unproductive cough; in the later stages, the lungs filled with a pinkish fluid that the patient coughed up as sputum. In more severe cases, the patient developed pneumonia and suffocated. The length of time between the onset of the flu and death was sometimes only a few days. For others, it was longer, and many also survived the flu. Some of our famous leaders contracted the Spanish flu and survived, including President Woodrow Wilson."

Preparing to conclude his presentation, John began, "Ladies and gentlemen, this has been a quick overview of the Spanish flu pandemic. It is my belief that what we are experiencing across the nation is the return of the Spanish Flu of 1918-19, but as a much stronger strain. I will have confirmation within a few days as to whether I am correct in my analysis. The bad news is that presently, we do not have a vaccine to battle this strain, and to date, none of the antibiotics has had any effect on the current influenza infections. I will take questions now."

"John, George White. I am counsel to the President. How long did you say that the Spanish flu lasted, and how did they contain it back then?"

"Ironically, George, the 1918-1919 flu disappeared as quickly as it appeared. In 1919, cities began to report fewer and fewer cases until one day there were no more reports and it was simply gone. We don't know how or why. It just disappeared," John explained, before turning his attention to the next speaker.

"Dr. Doyle, what about the second part of Mr. White's question? What precautions did people take to avoid getting the flu?" Ken Sitarek asked.

"The government cancelled all events where people would normally gather in large crowds, such as Broadway shows and theaters and sporting events. All citizens were asked to stay at home and if they had to go out, everyone wore face masks to avoid breathing in the virus. Some of these procedures helped, but the fact remains that we still had one out of four Americans affected by the flu."

The President then asked, "John, if your suspicion is correct and this is in fact the Spanish flu, how long before your people at the CDC develop a vaccine to protect those not afflicted?"

"Mr. President, it will be at least six months before we can have a vaccine available, and then it would only be in limited supply, probably enough to vaccinate healthcare workers and emergency responders, such as firefighters, police, and EMT's. It would take an additional three months to produce enough for the general population." "John, how many deaths can we expect during that waiting period?" the President asked.

"Mr. President, my best guess would be millions."

"Dr. Doyle, I am Dr. Carey, the Surgeon General. Can you absolutely say that your suspicion of Spanish flu is correct?"

"Dr. Carey, I am about 90 percent sure and with a few more days of testing, I believe my analysis will prove correct."

Bob Roche stood and thanked John Doyle for his presentation. He added, "John, I have a question that I am sure everyone has on his or her mind. Why do you think that this flu strain reappeared after almost ninety years?" "Bob, I don't have the answer to that question. It came about as quickly as it did back in 1918, but we have no information as to how. I will say that at the CDC, we have always believed that it would come back some day, but without samples of the original strain, we have been unable to develop any type of vaccine."

"Thank you again, John, for coming in today. We will be looking forward to hearing from you in a few days once your analysis is complete."

John Doyle packed up his laptop and left the Situation Room. Once the door had closed, Bob Roche re-addressed the council.

"Ladies and gentlemen, our intelligence is developing rapidly and we believe that this flu may have somehow been introduced to the public by a terrorist group operating out of Malaysia and North Africa. Henry Volner, our CIA Director, has learned through his informants in North Africa that there is also a connection in Scandinavia, possibly in Norway. Henry, do you have anything to add today?"

"No, Bob, you pretty well covered it. We're hoping that something will break soon."

"Folks, thank you for coming today. We'll meet again when we hear from Dr. Doyle at the CDC. Meeting adjourned."

DUBAI, UNITED ARAB EMIRATES

At the import/export warehouse in Dubai, Muhammad Sutwa was packing box after box of vials of the deadly virus for shipment to Casablanca. He looked up as his co-conspirator walked through the front door.

"Dr. Zayed, you are a genius. Our mission appears to be complete and a fantastic success, and all because of your work here."

"Mr. Sutwa, you are too kind. It was a team effort. The infidels will suffer greatly. They will be unable to fight us at this level. We are superior in every way. The stupid pigs have no idea what they are up against. Our new strain is weaponized and they will be unable to fight it without the original, which only we have. I believe we can tell Mr. Kabigting that this mission is accomplished. Millions of infidels will die and Allah will be pleased."

At that moment, Muhammad Sutwa's cell phone rang and he answered, "Praise Allah," when he recognized the incoming number on his display.

"Praise Allah," Kemal answered. "We have carried out a successful operation and now it is time to dismantle your lab and leave no trace of what you have accomplished."

"We are in the midst of doing that, Kemal, but we will also keep the strain for future operations."

"Thank you, Muhammad. Be safe and careful. We will meet in Malaysia and celebrate together."

Having informed Kemal, Sutwa and Dr. Zayed began the chore of packing everything that was in the lab and labeling the boxes "Best of Dubai." These would be shipped to a remote location outside of Dubai where, two days later, they would be unloaded for destruction and incinerated, all evidence destroyed.

"Dr. Zayed, say goodbye to your home of the last twelve months. Our limousine is waiting to take us to the airport. You shipped the cryogenic tube also, yes?"

"Yes, Muhammad, the diplomatic courier picked it up one hour ago. It is on its way to Malaysia as we speak." "Excellent, Dr. Zayed. Let's be on our way."

The warehouse on Al Rasheed Blvd. faded into the distance as the limousine driver transported his passengers to the airport. The basement lab, if ever discovered, would reveal only a few walk-in coolers and nothing else. The rest of the warehouse appeared as it was: a legitimate import and export business.

FIRST FAMILY QUARTERS

It had been two days since John Doyle had made his presentation to the National Security Council. Sean Doyle was getting impatient for a confirmation from John. As he paced up and down in his private study, the phone rang. He picked it up on the second ring.

"This is the President."

"Mr. President, an urgent call for you from Dr. Doyle at the CDC."

"Thank you, Ms. Woods, please put him through."

"Mr. President, John here."

"Good evening, John. Do you have news for me?"

"Yes, Mr. President, but I am afraid it's not good. Further etiological testing of the aerosolized samples has confirmed that what we are dealing with is, in fact, the Spanish flu. However, there is more bad news. The strain we're researching is much stronger than the original Spanish flu and more difficult for the patient to fight off. We lost half a million people back in 1918-19, but millions still survived. This new strain almost looks like it has been weaponized."

"Jesus Christ, John! Are you telling me that this strain has been produced by someone?"

"That's what it looks like, Mr. President. If this is true, then somehow we need to find the original strain in order to know how to combat the new one."

"John, any idea how this may have started or how it was distributed?"

"That is out of my realm, Mr. President. Your spy guys need to find that out. If they do, perhaps we can apprehend the people behind this and produce a vaccine much faster. Meanwhile--and I hate to say it--but we are in for one hell of an epidemic. While my people are working sixteen hours a day now, we're not making much progress."

"John, thank you for your efforts. I need to digest this and discuss it with my national security folks before I announce it to the country. Keep me apprised of any further developments, and may God be with you in your research, John."

"Thank you, Mr. President."

Maggie walked into the study as Sean hung up the telephone. "Sean, you look like you've seen a ghost. What's wrong, luv?"

"Cousin John just called and confirmed that we're dealing with a very deadly strain of the infamous Spanish Flu of 1918-19. He also thinks that it's been weaponized, which means someone has altered the makeup of the flu strain, making it stronger and more resistant to any drugs we currently have to fight it off."

"Sean, what are we going to do about this?"

"Maggie, I wish I knew, I really wish I knew."

Within minutes, the phone rang again. "This is the President."

"Mr. President, Ken Sitarek here. We just listened to a press conference held by Senator Atkins. He's calling for a special meeting of the leadership to discuss what we're doing about the crisis. He wants you to come up to the Hill, or they'll come to the White House, your choice."

"Ken, tell him we'll meet with him the day after tomorrow. I've received word from John Doyle confirming his suspicion that we have a reappearance of the Spanish flu. He told me that this strain is much stronger than the original; he suspects that someone has weaponized it. I need to get on the networks and speak to the nation about this, but first let's get the staff in here and decide exactly what I'll say at the press conference. Thereafter, can you set it up as soon as possible?"

"Certainly, Mr. President. I'll call the Senator and set up the meeting for Thursday. Where would you prefer to meet with the leadership?"

"Let's convene in the Situation Room."

"Will do, Mr. President."

Sean Doyle replaced the receiver and looked at his wife. "Maggie, this will be the biggest challenge of my Presidency: trying to explain to the nation what we have learned." After a very pensive pause, Sean looked at his wife and said, "Luv, I have been so preoccupied with this threat that I haven't asked you: how is Kevin doing? Any further word from Dr. Byrne?"

Maggie said, "He called this morning and said there was some improvement right after I flew back last evening, but doctors have observed that this often happens with this flu. He could have a relapse at any time, so I'm afraid it's no good news yet. But I'm confident that we'll hear some soon. I plan on flying back to Buffalo tomorrow."

"That's what I love about you, Maggie. You are the ultimate optimist."

The telephone rang once more and Sean answered, "This is the President."

"President Doyle, this is Sherry Katz. We have set up your appearance on the television networks for nine o'clock tonight. The networks were not happy to interrupt their schedules, but we told them that it was a matter of national security and they all agreed to ten minutes. Will that be enough, sir?"

"Sherry, I believe that will be more than enough. I am going to need you to come up here with the rest of the staff and help me prepare, if you don't mind."

"Not at all, Mr. President. I will be there in thirty minutes."

"Thank you, Sherry. See you then."

*   *   *

"Ladies and gentlemen, you are about to hear a message from President Sean Doyle in the Oval Office. We now go to the White House. Here is the President."

"Good evening, my fellow citizens. Tonight, I bring you very grave news. We are at a very serious crossroad in the history of

94

our country. Earlier this month, an unidentified illness appeared in New York City and San Francisco, before spreading throughout the country. We have experienced a high death rate from this deadly disease, now rising into the hundreds. Nothing the medical community has tried in the way of antibiotics has helped the situation. The disease has been resistant to all medication administered to the patients. The end result has often been death. In the more positive cases, the disease has run its course and the patient survives."

Here, Sean glanced away from the camera and placed his hand on the picture frame sitting on his desk. Looking at the photo of his son before returning his focus to the camera, he said, "My own son, Kevin, has been in the Erie County Medical Center's Intensive Care Unit for two weeks. The prognosis is that he may survive. The longer a patient lives, the better chance of his or her survival.

"I am here tonight to inform you that the Center for Disease Control in Atlanta has isolated the virus and has identified it as the same Spanish flu that caused close to forty million deaths across the world back in 1918-1919. Unfortunately, the Spanish flu disappeared then before scientists were able to develop a vaccine. The CDC has long been convinced that the Spanish flu would return some day; it appears they were right. We were informed that this new strain is much stronger than the original flu. The CDC is using its every available resource, with three shifts working around the clock, to develop a vaccine and we hope and pray that it will be soon.

"In the interim, I ask all of you, my fellow citizens, to be extremely cautious when out in public. Wear a HEPA mask—HEPA is the acronym for High Efficiency Particulate Air—to filter out any possible infection. Avoid large public events where you may be exposed to the flu. Whenever possible, stay at home and avoid any contact that may put you in danger.

"With the help of our Center for Disease Control, we will fight this disease and eradicate it. Thank you for listening. God Bless America."

The President's words sent the network's talking heads scrambling for details on the Spanish flu. Telephone lines at the White House were jammed with citizens calling for additional facts. The Internet was slowed considerably, and the CDC website was shut down for the evening; it simply could not handle the millions of hits it was taking. People were searching for any information they could find.

PANIC IN THE STREETS

On the evening following the President's talk from the Oval Office, the entire hour of *Dan Quigley Reports* was devoted to the Spanish flu and the current epidemic.

Quigley opened his show dramatically. "There is panic in the streets of America tonight. After President Doyle's address to the nation last night, a frenzied rush to find as much information about the Spanish flu ensued. The horror stories coming out of the archives have added fuel to the fire and our citizenry is beginning to panic. The fact that scientists and other medical professionals do not have a vaccine to inoculate people has communities terrified. The number of Spanish flu cases has risen dramatically, along with the death toll. There are now 1,251 cases reported throughout the New England area and there are 2,184 cases in the western states. There were demonstrations in Boston, New York, Chicago, and Los Angeles today demanding that the government do something about the crisis.

"On another front, the CDC today called to quarantine certain areas of the country that have been hit the hardest. Most localities have a designated, quarantined hospital where all flu victims are sent so that neighboring facilities are not contaminated. All patients admitted to other hospitals are initially screened to ascertain whether they have any flu symptoms and if so, are immediately sent to the designated hospital for treatment. President Doyle's own son is in one of those quarantine facilities in Buffalo, New York, where forty deaths have already been reported.

"The CDC has recommended cancelling all public events, and has suggested that everyone wear masks, reminiscent of the SARS scare a few years ago. It has also implemented strict, protective measures for the healthcare workers who are treating the victims.

"Reports from the World Health Organization indicate that the flu has now spread to Europe. Like the Spanish Flu of 1918-1919, most fatalities around the world have been in the twenty-to-forty-year-old age group."

Dan hesitated for a few seconds, adjusting his headset. "We now have a late-breaking story from our Washington Bureau. Jane Temple, can you hear me?"

"Yes, Dan, I can. We now have video footage as well."

"Jane, what can you tell us about this breaking news out of Washington?"

"Dan, we have it on very good authority that the CIA has identified a terrorist cell that appears to have operated out of Norway, cooperating with another cell in the United Arab Emirates. Our sources tell us that these terrorist cells could have something to do with the current Spanish flu crisis."

"Do we know, Jane, how these cells may be involved?" Dan asked.

"Dan, it is merely speculation at this time, but these cells could have been responsible for manufacturing the current flu strain and may have been instrumental in its distribution here and abroad. We do not have confirmation of that, however."

"Thank you, Jane, for that report. Ladies and gentlemen, are we looking at a terrorist attack here? Stay tuned to CNN for further developments."

*   *   *

The following day, Congressional leaders arrived at the White House for their briefing on the crisis. Bob Roche was chosen to give the presentation to the Senators and Congressmen and women. Bob did not pull any punches with these tough politicians.

"We are facing something that we presently cannot control. Unless the CDC can come up with a vaccine and very soon, our nation will suffer the worst crisis in its history, including all of the wars, terror attacks such as 9/11, and the Spanish flu pandemic back in 1918-1919."

Senator Atkins asked, "Now Mr. Roche, we know how hard your staff is working to tie down this terrorist connection, but what kind of progress are you making or is this top secret?"

"Senator, as members of the U.S. Senate and Congress, we are not holding anything back from you. It may be secret to the general public, but we have no intention of keeping you in the dark, sir. The fact is that we have identified a terrorist cell operating in Norway. You may wonder, 'Why Norway?' We understand from Dr. Doyle at the CDC that an expedition was led there nearly ten years ago to explore the possibility of finding the Spanish flu strain in bodies buried below the permafrost level."

Senator Atkins put both hands up to indicate a stop and said, "Whoa, whoa, whoa, Mr. Roche! You're beyond my comprehension level! What does this have to do with the terrorists?"

"Well, Senator, we know this: the current flu strain has somehow been weaponized. We suspect that the terrorist cell found the original strain and cultured it to what we have today."

Congressman Marino of New York City asked, "Mr. Roche, what exactly are we doing with this information?"

"Sir, Dr. Doyle is putting together an expedition to Norway to investigate our suspicions. We already know the locations of some of the graves from the failed expedition ten years back. It is a shot in the dark, but a better option than anyone else has been able to come up with." "Mr. Roche," Senator Atkins said, "I want to thank you, on behalf of the leadership, for your straightforward approach to this situation. This is what we needed to report back to our constituents. We won't mention terrorism until you allow us to, but we will still be able to relay that the CDC is doing everything possible to develop the vaccine. I guess 'patience' will be the word of the day from now on. Thank you, sir, and good day.""Thank you, Senator."

A Presidential aide entered the room and whispered to Bob Roche that the President wanted to see him in the Oval Office. Bob excused himself from the meeting and made his way to President Doyle's office.

"Come on in, Bob."

"You wanted to see me, Mr. President?"

"Yes, Bob, good news. My son Kevin has improved significantly. He is alert, sitting up, and taking nourishment on his own."

"Sir, that's wonderful news! I'm very happy for you. Let's hope he's back to normal soon."

"Thanks, Bob. Now, tell me how the meeting went with the leadership. Sorry I was called away to take that call about Kevin, but when I left the room, I had the impression they were going to put you over the coals."

"On the contrary, sir. They were attentive and appreciative that we were above board with them. Senator Atkins especially complimented our approach. I think he was simply relieved to be able to go back home and report something positive."

"What might that be, Bob?"

"Mr. President, I told them that the CDC will be heading up an expedition to Norway to look for the original strain of the flu virus."

"Oh, that's a good decision, Bob. Glad you passed that on to them. What about the terrorist issue?"

"The Senator agreed to keep that quiet until we are ready to announce it."

"It sounds to me, Bob, that we're all on the same page. It's up to John Doyle to come through now."

MEET THE PEOPLE

"Good morning, everyone. I'm your host, Tim Clark, and this is *Meet the People*. Our subject today is the Spanish flu epidemic and what is being done to control it. Our guests today are Dr. John Doyle, Director of the Center for Disease Control in Atlanta, Georgia, and Dr. Richard Carey, Surgeon General of the United States. Good morning, gentlemen."

"Good morning, Tim," both men responded in unison.

"Dr. Doyle, let me begin with you. We understand that you suspect this virus is the Spanish Flu of 1918-1919 reappearing after all these years. How did you determine that initially?"

"Tim, I've studied the Spanish flu my entire career. In fact, I did my thesis many years ago on infectious diseases that never had a cure. The Spanish flu was the disease that I concentrated on most; I've been researching this virus on a regular basis ever since."

"Is it true, Dr. Doyle, that your preoccupation with the Spanish flu was a result of your grandparents succumbing to the flu back in 1919?"

"That certainly had an influence on me, but I would not say it was the only reason. You see, the flu killed so many people worldwide that it stands out in history as the most deadly and most devastating plague of all time. Even the Black Plague did not approach the destruction of human life that the Spanish flu caused, and yet very few people, until this past month, were even aware of the Spanish flu."

"Dr. Doyle, what can you tell us about the progress in developing a vaccine for this new strain of the flu?"

"As you may know, Tim, a vaccine was never developed for the original Spanish flu and after killing millions of people, it just disappeared. About ten years ago, an expedition to Norway was led by a doctor from Canada who attempted to exhume the bodies of Spanish flu victims who were believed to be buried below the permafrost level." "And what success did the doctor have, Dr. Doyle?" "Unfortunately, the flu strain was unable to be recovered, as the bodies were not buried completely below the permafrost. If they had, the plan was to extract samples of the flu strain and bring them back to the States to develop a vaccine.

"Next week," Dr. Doyle continued, "I will lead another expedition to Longyearbyen to explore once more whether we can locate any bodies below the permafrost. If we are successful, we will then seal the samples in cryogenic tubes and bring them back to Atlanta."

"Dr. Carey, let me turn to you for a moment. Assuming that Dr. Doyle here is successful in developing a vaccine, how long do you think it will take to get the vaccine out to the general public?"

"Our best estimates, Tim, are that the vaccine will take at least six months to develop and that we will not have enough for the general public until three to six months beyond then."

"Dr. Carey, are you saying we may have to wait for a year to control this virus?"

"That is a firm possibility, Tim, I'm sorry to say."

"Once the vaccine is available," Tim asked, "how will it be distributed?"

"The distribution procedures have long been in place. Ever since the threat of smallpox, local health departments across the country have drawn up implementation plans to inoculate an entire county of one million people over a seven day period."

"And how would the Federal Government get the vaccine out to the local municipalities?"

"The same plan that we would use for the National Pharmaceutical Stockpile would be implemented to distribute the vaccine. This is one area where we have been prepared for many years now," said Dr. Carey.

"It sounds like the distribution would run smoothly, Dr. Carey, but we need that vaccine developed quickly. Gentlemen, thank you for appearing this morning on *Meet the People*. To all of you out there, thank you for watching. This is Tim Clark. See you next week on *Meet the People*."

THE CABINET ROOM

President Doyle began his Cabinet meeting by saying, "Before we hear reports from the FBI and CIA, I wanted to apprise everyone of my recent conversation with Dr. John Doyle at the CDC. John tells me that the epidemic has now spread to the following countries: Canada, the U.K., France, Italy, Spain, Switzerland, Germany, and Japan. Estimates of over twenty thousand victims throughout the European Union and Japan have been reported. With that many victims, the death toll will rise rapidly.

"John also reported that his team will leave tomorrow for Longyearbyen, Norway to begin the search for any bodies buried below the permafrost. As you may know, this location was a mining community, and many miners came there from Europe in the early 1900's looking for work. In 1918, the flu spread rapidly through the community, carried there by these migrant workers. John is not sure how many, if any, graves he will find, but he does know of some that were already opened during the expedition in 1994, so he assumes there will be more. Mr. Volner, would you like to begin the CIA report?"

"Thank you, Mr. President. We have learned from our informants that a terrorist cell directed from somewhere in Malaysia was operating in the same area of Norway where Dr. Doyle will be traveling. Another cell was active in the United Arab Emirates in the city of Dubai. We believe the two were working together and that they may have produced the flu strain we're fighting. Working with the FBI, we plan to raid the warehouse where they are suspected of operating. We should have more information for you by tonight."

"Thank you, Mr. Volner. Mr. Graham, what do you have for us from the FBI?"

Ted Graham was a hulk of a man. A middle-linebacker for Purdue in college and an officer in the Marine Corps during Desert Storm, Graham joined the FBI soon after his return from the Persian Gulf. He was a no-nonsense guy and as Director of the FBI, he was being strongly considered for the position as the next Director of Homeland Security when the current Director retired in two years. Ted rose to speak, and his six-foot-six frame cast a shadow across the table from the sunlight flowing through the window behind him.

"Folks, we honestly don't have a lot to report to you, at least nothing earth-shattering. You heard from Mr. Volner that we will be raiding this warehouse in Dubai in a few hours. On the home front, our agents are convinced that the flu virus was distributed by terrorist agents who were passengers on various airliners. One flight in particular was Northeast Airlines 897 from Tampa, arriving at LaGuardia in New York City a few days before the first victims were taken ill. The initial report of the patients by a Dr. Simpson at St. Vincent's Hospital identified that the only commonality among these victims was that they were all staying at the Roosevelt Hotel in Manhattan. Well, the fact is that they were also on flight 897 together and flew into LaGuardia not as a group, but on the same plane.

"We have recently recovered an overnight bag that was found after the passengers were deplaned. It was in an overhead compartment and had a few items in it, including a shaving kit with razor blades. That put up the red flag a little late, but we have sent the items to the

CDC in Atlanta and they have reported back to us that the shaving cream container had a false bottom in it. They are testing it right now to see if anything was dispersed from it while in flight.

"We have also contacted San Francisco International Airport and advised them to check their inventory of items to see if they have recovered anything suspicious. Of the ten original victims in the Bay area, six of them were on the same flight from Malaysia, with a stop in Honolulu, and arriving in San Francisco the day before they were admitted to the hospital. The coincidence is too strong to ignore the fact that we may have had dispersal devices on numerous aircraft over the past month."

"But Director Graham," the Surgeon General asked, "how could they have gotten them past TSA and onto the plane?""That is exactly what we are investigating, Dr. Carey. We hope to have an answer for you very soon."

President Doyle thanked Director Graham and Director Volner and suggested that they meet again the next day for another update.

*　　　*　　　*

The following morning, the FBI and CIA reported that a warehouse in Dubai had been raided. A hidden room below the structure with two walk-in coolers appeared to have been recently vacated. The FBI arrested three suspects and after intense questioning, they confessed to being members of an organization that had former ties with al-Qaida. One of the suspects told agents that his cell had exhumed bodies from graves somewhere in Norway and had shipped them to Dubai in cryogenic containers large enough to hold the bodies and keep them in their frozen state.

The room below the warehouse was used as a laboratory where technicians took samples of the flu from the preserved corpses and then cultured them and produced the flu strain. He did not know where the product was shipped to from Dubai. Upon further inspection, the import/export company records showed numerous shipments to a location in Casablanca. FBI agents were dispatched to Morocco to investigate further.

NORWAY EXPEDITION

The outdoor temperature at St. Gustaf's Cemetery was only 18 degrees when John Doyle and his team arrived two days earlier. Fortunately, it was not late in the season and they would be able to unearth the graves without much trouble until they reached the permafrost level. The graves of the seven miners who had died in the fall of 1918 were located by the CDC Team and every precaution was now being taken to very carefully exhume the bodies. Hazardous materials personal protective equipment was provided for all team members, who each wore fully encapsulated level "A" suits, and self-contained-breathing-apparatuses, or SCBA's, as they were known. This protection was necessary for the members completing the exhumation, as well as for the bodies that had hopefully been preserved. There was no desire to contaminate the miners. The team wanted to exhume the bodies intact; assuming they were frozen, the bodies would be well-preserved. Once the exhumation was complete, the corpses would immediately be placed into cryogenic tubes and shipped back to Atlanta.

The team had been digging for over an hour when John Doyle arrived at the scene.

"How are we progressing, Dr. Austin?" John asked. Austin had been with the CDC for ten years and an assistant to John for the past four. He looked at John Doyle and said, "We're about halfway down, Dr. Doyle. I would say about another hour and we should be at the permafrost level and then we will know if this expedition is a success."

"Dr. Austin, I'll be in the tent, trying to keep warm. Give me a signal as soon as you know something."

"Will do, Dr. Doyle."

Forty-five minutes later, John's attention turned to Dr. Austin, who was waving at him somewhat frantically. John bolted from his table and trudged through the snow over to the set of graves.

"Have you reached the permafrost, Dr. Austin?"

"Dr. Doyle, I'm afraid I have bad news for you. We have indeed reached the permafrost level, but there are no bodies in these graves. There are wooden boxes, but they're empty. It appears that someone has beaten us to them, Doc."

John peered into the first grave. "Shit. I should have suspected this. The FBI did tell us that the terrorist cell was operating somewhere in Norway. We're not dealing with stupid people here. They had to know about the 90's expedition. It was well-documented at the time."

"What do we do now, Dr. Doyle?"

"First thing, Dr. Austin, is for me to call and inform the President. Then we're going to search throughout this cemetery."

"And what are we searching for, Dr. Doyle?"

"Our team will scour St. Gustaf's Cemetery until we find any graves dated late 1918 or early 1919. Maybe we'll find another victim or two who died of the Spanish flu." "But how will we know, Dr. Doyle? We can't just dig up any grave we find without permission. How will we know how these people died?"

"Dr. Austin, we're going to need a little luck and a lot of help from God. Get our team on it right away and let's see what we can find."

John Doyle hurried back to his tent, where the temperature was nearly fifty degrees warmer. "Shit," he exhaled again, his favorite curse word, and reached for his satellite phone. As he dialed the private number, he thought about the time difference. The President would be starting his day back in Washington.

"This is the President."

"Good morning, Mr. President. I hope I didn't interrupt your breakfast."

"Not at all, John. I've just about finished my morning bagel and I'm almost done with my coffee. Then I'm headed downstairs to the Oval Office. Tell me something good, John. You located the bodies and they are below the permafrost?"

"Not exactly, Mr. President. We've located the graves and were successful in excavating down to the permafrost, but the bodies are no longer there."

"What the hell? John, are you saying someone took the bodies?"

"Yes, Mr. President, that's exactly what I'm saying. The wooden coffins were still in the graves, but they were all empty. It appears the terrorist cell got to them before we did. My suspicion is that they probably shipped the bodies frozen to Dubai and were able to manufacture the flu virus in their lab."

The President let out an audible sigh and said, "John, what's the next step? We have people dying by the hundreds. We need something positive to tell the general public."

"Yes, sir, I know. Our team is searching the cemetery as we speak for graves dated 1918 or 1919. Then we will check with the caretaker for records to determine who is buried there and how he or she died."

"John," the President asked, "do you really think that we might find another corpse containing the flu virus still frozen and preserved?"

"Yes, Mr. President, I don't believe that these are the only seven graves that held flu victims. If the terrorist cell was successful in the exhumation and manufacture of this weaponized flu strain, then we have an excellent chance of locating and exhuming a body to manufacture a vaccine."

"John, I wish I had your confidence, but I trust your judgment and expertise. I am relying on you to come up with a solution to this tragic event."

"Thank you for your confidence, Mr. President. I'll get back to you as soon as we have something."

Sean Doyle replied, "Thank you, John," and put the telephone down.

Sean turned back to his now lukewarm coffee and raised the television volume in time to catch a CNN report regarding John's expedition.

"We have just received word that members of Dr. John Doyle's expedition team in Norway have discovered the graves they were looking for. After unearthing the graves, however, and finding the coffins, they have reported that there were no remains in the crude wooden boxes. Dr. Austin, the scientist in charge of the exhumation, has informed CNN that the team will continue to search the cemetery for other possible victims of the Spanish flu. Later."

"Shit!" Sean bellowed, and slammed his coffee cup down on the table, spilling the remaining contents. "How in the hell does CNN get this information so quickly? You'd think they had a member on John's team!"

Sean had a very rare craving for a cigarette, a habit he had given up over twenty-five years prior. The craving always came back during times of tremendous tension.

Maggie leaned over her husband, and wiped up the spill around his place setting. "Now Sean, you watch your blood pressure. We don't want you to have a stroke. The nation needs your level-headed leadership and I need you more than ever, so please calm down." She bent over and kissed him on the cheek. "I love you," she whispered to her husband. "I love you too, Maggie. I'm just so damn frustrated with this entire situation. We need something positive and we need it soon or we are going to have a country completely out of control."

STATE OF EMERGENCY

Sherry Katz stepped up to the podium and the news room became very still. "Ladies and gentlemen of the press: Here is the President of the United States."

Sean Doyle walked into the room from the right of the podium and adjusted the microphone.

"I have always believed that the press and I have had a good relationship, and I hope that continues. I will add, however, that I never dreamed we would be meeting on such a regular basis." There was a murmur of agreement from the press corps. The President reached up and smoothed his club tie before continuing.

"If you will allow me, I'd like to make a brief statement before I take any questions. Early this morning, Dr. John Doyle, the Director of the Center of Disease Control, telephoned me from Norway to report the progress of the expedition there to find samples of the Spanish flu that is presently and ferociously attacking our country. I am sorry to say that we do not have any good news yet, but we are confident that Dr. Doyle and his team will ultimately be successful. The number of cases of the flu in the United States has quintupled just this past week and we now have nearly twenty thousand deaths attributed to the virus. The European Union has reported to us that their death toll is over seventeen thousand. The other major countries around the world are reporting similar numbers. "As of tonight," the President continued, "I am declaring a National Emergency throughout the country. This declaration will impose severe, yet necessary, restrictions on our society, but will also allow the local governments to apply for Federal assistance through our Homeland Security Department."

"Additionally, it has been suspected for some time that the current virus situation is the result of a terrorist plot and subsequent attack. Directors of the CIA and the FBI have confirmed that suspicion: the flu was, in fact, spread by a terrorist cell formerly connected to the al-Qaida organization. Our intelligence has uncovered a location in Dubai, United Arab Emirates, where we believe this flu strain was produced. It is unfortunate that the people responsible had already fled when our agents arrived. They are on the run, but we will track them down and bring them to justice, so help me God. Our agents are hot on their trail; it is only a matter of time before we have them apprehended. I want to ask all Americans to have patience, though I know how difficult that is for us at this time. We need time to battle this enemy and bring this situation to a rapid conclusion. I will take questions now."

"Mr. President, Connie Fletcher with the London Times.

Is it true, sir, that your Dr. Doyle and his team of experts located graves in Norway, but that they were empty when they were uncovered?"

"Yes, Ms. Fletcher, that is correct. The graves were empty and the team is seeking other graves to locate additional victims of the 1918-1919 Spanish Flu."

"Just a follow-up question, sir. Do you really expect after all these years that Dr. Doyle will be able to locate victims and still have a viable flu sample?"

"Ms. Fletcher, I have every confidence in Dr. Doyle. If there is anyone on this earth that can solve this dilemma, it is John Doyle. Next question."

"Mr. President, Dan Quigley of CNN. Reports coming out of Europe indicate panic in the streets, and the paranoia that often comes with this type of situation. There are close to seventeen thousand dead over there and, as you mentioned earlier, twenty thousand dead in the U.S. I would say that throughout the world that figure could be approaching a million within a month. You have just declared a state of emergency. Would you categorize whether what we have—or may be headed for—is a pandemic?"

"Dan, what we have is a definite epidemic. I am not ready to classify it as a pandemic. Our citizens are bravely handling this crisis like true Americans. We will fight this enemy just as we have every other enemy over the past two centuries: with perseverance and bravery. We will overcome this. Next question."

"Mr. President, Josh Gates of ABC News. I've noticed that you do not wear a mask when out in public. Most citizens now have and wear masks. Don't you think that you are sending the wrong message?"

"Good question, Josh. I probably was creating a false sense of security among the American people. I want all of our countrymen to wear protection. After I experienced my son being stricken, I decided that I will wear a mask whenever I am out in public. Just like you, Josh, I would like to be around to enjoy my family. Thanks for asking. That's all for now, folks." The President left the podium and quickly exited through the press room door.

Once back in his office, the President motioned to Sherry to follow him in.

"Sherry, that was an embarrassing question for me. I'm not blaming you, but next time could you brief me on exactly what to expect from the press? I could have circumvented that question by announcing that I would be wearing a mask before I was asked about it."

"Mr. President, I am so sorry. I should have guessed that they would ask you that. I promise I won't let that happen again."

"Thanks, Sherry. I learned a lesson in there and we can both learn from it."

At that moment, George White entered the Oval Office, with Ken Sitarek right behind him. "Mr. President," George said, "you might want to sit down. We have just received word from Dr. Doyle in Norway."

The President seated himself at his mahogany desk. "What is it, George? Tell me, please."

George stepped forward just as Bob Roche entered the office with a confident smile on his face. President Doyle caught the look and turned back to George with anticipation.

"Mr. President," George began again. "Dr. Doyle called while you were holding your press conference and informed us that his team has found another grave and it is below the permafrost level. They have confirmed that there is a perfectly preserved body within, which they have removed and placed into a cryogenic tube to keep it preserved. They will be flying the body back to Atlanta in the morning to begin their examination to locate the flu strain."

"That is wonderful news, George. I knew John would never let us down. One thing, though: Why does everyone look so happy? I understand you would be elated, but Bob here looks overjoyed."

George hesitated and then glanced at Bob Roche. "Do you want me to tell him, or do you want to, Bob?"

"No, George. You seem to be doing fine yourself."

The President said impatiently, "Well, someone tell me!"

This time George sat down. "Mr. President, Dr. Doyle is not sure of this. He wants to check DNA when they return to the CDC, but the name of the person in the located grave was Matthew O'Bannon, and he was buried in 1918. The paperwork at the cemetery office only had his name, death date, and occupation, which was merchant marine."

"Oh my God!" the President exclaimed. "This could not be just a coincidence! The DNA, of course, will prove it, but it has to be our Great-Uncle Matt, who never returned from World War I! Aside from a letter that my great grandmother received almost one year later, he was never heard from again. The family had already lost other children to the flu, but they never knew what happened to Matthew; he had simply disappeared. If it is him, then we will know that he, too, was a victim of the Spanish flu, just like his brother, sister, and brother-in-law. Let's all pray that the virus is intact and that John can begin producing a vaccine. If the body is Uncle Matt's, that would be a bonus to our family after almost a hundred years."

FBI HEADQUARTERS

Ted Graham was always in his office by 6:30 a.m. and today was no exception. The extra ninety minutes before staff arrived allowed him to get a lot of paperwork completed before the phones began to ring and appointments and meetings had to be attended. It was 6:45 when the phone startled Ted as he was attempting to complete an Excel spreadsheet.

"Hello, Graham here."

"Director Graham, this is Agent Terry Crowley. Sorry to interrupt, sir, but this is important and the operator knew you were there so she put me through."

"What can I do for you, Agent Crowley?"

"Well, sir, I am at San Francisco International Airport."

"You're up kind of early, are you not, Agent Crowley? What is it, about quarter to four in the morning?"

"Yes, sir, it is, but we just stumbled onto something regarding the terrorist connection to the flu. At LaGuardia we discovered that

119

a men's shaving cream container was used as a device to release the virus by aerosol, so we've been checking out other airports for leads."

"Yes, Crowley, I'm aware of the investigation. Why did you go to San Francisco from LaGuardia?"

"Sir, after getting the report on the LaGuardia device and learning that the first three flu victims were on the same flight, we began to check all flights. A flight originating in Malaysia with a stop in Honolulu arrived in San Francisco, and the following day there were ten flu victims admitted to the hospital here. Seven of those were on that flight from Malaysia, so we brought our investigation here. That's why I'm calling, sir. After intensive questioning and legwork, we've learned that each of these overseas flights has a standard procedure of spraying a deodorizer throughout the interior of the aircraft prior to landing. Since there were no items found on the JAL flight that would indicate an aerosol device, we took a look at the cans used to disperse this deodorizer. Sir, we sent three of the cans to our lab out here in the Bay area; they have determined that there is the definite residue of a virus that they cannot identify. We've sent the cans to the CDC and should have a report by later today."

"Agent Crowley, that is excellent investigating. Were those cans right off the flight from Malaysia that you mentioned?"

"No. That's the reason I'm calling you direct, sir. These cans came in on a flight from Taiwan the day before yesterday. God knows how many have been used on any number of foreign airlines, and domestic flights as well."

"Thank you for the heads up, Agent Crowley. We have a lot of work to do. Keep us apprised as soon as you get further info."

Director Graham hung up the phone and hit the speed dial button for Bob Roche at the White House. Bob answered on the first ring.

"Roche here."

"Bob, this is Ted Graham. Figured you would be in this early, too."

"Always, Ted. What's up?"

"Just received a call from one of our special agents doing some investigating out in San Francisco. We'll confirm this later today, Bob, but it looks like we are still being infected by this virus on a daily basis and I'm not talking about one person passing it on to another." "What do you mean, Ted?"

"We've discovered that a common aerosol can that dispenses a deodorizing mist to freshen the airliner cabins may be the terrorists' weapon of choice. Hell, they don't even have to be on the flight. Just place the canisters with the regular deodorizer or replace the valid cans before they are loaded on board."

"Ted, let us know as soon as you get confirmation. If this is true, we need to put new directives into motion and as quickly as possible."

"I agree, Bob. With your approval, we will send out a notice to all airlines requesting that no type of aerosol can or device be allowed on any flight, domestic or international."

"You have it, Ted. I'll inform the President as soon as we hang up."

"Thanks, Bob. Talk to you later today."

Bob Roche glanced at the notes he had taken during the conversation, and then pushed the phone button that would connect him directly to President Doyle.

"This is the President."

"Mr. President, I had hoped that you would be at your desk this early. Bob Roche here. Just spoke to Ted Graham and we've determined that aerosol canisters aboard airlines were used to spread the virus. We'll have definite confirmation of this from the CDC this afternoon, but in the meantime, I authorized Ted to go ahead and order all airlines to discontinue the use of these deodorizers or to refuse to even fly an aircraft with an aerosol device on board."

"Good decision, Bob. You have my unqualified support on that. Guess we'd better have another National Security Council meeting. Set it up for later today, after we receive confirmation from the CDC."

"Yes, sir. I'll try for five o'clock."

"Oh, and Bob? Pass that information on to your contact in London. What's his name . . . Martin Harrington?"

"That's right, Mr. President. I'll call Marty right away."

*　　　　*　　　　*

Marty Harrington had just returned from lunch when he received Bob Roche's call.

"Well, I'll be damned. Clever, rotten bastards they are now. Are they not? No wonder the damn thing has spread so fast and to so many countries. This is a bloody disaster, Bob. We need your CDC boys to come up with a vaccine damn fast or we are all going to be dead. It's like the damn bubonic plague."

"I hate to tell you, Marty, but the Spanish flu killed millions more than the plague did. We are in for a long haul here and for so many deaths, it will be unimaginable. It is possible that the terrorists already have a vaccine developed to protect themselves. Can't imagine they would have brought this havoc on around the world without protecting themselves."

"Got that right, old chap. They might be rotten, but they sure as hell are not stupid. Talk to you soon. I will inform the Prime Minister straight away. Thanks for the call."

"Talk to you soon, Marty."

"Hope it is real soon, Bob, and with a solution, no doubt."

NATIONAL SECURITY COUNCIL

Sean Doyle convened his National Security Council meeting at seven o'clock in the evening.

"Folks, I appreciate you all coming out this evening. I'm afraid we'll be having a lot of these late in the day meetings in the future. No doubt, you've all heard the latest developments in our flu crisis. It appears that the situation will only get much worse before it gets better. We're going to have a lot of dark days ahead. Our first big break has come from St. Gustaf's Cemetery in Norway. It is quite ironic that the body exhumed was that of my great-uncle, Matthew O'Bannon. I've received confirmation of that from Dr. John Doyle at the CDC. We now need another break in extracting the flu strain from Matthew's body and comparing it to the current weaponized strain that is rapidly killing people worldwide. Our best guess for developing a vaccine is six months. Considering that we have had twenty thousand deaths in just over five weeks, the death toll is going to rise to enormous numbers by the time we are able to inoculate the country. I will take your reports now."

Director Graham of the FBI was first to speak. "Mr. President, as I reported to you this morning, we have discovered what we think was the device to initially spread the flu. The canisters from the airlines at San Francisco were sent to the CDC and we have received confirmation that they did, in fact, contain the flu strain. This also confirms that these were the devices used to spread the flu on international flights. The terrorist cells that we have been investigating are our suspects in this, and they did not have to be on the plane, as they were back in 2001. The flight attendants were just doing what they have always done in spraying the cabin before landing."

The President nodded and said, "Ted, do we have any further developments on finding these terrorist cells?" "Sir, as you know we raided the facility in Dubai, but they had already cleared out. We have, however, located their receiver's address in Casablanca. That location was also vacated. In checking with one of the major air freight carriers, we found that most of the containers shipped to Casablanca were then shipped to locations throughout the Far East, mostly in Malaysia, Japan, and Taiwan, with some going to Florida. We are investigating the Florida location as we speak. The most unusual part of this entire scenario is that no terrorist organization has come forward and taken credit for this epidemic."

The President frowned and said, "Thank you, Ted. It sounds like your agents have their work cut out for them. We need answers and we need them yesterday. Who's next?"

Dr. Carey, the Surgeon General, leaned forward and said, "Mr. President, I'm afraid the news from the Northeast is not good at all. New York City and Philadelphia have been hit the hardest, with one third of the deaths coming from those two cities. My office has ordered all hospitals quarantined, as well as any other health care facility that has reported any flu cases. Our ability to control this epidemic is extremely limited. The patient either survives after one horrific bout of anywhere from a few days to a few weeks, or succumbs. Death usually occurs quite soon after being diagnosed. The longer the patient survives, the better the chance he or she has of beating the flu. We need a vaccine and we need it soon."

"Thank you, Dr. Carey. Your staff is doing a superb job under monumental circumstances. We pray to God that we will get you that vaccine soon."

Bob Roche spoke next, after reading a note passed to him by one of his staff. "Mr. President, I have word here from the FAA that most of the major airlines have informed us that they will discontinue all flights to the largest cities in the U.S. and all international flights as of tomorrow morning at 7:00 a.m. They are also asking for financial relief, just as they did after 9/11. In only two weeks time, air traffic has dwindled to mostly business travel. People are simply too terrified to travel anywhere."

The door to the Cabinet room opened and George White entered with a grim look on his face; he looked as though he had just experienced a tragic event.

"Mr. President, I'm sorry I'm late, but I have very disturbing news, sir. House Majority Whip Joe Leblanc and three of his staffers have all succumbed to the flu. Leblanc passed away about an hour ago and his staffers all died within the last twenty-four hours. One commonality in the four deaths: they were all in their thirties. Congress has called an emergency joint session for tomorrow morning. Not sure what their agenda is yet, but we're in contact with the Speaker to find out what it is."

The President sighed and massaged his temples, attempting to rub away the stress building behind his eyes. "This is terrible news, George. Have Aggie get Mrs. Leblanc on the phone as soon as we adjourn here so I can offer my condolences. Does anyone have any good news? If not, let's adjourn for the evening."

With that, the meeting broke up and everyone left the room except for the President and George White.

"George, let's get that agenda as soon as we can. I want to know what the Congress plans. I certainly don't want to get blindsided tomorrow. We have enough issues to deal with as it is."

"Will do, Mr. President. It may be late, though, when I get back to you."

"George, no matter what time it is, call me in my family quarters."

"Yes sir, I will."

CAPITOL HILL

The gavel banged loudly three times at exactly nine o'clock the following morning and the joint session of Congress was brought to order. The Speaker of the House introduced Cardinal James O'Malley of the Washington Diocese to give the invocation. After a brief prayer, the Speaker then asked for one minute of silence for the Majority Whip, Congressman Leblanc, and his three staffers. Everybody in attendance wore a HEPA mask, protecting them from the flu virus.

Senator Atkins asked for permission to speak and was given the floor.

"Ladies and gentlemen of the House and Senate, we have gathered here today at this terribly tragic time in the history of our country. Over twenty thousand of our citizens have been taken from us by an evil force. True, we have been in a state of war with terrorists around the globe since President Bush first declared war back in 2001. This new battle is worse than we have ever experienced, and it will continue to get worse before we can adequately fight this disease.

"To date, there is no cure for the Spanish flu that we know of and the CDC advises it will take months before we are able to develop the vaccine and begin inoculation. Meanwhile, thousands more of our countrymen and women will die. We must make every attempt to avoid this horrible disease as we wait for the vaccine," Senator Atkins emphasized.

"I am introducing a resolution today that asks the President of the United States to impose a thirty-day curfew on all public gatherings of any type. Understanding that we are already in a state of emergency throughout the land, this resolution takes us a step further in fighting the spread of this influenza. If enacted, this resolution could eliminate the possibility of spreading this communicable virus from one person to another. To put it bluntly, people will be asked to go only to work and to stay at home otherwise, avoiding all unnecessary contact with each other.

"Mr. Speaker, I would ask that the House approve my resolution and Mr. President of the Senate, I would ask our colleagues to approve it as well. Thank you for recognizing me."

Senator Atkins sat down and there was an immediate round of applause from both sides of the aisle. It was obvious there would be little discussion on the resolution and approval seemed a sure thing.

The resolution was passed unanimously by both the House and the Senate and was sent to the White House for the President's signature. Before adjourning, the joint session of Congress also voted to suspend all meetings of both the House and Senate during the thirty-day period, except for an emergency situation.

Thereafter, all congressmen and women and senators left for their home districts to be with their families during this time of crisis.

President Doyle received the resolution one hour after it was passed and signed it immediately. A press conference was held to announce it to the nation and the President emphasized very strongly that the curfew would be enforced to the letter of the law. All citizens were not to participate in any type of public gathering and were to wear masks at all times when in public or at their workplace.

CNN: ATLANTA

"This is Tom McGinnis at CNN headquarters in Atlanta with the six o'clock report. We have breaking news coming to us from our reporter in Dubai. John Brennan, what can you tell us about this?"

"Tom, we have received a report from the Islamic Satellite TV Network that a breakaway group of al-Qaida has contacted the Islamic Network and is taking credit for the flu epidemic. In a prepared statement, they first praised Allah for his blessings and for guiding them to the destruction of the infidels. The infidels they refer to, of course, are the United States, the United Kingdom, and their allies. In the statement, they claimed they are responsible for what they are calling the 'St. Gustaf flu epidemic.' This obviously is a reference to the cemetery where the flu strain was harvested in upper Norway. They also claim that as a breakaway group, they are much stronger than al-Qaida, and they criticized Osama bin Laden for what they called his 'inept attempt to follow through with his threats after the 9/11 victory.'

"In a related story, Tom, we also have word from the Islamic network that al-Qaida has promised more terror threats, saying 'we will attack the American pigs while they are weakened by this epidemic.'"

"John, thank you for that breaking news report. We will be back to you in the next hour for an update."

"Thanks, Tom. This is John Brennan reporting from Dubai."

"Back to the home front. We have heard from reliable sources at the CDC here in Atlanta that the death toll could rise to one million within six months time. If you recall, that is the time frame that experts have informed officials that it will take to develop the vaccine. More on this later in *Dan Quigley Reports* in the next hour.

"On signing the curfew resolution passed by Congress, the President today asked all public venues to cooperate with officials in maintaining the curfew. The theater district in New York City has closed down indefinitely, along with Radio City Music Hall and all other entertainment venues in New York. The New York metropolitan area has been hit the hardest, with as many as four thousand deaths in five weeks time.

"We now have more breaking news from right here in Atlanta at the Center for Disease Control. We understand that Dr. John Doyle, the Director of the CDC, is about to hold a news conference and we will take you there right now."

Standing in his white lab coat, John Doyle adjusted the microphone and began to speak.

"Ladies and gentlemen, we are here to announce that we have isolated the flu strain and have frozen it while we continue to develop a vaccine. This evening we were able to identify the strain from the body of Matthew O'Bannon, who died in Norway in the fall of 1918. His body had been buried below the permafrost level and was preserved. We shipped the body back here to Atlanta in a cryogenic container, where we then isolated and extracted the flu strain from his remains. Our next procedure is to compare our strain to the weaponized strain that the terrorists developed in their lab in

Dubai. Hopefully, we will soon have a vaccine that will combat this weaponized version. I will now take any questions."

"Dr. Doyle, Sam Piza from the Associated Press. A terrorist group just tonight is taking credit for this epidemic and they are calling it the 'St. Gustaf flu.' Can you explain why?"

John smirked and said, "Sam, what we are dealing with is the original Spanish Flu of 1918-19. As I have explained, the terrorists have weaponized the flu strain, making it much stronger than the original and more difficult to combat. While they have named their weaponized version the 'St. Gustaf flu,' it is still the Spanish flu, only more deadly."

"Dr. Doyle, Claudia Engles from MSNBC. Is it true, sir, that it will take the CDC at least six months to develop the vaccine to fight the flu and can we expect up to a million deaths by the time we are ready to distribute the vaccine?"

"Claudia, both questions are difficult to confirm. The six month period to develop the vaccine is a guesstimate at best. Depending on how well the President's directives are carried out, the death toll could be much smaller than some are predicting. We are not sure of anything right now, except that we do have the strain isolated and will begin developing the vaccine immediately. There is always a very slight chance that we will get lucky and this flu will go away as quickly as it came. It will not be distributed by the terrorists any longer, now that we have confirmed how it was transmitted: via standard airline aerosolization procedures."

"Dr. Doyle, Mark Gibbs from CNN. Can you tell us if the general public will be kept informed as to the progress of your development? Will you be holding regular press conferences such as this one so you can keep the panic down to a somewhat manageable degree?"

"Yes, Mark, we will be keeping you informed on a regular basis. In addition, anyone can go to our web site at the CDC and click on the Spanish flu icon for continuing updates." With that, Dr. Doyle stepped away from the podium.

"That's all from Dr. John Doyle at the CDC. This is Tom McGinnis back at CNN headquarters in Atlanta. You have been watching a news conference at the Center for Disease Control here in Atlanta where Dr. John Doyle announced that the CDC has isolated the original Spanish flu strain in the exhumed body of Matthew O'Bannon, who died in 1918 in upper Norway. Mr. O'Bannon had been reported missing while working aboard a freighter and his family never heard from him again. He was the great-uncle of Dr. John Doyle and President Sean Doyle. Thank you for watching. Stay tuned for *Dan Quigley Reports*."

THANKSGIVING EVE

The President began his Cabinet meeting by thanking everyone for the countless hours they had put in over the past eight weeks.

"Folks, I cannot tell you how much I appreciate the time and effort that has been put forth by all of you during this, our worst crisis ever. There is no estimate how long this pandemic will last. We need to continue to be vigilant and strong during these trying times. Tomorrow is Thanksgiving and as you spend the day with your loved ones, be thankful that we are a strong nation. We will defeat this enemy. Mr. Secretary of the Treasury, do you have a report for us?"

"Yes, Mr. President, but it is not what you want to hear, I'm sure."

Adam Wainright was a former vice-president of one of the largest accounting firms in the country. His appointment by President Doyle had received unanimous approval and he was considered a probable candidate to be the next Chairman of the Federal Reserve.

"Mr. President, this pandemic is wreaking havoc on our economy and as you know, the stock market is in its worst shape since the crash of 1929. The New York Stock Exchange is down day after day and the NASDAQ is close to self- destructing. The Dow Jones has also experienced devastating losses. There simply is no confidence in any of the stock and bond markets. We are close to a crash; I cannot guarantee that there won't be one. We need a miracle to climb out of this one."

"What would you suggest, Adam?" the President asked. "Mr. President, we need something very positive to come about regarding the flu. Some good news on any front might help the situation."

"Mr. Sitarek, what do we hear from our national security people that could influence the stock market?"

"Sir, they have still not located the terrorist cells in Malaysia. One victory in this war against the terrorists would be positive enough to start generating some confidence in the stock market. The FBI and the CIA have been chasing numerous threats that we believe have originated from various terrorist groups. We have two of our largest agencies spread very thin at this point."

The President leaned back in his chair. He looked over at the Secretary for Homeland Security and asked, "Chuck, what kind of leads is Ken referring to?"

"Mr. President, they are not leads, as much as they are threats. Some may be legitimate and others may simply be copycats, similar to those we received back in the 90's.

Though there have been numerous anthrax scares and bomb threats, nothing has occurred yet. I believe it is only a matter of time, though. As Mr. Sitarek points out, we are spread very thin."

"Dr. Carey, I understand that our Secretary of Health is ill and has asked you to report for him."

The Surgeon General straightened in his chair and said, "Yes, Mr. President, that is correct. It has been eight weeks since the first diagnosed case of the Spanish flu was diagnosed at New York's St. Vincent's Hospital. We now have a reported three hundred thousand cases confirmed and thirty-nine thousand deaths, sir. Dr. Doyle reports that they are making progress on the vaccine, but still do not have the weaponized strain completely contained. He is estimating another two-to-three weeks before they can begin production of the vaccine for distribution. It will take another four months to develop enough vaccine to inoculate our first responders, including all healthcare workers, firefighters, police, EMS personnel, and our hazmat responders. He also predicts it would be at least two-to-three months beyond that to have enough of the vaccine to distribute to the general population."

"Dr. Carey, do you realize how many dead we may have by then, including other countries worldwide?"

"Yes, sir, I do. It will be catastrophic. My best guess is that we will have over one million dead here in the U.S. alone."

The President looked around the room at the somber faces, and all he could say was, "God help us all."

The meeting adjourned and the Cabinet left for home, while Sean Doyle headed up to the family quarters.

THE EUROPEAN UNION

Prime Minister O'Keefe of Great Britain had recently returned from a meeting of the European Union countries and was preparing his report to Parliament. The flu was ravaging every country in the Union. Although England and Scotland had twenty thousand deaths so far, they were handling it as best as they could. No rioting in the streets. No looting or any other type of major crimes had been committed. The same could not be said for the countries outside the United Kingdom. Italy had rioting in the streets and demonstrations against the United States for bringing on this horrible disease.

France was not much better. The French and the Americans had always agreed to disagree and this crisis was no different. The French blamed the Americans for bringing this curse on the world. They believed the American President was to blame for his strong stand against terrorism and that he needed to try to understand the Muslims. France had forty thousand cases of the flu with ten thousand deaths so far. The entire country was in turmoil.

Germany and Switzerland were no better off. The rioting and looting had begun a month earlier and were still rampant. These countries, however, supported President Doyle fully and offered any expertise the U.S. government needed in developing a vaccine.

Ireland, always a U.S. supporter, was hit by the flu in a devastating way. With a population of only eight million people and with one million of those living in Dublin, the city had become a quarantined zone. The majority of Dubliners were young people in the twenty-to-forty-year-old age group, the same group most affected by the flu. Ireland reported approximately 100,000 diagnosed cases, with eighty thousand of them in the City of Dublin. There were also twelve thousand deaths in Dublin alone.

Spain, where the original flu was named in 1918—although it was a misnomer—had relatively few cases of the new strain compared to countries of similar populations. There were only fifteen thousand cases diagnosed and only 2,300 deaths.

The eastern European countries were being affected by the flu at an alarming rate and the former Soviet Union countries reported close to one million diagnosed cases of the flu. The number of deaths there, though, was unavailable.

As he finished his report, Prime Minister O'Keefe wondered if life would ever get back to normal. It was becoming increasingly obvious that the terrorist threat would be there for many years to come. Eradication of this scourge could take decades, rather than years.

THANKSGIVING

Sean and Maggie were in the family quarters of the White House on Thanksgiving morning doing what they loved to do, though usually on a Sunday morning. The newspapers were spread everywhere and although it was not Sunday, it was a holiday and the President was not to be disturbed unless there was a crisis. Just as the Macy's Thanksgiving Day Parade was about to begin, there was a knock on the door of the living room.

"Tell me Maggie, please, that that is not the Secret Service out there, wanting my attention to something. I know it's impossible, but I wish they could at least leave us alone for even a little while, especially on Thanksgiving."

Sean stepped over to the door, and opened it to a boisterous chorus of "Surprise!" Standing in the doorway were his two sons, Kevin and Brendan, and Kevin's wife Barb, and their two children.

"Wow! What a wonderful surprise! Come on in everyone! Happy Thanksgiving!" He turned to Maggie with a look of suspicion. "You knew about this, didn't you?" "Who me?" she gently protested.

Both the wide grin on his face and the strength of his hugs revealed that Sean was obviously very happy with Maggie's big

140

secret. Here was his family at the White House for Thanksgiving dinner and for all those years that he did the cooking, now he didn't have to raise a finger. He looked at Kevin and saw that he had lost at least forty pounds from his bout with the flu. *Thank God,* he thought, *that Kevin survived. So many more did not and will not before this is over.*

The grandchildren headed for the television room to play video games, and the men headed to the other television in the living room to watch the upcoming traditional Thanksgiving Day football game, Detroit versus Green Bay. Maggie and Barb sat in the kitchen area, enjoying the wonderful scents of Marcus' cooking and catching up on what was going on back in Buffalo.

Shortly before dinner was served, President Doyle was summoned to the telephone for an important call. He picked up the phone in his study and said, "This is the President."

"Mr. President, this is the Vice President. Sir, I called to let you know that our daughter, Emily, passed away thirty minutes ago from the Spanish flu."

Sean was too stunned to reply immediately. Jim Schultz was not only his Vice President, but also a good friend. He gathered his thoughts and said, "Jim, I am so sorry. I am at a loss for words to comfort you. I'm shocked. Please let me know whatever Maggie and I can do for you and Jane."

"I will, Mr. President. Please pray for the repose of her soul."

"We certainly will, Jim, and we will be at your side at the funeral."

"Thank you, Sean. I know you'll do everything a good friend can." The Vice President hung up and Sean Doyle stood there for a full minute, numbed by what he had just heard. How guilty he felt.

Here he had his son back from the dead and at the White House for Thanksgiving dinner, and his Vice President had his only daughter taken from him. Life was not fair.

Sean returned to the living room as Marcus entered and announced, "Dinner is served." The entire family rose and filed into the dining room.

Maggie looked at Sean and thought that he looked like he had seen a ghost. She grabbed his hand and whispered, "What's wrong, luv?"

"Let's sit down first, Maggie. I have terrible news."

At the table, the diners readily found their seats, as Marcus had put little name cards at each place. Once seated, everyone turned to Sean, whom they assumed would say grace. The President looked around the table at his family and then said, "That phone call I just took was bad news. The Vice President called and informed me that his daughter, Emily, passed away a half an hour ago from the Spanish flu. I promised him that we would pray for her soul, so as we thank God for our Thanksgiving feast and for saving Kevin from the same fate, let us all offer a prayer for Emily."

The news of losing Emily cast a shadow over the Thanksgiving dinner and the family reunion that Maggie had planned so well. Sean noticed, though, that Kevin was eating like he had never seen or tasted turkey before. He jokingly said to Kevin, "Mr. Doyle, you eat like you are going to the electric chair in the morning."

Kevin laughed and said, "Just trying to make up for all those days I was on IV and didn't know where I was. This dinner is fantastic! I can't get enough of it!" "That's pretty obvious," Sean laughed.

With dinner finished and dessert and coffee served, the family decided to retreat to the movie room to watch an old movie. The boys were all unanimous in their choice. It was a Thanksgiving tradition to watch the John Candy movie, *Planes, Trains, and Automobiles.*

Afterward, Sean thought to himself, *what a great stress reliever that movie was, continuous laughing for over ninety minutes. So glad we did that. There is nothing better for the soul than a good laugh.*

NATIONAL CATHEDRAL

It was the Saturday after Thanksgiving, and Vice President Jim Schultz and his wife Jane led the entourage into the National Cathedral behind the casket bearing their only daughter, Emily. Directly behind them were their two sons, with their wives and children. Next in line was the President of the United States, his wife Maggie, and their family. The Doyle children were close to the Schultz family and had stayed in Washington for the funeral. All attendees at the funeral wore HEPA masks to protect them from transmission of the flu.

Cardinal O'Malley officiated at the funeral service, and gave the eulogy as well.

"A graduate of Georgetown University and a former member of the Peace Corps, Emily Schultz dedicated her life to helping others. She worked tirelessly in the Congo with malnourished children, nursing them back to health. She assisted in the AIDS program clinics throughout many African countries. Upon returning to the United States two years ago, Emily worked at a local health clinic as a physician's assistant. It was there that Emily contracted the flu virus that is sweeping the country.

"Only thirty-two-years-old, Emily succumbed within four days. She is God's angel now, just as she was an angel on earth caring for others. We don't know why God takes our children from us at a time in their lives when they are only beginning their young professional lives, but we do know that she is happy now and doing God's work from above instead of among us. We are honored to have had Emily for the short time that God shared her with us."

As the President looked around the Cathedral at the masked faces, he saw that many friends and family were adjusting the coverings as they wiped tears from their eyes. Sean thought, *God, will this ever end, all of this sickness and death? We need a miracle. We need a vaccine and we need it fast. So many families are being torn apart. Please God, help us out of this.* Sean blessed himself and stood for the next prayer as Maggie's hand reached over to take his.

                    *   *   *

The funeral procession left the National Cathedral and proceeded to Andrews Air Force Base where Emily would be put aboard a flight back to Chicago for burial. Her parents accompanied the casket aboard the 747 aircraft and turned to give a slight wave to those assembled.

Returning to the White House in the Presidential limousine, Kevin turned to his father.

"Dad, I cannot believe how lucky I am to have a second chance. I still don't understand why I survived and my friends did not."

Sean leaned toward the jump seat and said, "Kev, I believe that God decided you had more to do here on earth, including raising those two young sons of yours with Barb. Yes, you were lucky, but God obviously decided it was not your time. Let's hope this epidemic ends soon and we do not have to attend any more of these funerals."

"Dad, it had better be soon. We already have panic in the streets. People are beginning to blame you for not doing enough. Sometimes our citizenry can be so stupid and naive. Don't they know you are doing all you can?" "Kevin, when you are losing your children to a disease that no one understands and you don't see any hope on the near horizon, you always turn and look for someone to blame. They are blinded by their grief. As their President, it is my responsibility to find a way out of this and by the help of God, Kevin, I will."

NEW YORK CITY

New York City Mayor Michael Lundquist left the New York Stock Exchange and told his driver to head down Wall Street and then over the Brooklyn Bridge. The mood at the exchange was one of sheer panic. Brokers were all of the same opinion: a crash would occur. Every day brought more and more losses and few, if any, gains. The country was panicked by the flu; the market was crumbling and the economy was in dire straits.

Mayor Lundquist adjusted his mask and glanced out the limousine window to see citizens going about their routines covered in masks of all types and sizes. Some had even taken to covering their entire face, leaving only their eyes showing behind the mask.

As the limousine left Manhattan and crossed into Brooklyn from the Brooklyn Bridge, one of the most famous structures in the world, Mayor Lundquist instructed his driver to head for the residential areas. Driving by funeral homes, he was shocked at what he saw. Every establishment had semi-trailers in its parking lots; the refrigerated trucks obviously held the deceased victims of the flu. Deaths were occurring at such a rapid rate that the funeral homes were unable to keep up. The trailers held the bodies until they could be prepared for burial. Funerals were not only taking place during the morning, which was standard procedure, but now were held in

147

the afternoons and evenings as well. The death toll in New York's five boroughs alone was quickly approaching six figures.

Turning into one of the older neighborhoods, it was immediately obvious to the mayor that this street had been hit severely by the flu. In the window of nearly every third house was a white ribbon with an angel attached, indicating that a person from this home had been taken by the flu. The next house had three ribbons in its window, and the mayor felt a large lump in his throat as he drove by. Startled by the ringing of his car telephone then, he retrieved it from the holder.

"This is Mayor Lundquist."

The Chief of Police was on the line. "Mr. Mayor, we need you at the Emergency Operations Center immediately, sir! We have just had a bombing and it has terrorism written all over it!"

"Chief, where did this take place?"

"Right next door to the New York Stock Exchange! We have twenty fatalities and another thirty-four missing!" "Oh my God, Chief! I was there about an hour ago! I will be right there as soon as we can get back over the bridge."

"Thank you, sir. Meet you at the EOC."

The mayoral limousine sped away, and the driver placed a portable red light on the roof. With the sirens of the accompanying police escort blaring, the driver raced back into Manhattan. As the vehicle approached the Brooklyn Bridge, large black clouds of smoke were visible over Wall Street. The mayor wondered to himself, *will our country ever get back to normalcy again? First the Spanish flu and now bombings. Who knows what else these bastards have in store for us.* He turned on the television in the limousine to hear Dan Quigley describing the scene on Wall Street.

"The building where the bombing took place is two doors from the Stock Exchange and is burning as the New York firefighters direct hoses on the flames from three snorkel trucks. The façade of the eight story building is completely gone."

It reminded the mayor of the initial video footage he had seen of the Oklahoma City bombing.

Quigley continued, "Wall Street has been closed to all traffic," as the mayor's limousine sped past drivers who veered to the right and stopped, hearing the siren.

Mayor Lundquist adjusted the volume on the television just as the scene switched from Wall Street to a view of the Capitol in Washington.

"The letter arrived this morning in the offices of the Speaker of the House. Test results will be available late this afternoon, but the suspicion is that the envelope did contain anthrax," the reporter revealed. "The offices have been closed indefinitely and the employees who came in contact with the anthrax were decontaminated by the hazardous materials response team, sent home with a prescription of Cipro, and advised to see their doctors."

Reeling from the news of these events, Mayor Lundquist arrived at the Emergency Operations Center, and headed into the EOC press room for his briefing by the Chief of Police.

OVAL OFFICE

Sean had just watched the same report from CNN regarding the bombing on Wall Street and the anthrax threat at the Capitol. Bob Roche and Ken Sitarek both began to speak at once before Ken said, "Go ahead, Bob."

"Mr. President, what I was about to say is that our intelligence did tell us that we could expect these kinds of terrorist acts. The problem has been that we did not know where or when. Now that we have had two in as many hours, my recommendation would be that we go to threat level Red."

Sean nodded and said, "Bob, I don't disagree with you, but before we do that, are we saying that more of these acts are imminent?"

"Absolutely, Mr. President. We have no doubt that this is just the beginning of more attacks."

"Okay, Bob. Call the Director of Homeland Security and tell him we are going to threat level Red. Now Ken, what do you have?"

"Mr. President, I have some good news, believe it or not. Dr. Doyle called just before our meeting and informed me that his team has made significant progress with positive results in eliminating the weaponized strain."

Sean beamed. "Now that is good news. When does he expect to have the vaccine ready?"

"Best guess is about four months, possibly five, to have enough for distribution to the first responders and the healthcare workers. It would still be six months to inoculate the general population."

Sean sighed and said, "My God, we could have a million people dead by that time."

Ken nodded his head in agreement and said, "Yes, Mr. President, I'm afraid that's true. The people at the CDC are doing everything they can to speed up the process, but this takes time. Even a year ago when the flu season hit with a vengeance and the supply of vaccine was used up, it still took a long time to re-supply. This is a lengthy process."

"Ken, I think it would be better to keep a lid on this for now. We don't want to get hopes up too soon. Let's keep it quiet and wait for the right moment to announce it to the country."

The telephone on the President's desk interrupted the conversation. "This is the President."

"Mr. President, Dr. Doyle from the CDC is on the line."

"Thank you, Aggie." Sean pushed the speaker phone button so Ken and Bob could hear what John Doyle had to say. "Hello, John. That was great news you had for us. We were just discussing your recent success in eliminating the weaponized strain. I knew you could do it."

"Thank you, Mr. President. It is going to take months before we are ready to inoculate, but I know that you were aware of that. Right now, however, we have another crisis, sir."

"What's that, John?"

"Mr. President, we've finished analyzing the anthrax spores that were taken from the Capitol earlier today. This is an unusually strong strain of anthrax, the most potent we have encountered to date. These spores will cause many deaths if people are exposed to them. The spores have a resistance to some of our stronger antibiotics, such as Cipro."

"That isn't good news, John. You should know that we have discussed going to threat level Red. Our intelligence tells us that this will not be an isolated attack at the Capitol Building. We do expect more attacks, though where and when are the questions of the moment right now."

"Mr. President, we will do everything possible to help in this battle, but we are spread quite thin right now because of the vaccine development."

"I understand, John. Please keep me informed as to the progress. Thank you for your diligence in getting this flu strain killed. We'll talk again soon."

"Thank you, Mr. President."

"Well, gentlemen, you heard John. This just doesn't get any easier for us, does it?"

Bob Roche replied, "No sir, it doesn't, and it appears that we're going to be fighting these terrorists on numerous fronts for the long run. I'll head over to the Office of Homeland Security and brief the director."

"Also Bob, have Sherry arrange for a press conference and have the Secretary of Homeland Security announce that we are going to threat level Red."

"Yes sir, Mr. President."

Bob Roche left the Oval Office and Sean turned to Ken Sitarek. "Ken, call the Cabinet together for a meeting tomorrow morning. We need to make sure everyone is on the same page when questioned about this threat level Red situation."

"Certainly, Mr. President. I'll let Aggie know when it's set up."

Ken left the Oval Office and Sean Doyle began to wonder why he ever wanted to be President.

TORONTO

Dr. John Cooper, Chief of Staff at Toronto General Hospital, brought his staff meeting to order for their daily briefing.

"My friends, we have some good news this morning. For the first time since this flu pandemic began, we are able to report a twenty-five percent decrease in the number of new cases. This is significant; I would not have expected any type of decline as long as the strain was weaponized. I have put a call in to the Center for Disease Control in Atlanta and have asked Dr. Doyle if he could send a team up here to give us an opinion. Dr. Doyle has told me confidentially—and this information is not, I repeat, not to leave this room—that he and his staff have had success in isolating the strain and are now developing the vaccine. The Americans do not want to announce any detailed information until they have a more solid schedule of when the vaccine will be available for inoculation. "Meanwhile, the 1918-19 pandemic statistics show that the flu disappeared then as quickly as it appeared. We can only hope that history may repeat itself."

The team from the CDC arrived at Toronto General Hospital that afternoon and began their research immediately.

Toronto, a city of four million, had been hit severely by the flu pandemic. A hub for overseas flights, nearly every major airline in the world flew in and out of Toronto. Now that it was known that the terrorists had spread the flu strain aboard aircraft, it was apparent why Toronto had seen so many cases of the flu. Canada's largest city and financial capital of the country had over sixty thousand victims of the flu. The deaths that occurred there followed the typical course: most were in the twenty-to-forty-year-old age range and included Yuri Malovich, the star center of the Toronto Maple Leafs hockey team, and Joe Miller, an assistant coach.

TOKYO

Muhammad Sutwa had been traveling from one country to another since leaving Dubai and then Casablanca. His cell in Dubai had completely disbanded after he and Dr. Zayed closed the warehouse and shipped the remaining flu strain. He was traveling with a false passport that identified him as a British citizen by the name of Marcus Schoenfeld. His work visa, which he had obtained in Dubai, listed his occupation as an import/export agent for a company based in Hong Kong.

Sutwa had encountered some close calls as he traveled around the globe. He was detained for two hours in Hanover, Germany for suspicion and then released. He was stopped at the gateway on a flight out of London and was scanned and searched. He believed his release was expeditious because of his British passport, but the extra security precautions indicated to Sutwa that authorities were judiciously checking all travelers who had import/export backgrounds.

Waiting for the last flight out of Tokyo to Malaysia, Sutwa was excited knowing he would be welcomed by Kemal for the successful operation he had conducted. After months of traveling, he was tired and wanted to be back in Malaysia to stay. *Enough of this running around the world and taking all of these chances of being captured.*

In Sutwa's mind, he had accomplished his mission and he deserved to retire from this rat race of attacks on the infidels; leave that work up to Kemal and his numerous cells. Sutwa would be rewarded by Allah for having been the instrument that killed millions of the non-believers.

As the loudspeaker announced, "Japan Airlines flight 348 is now beginning to pre-board first class passengers," Sutwa stepped into line with his identification and boarding pass in hand. He handed the agent his boarding pass and felt a hand on his shoulder. He turned to see two Japanese security officers.

"Mr. Schoenfeld, would you please step out of line and come with us?"

"Officer, there must be some mistake. I am about to board my flight."

"Mr. Schoenfeld, please do not resist. If you miss your flight, we will arrange for you to be on a later one. Now please come with us."

Sutwa was taken to the security office at New Tokyo International Airport, where he met two gentlemen who he immediately assumed were American. Sutwa had seen enough movies over the years, including *Men in Black*, to educate himself on the appearance of an FBI agent. These two had that image that he had seen so often on the big screen. The taller of the two Americans stepped forward and introduced himself as Agent Terry Crowley of the Federal Bureau of Investigation. The other man was introduced as Colin Fargo of the Department of Homeland Security.

"Mr. Schoenfeld," Agent Crowley said, "we have a warrant for your arrest as a suspected terrorist, and the Japanese government will allow us to take custody of you and fly you back to the United

States where you will be given all of the rights you are entitled to under our laws."

Sutwa was too shocked to speak at first. He finally calmed down long enough to ask, "What am I being charged with?"

Agent Crowley answered, "Terrorism and the distribution of a weaponized flu strain meant to kill innocent people." With that, Agent Fargo stepped forward and clasped handcuffs on Sutwa.

Forty-five minutes later, the two FBI agents boarded an American Airlines flight with their captive and headed for Washington, DC. The Japanese News Agency read a press release from Prime Minister Myaki that said an arrest had been made in the flu pandemic investigation. The suspected terrorist was en route with the American FBI to the United States for further questioning. He was identified by the Prime Minister as Marcus Schoenfeld, a British citizen, but was suspected to be Muhammed Sutwa, a terrorist cell leader who authorities believe ran the operation to develop the weaponized flu strain that was killing thousands of people worldwide.

*   *   *

It was five o'clock in the morning on the east coast when the telephone rang in the Presidential family quarters. A sleepy Sean Doyle answered on the second ring to hear the British Prime Minister O'Keefe say, "Sorry to wake you so early, Mr. President, but I knew you would want to hear this news."

Sean was wide awake and said, "What is it, Mr. Prime Minister? You have my attention."

"Mr. President, our intelligence agency discovered by going through our passport records that we had issued a British passport to a Mr. Marcus Schoenfeld. When running it through our computers, the photo matched that of your terrorist wanted in Dubai for the manufacture of the weaponized strain."

"That is wonderful news, Mr. Prime Minister."

"It gets better, Mr. President. Your FBI, on a tip from Agent Marty Harrington, has just apprehended the suspect, real name Muhammed Sutwa, at the New Tokyo International Airport and are transporting him back to the States."

Sean was now out of bed and pacing back and forth, while Maggie was trying to figure out what this conversation was all about. Sean was saying, "I don't know how to thank you enough for this splendid work by your people. Mr. Prime Minister, this is a giant step in the right direction. Thank you again. Speak to you soon, I hope."

Sean hung up the phone and filled Maggie in on this development and then called his press secretary to set up a press conference for mid-morning.

"Maggie, I think it is about time that we give this nation some good news for a change. I think this calls for a full-blown, back home breakfast instead of the usual bagel and coffee."

Maggie smiled and said, "Sean, you can have whatever you want. I'll tell the kitchen to get it started."

BUFFALO

Built in the 1920's, the Peace Bridge is a major border crossing connecting the United States and Canada. The bridge crosses from Buffalo, New York, and over the Niagara River to Fort Erie, Ontario. Security at the bridge had always been good, but since the advent of terrorism and now the threat level being raised to Red, the Border Patrol was at a very high state of readiness. The United States Customs Service was conducting more random searches of vehicles than ever before. All truck traffic was held up on both sides of the bridge as each and every trailer was inspected.

In addition to vehicular traffic, it was not unusual for pedestrian traffic to cross the bridge as well. The woman waiting in line to cross the Peace Bridge appeared to be in her twenties. As she approached the customs agent, she gave him a big smile and said, "I am so excited about seeing that new casino over there in Fort Erie."

The agent said, "May I see your identification, please?"

The young woman reached into her pocket, appearing to retrieve her driver's license. Instead, she reached in and pulled on a trip wire. It immediately exploded, killing her, the agent, and ten other people waiting in line. The explosion also blew up two cars that were in line at the next station. The bridge manager saw the entire incident from his third story window in the Peace Bridge offices. He grabbed his telephone and dialed 911.

When the dispatcher answered, the manager said, "This is the Peace Bridge Authority. We have just had a suicide bomber explode at our crossing, killing numerous people!" The dispatcher answered, "Sir, please stay on the line while I activate the fire department and the hazmat team."

The Buffalo Fire Department was dispatched, along with their hazardous materials response team. The County Domestic Preparedness Task Force, which had trained in response to weapons of mass destruction, was also dispatched to the scene.

The next call to the dispatcher was from a cell phone, number unknown, and a person with a thick, Arabic accent announced that his organization was responsible for the Peace Bridge bombing.

"Tell your President we are hitting his hometown and we will not stop. We will attack again." The caller then hung up.

As the first responders arrived at the Peace Bridge, they encountered complete chaos. Traffic was backed up on the Niagara section of the New York State Thruway for two miles. The bridge had been closed immediately after the bombing and attempts were being made to divert traffic by closing the I-190 ramp leading to the bridge.

Although the firefighters' first response was to put out the car fires, they also remembered their training in a terrorist situation. Where there was one explosive, there was also the possibility of a secondary device left there to explode after the responders arrived. The second bomb is intended to kill the responders. Fire Commissioner Margaret Keane ordered all of her firefighters to approach the scene with extreme caution and to allow the Erie County Bomb Squad from the Sheriff's Department, along with their bomb-sniffing canines, to begin inspecting the bridge for other devices.

Since this was a suicide bomber, she could have placed a device somewhere in the area before blowing herself up. Fortunately, that was not the case. The firefighters were able to contain the fire, while the Medical Assistance Response Team set up triage for the wounded and the Disaster Mortuary Operational Response Team, or DMORT, a team of emergency response morticians, set up a temporary morgue until the medical examiner could make his pronouncements.

President Doyle was notified within minutes of the bombing in Buffalo by the Director of the FBI. While on the phone with the Director, two other calls came in within two minutes of each other. There had been another suicide bombing at the border crossing in the Detroit area. The next call was from the Governor of California. A suicide bomber blew himself up at the halfway point of the Golden Gate Bridge in San Francisco, damaging the structure and blowing a hole in the surface while destroying three autos and killing ten people.

Sean Doyle could only think, *When will all this end?*

TERROR EVERYWHERE

The suicide bombings at the three bridge sites were not the work of al-Qaida, according to the FBI. The director reported to the President that this was not the modus operandi of the al-Qaida organization. They preferred bigger, bolder attacks, as they did in the World Trade Center and the USS Cole. Killing only a few people did not have enough impact for them. The goal was to kill thousands, not a few dozen.

The breakaway group responsible for the current pandemic, however, did not agree with that philosophy. They were intent on creating total chaos, no matter what it took. The weaponized flu virus was successful; they could now concentrate on other attacks, such as the three suicide bombings. They also had more in store for the United States.

*   *   *

On the morning following the bombings, Sean entered the Oval Office to find Ken Sitarek waiting for him. Ken stood as Sean walked in and said, "Good morning, Mr. President."

"Good morning, Ken. I hope you have some good news for me."

"Sir, I'm afraid not. CNN has reported this morning that they received a letter in their mailroom with suspected anthrax spores in the envelope. The letter stated that other letters have been sent throughout the nation. We could be looking at a hoax here, as we have seen in the past, or it could be the real thing."

"Ken, turn on the television and find out what the situation is, and then get me Bob Roche on the line."

The President shook his head in wonderment. First the Spanish flu, then suicide bombings, and now possibly, anthrax. Ken handed Sean the phone and said, "Bob is on the line, Mr. President."

"Good morning, Bob. Have you heard about the situation in Atlanta at CNN?"

"Yes, Mr. President. I just got off the phone with Director Graham of the FBI. He tells me there is another possible anthrax situation in Tampa at their post office there."

"Bob, I thought we had all of the postal service centers equipped with special equipment to discover anthrax."

"Yes, sir, we do, but it appears the one in Tampa had been out of service for about two weeks now. They had gone back to the old system while repairs were being made and the anthrax powder came through the line. The Tampa site is completely contaminated."

"Bob, how can we be sure that it is, in fact, anthrax?"

"Mr. President, we are certain of it. Since the new detection device has been on the market, it has been ninety-eight percent accurate when tested. The FBI has closed the Tampa facility indefinitely and all the workers have been decontaminated and sent home with Cipro. They were told to watch for any type of cold or flu symptoms."

Sean looked at Ken and said, "Oh, great. Now they have to watch for flu symptoms. Half of the people in the country are already looking for those! Bob, please keep me informed on the progress. I also need to see the report on the suicide bombings yesterday. Do we know yet who is responsible?"

"Henry Volner from the CIA said that he and the Director Graham are in agreement that it's the same group that has spread the flu. The terrorists also left a message in Buffalo calling from a cell phone that they are hitting your hometown, Mr. President, and that they will continue there."

"Not if we get those bastards first, they won't!" Sean was furious over the recent developments. He was beginning to let his old Irish temper surface. He almost yelled into the phone. "Bob, you tell those two directors at the CIA and FBI that I want some answers and I want them soon!"

"Yes, Mr. President, I will pass along your message."

Sean hung up the phone and Ken turned up the volume on the television. Dan Quigley was reporting that the powder found in the CNN mailroom was indeed anthrax and that another incident had taken place at the Tampa, Florida post office. As Quigley was about to question the reporter in Florida, he was interrupted with a breaking news story. Anthrax had been discovered in Baltimore in the HVAC system of Baltimore's City Hall. All employees in the building had been quarantined until they could be decontaminated, sent home with antibiotics, and given the usual protocol to wait and watch for cold or flu symptoms.

Sean was boiling mad now, and could no longer hold his temper. His face was a deep scarlet, indicating the rise of his blood pressure.

"Ken, we have got to find these bastards and bring them to justice! We are going to have absolute chaos in this country! People can only take so much!"

Sean had just uttered these words when another late-breaking story came on the television. A large crowd with their faces covered with HEPA masks to protect them from the flu, was protesting at Peachtree Center in downtown Atlanta. The media estimated the crowd to be about fifteen hundred people. They carried placards that read, *"Find the terrorists Doyle or get out"* and *"Impeach Doyle."* A third sign, which Sean could barely make out, read *"We want our country back."*

The Atlanta Police were out in full force to keep the demonstration calm; however, a few of the protestors attempted to push through the barricade in front of CNN Center and then all bedlam broke out. Police officers swung at the crowd with their clubs, but the officers were obviously outnumbered and were overwhelmed within minutes. As the police attempted to move back, two officers were trampled under the surging crowd. The Georgia State Police were on their way to help. By the time they arrived, three policemen were dead and twenty-five protestors had been shot, with four dead.

The fire department had also been called to help disperse the crowd with high-powered fire hoses, while the State Police rounded up protestors and put them into waiting vans for a trip to the holding center at the city jail. The entire scene had been televised nationally and similar protests broke out simultaneously in other cities throughout the Northeast. It was still early in the west for any organized disturbance, but fearful that riots would take place, law enforcement officials in most of the major cities were preparing for the worst.

By noon, additional reports of anthrax were reported in Oklahoma City, San Diego, and Salt Lake City. The entire country was in a state of shock. The United States was being attacked on all fronts, and with numerous weapons, but it did not have much to fight against. The terrorists were winning each battle and were also winning the war. Panic in the streets had turned to mass protest and authorities were at a loss as to how to calm the fears except to continually report that they were making progress. However, the problem was that they did not believe it themselves. Curfews, previously implemented all over the country to help halt the spread of the flu, were now enforced to control the mayhem.

Christmas was only three days away and the stores were empty. There was plenty to buy, but no one to shop. People were afraid to go out to any place where there was a crowd, for fear of getting the flu or of getting caught up by an angry mob. The Christmas sales were certain to be the worst they had ever been in the history of keeping such records.

THE HOOVER BUILDING

Agent Crowley entered the nerve center of the FBI shortly after eight o'clock on the morning of the anthrax attacks. The long flight from Tokyo had taken a toll on Crowley. He could never sleep on planes and the jet lag he was experiencing was the worst he could remember. He hoped that his prisoner was equally exhausted by the flight. Maybe he could make some progress in getting Sutwa to talk and make a deal. Director Graham had given Crowley specific orders to arrange any kind of information gathering deal possible. The President wanted answers and the pressure at the Hoover Building was intense.

Terry Crowley walked into the interrogation room set up for the interview and found Marty Harrington, of British Intelligence, waiting for him.

"Good morning, Terry. You look like hell."

"Thanks, Marty, I feel worse than I look, though, if you can believe that. This jet lag is brutal."

"Ah, yes, I suspect I'll look badly, too, when I get back home in a few days."

Marty sat down at the table and said, "I guess we should put together a game plan here. What do you say?" Terry set a file down on the table and said, "Marty, the director has given me explicit instructions to make any kind of deal with this dirtball that we possibly can. The President is demanding results."

"Can't say as I blame him, Terry. If you want, I can play good cop with this guy. He has to know that I cannot have any jurisdiction here, and maybe he'll open up to me. Let's see what develops."

Terry picked up the phone and asked for the prisoner to be brought in for questioning. Muhammad Sutwa, alias Marcus Schoenfeld, was escorted into the room five minutes later, handcuffed, in leg irons, and wearing an orange jumpsuit. Terry, of course, had already spent the lengthy trip with Sutwa, but Marty Harrington was meeting the terrorist for the first time. His first thought was, *my God, he doesn't look like your average terrorist. I would have guessed he was British and that the name Marcus Schoenfeld was his given name.*

Terry began the interrogation by asking the prisoner to state his full name, address, and occupation.

Sutwa answered, "My name is Marcus Schoenfeld and I am a British citizen. You have no right to detain me."

"Well, Mr. Sutwa or Mr. Schoenfeld or whatever you want to call yourself, we are not going to get anywhere with that attitude, now are we?"

Marty Harrington introduced himself as a special agent from British Intelligence and explained that he was there to protect Mr. Schoenfeld's rights as a British citizen. That statement seemed to relax Sutwa a little and there was a trace, however faint, of a smile.

Terry continued with questioning and Sutwa was not cooperative. "Mr. Sutwa, you are suspected of running a terrorist cell in Dubai.

We know that you spent considerable time in the United Arab Emirates. What exactly did you do while you were there?"

The terrorist answered, "I was in the import/export business, very legitimate."

Terry smiled and said, "Mr. Sutwa, you and I know that that is not the truth. We both know what you really did in Dubai and we're going to get you the death penalty for the havoc you have spread throughout the world with your 'St. Gustaf's Flu,' as you call it."

Stone-faced and appearing to be completely at ease, the accused terrorist smiled at Agent Crowley and said, "I know nothing of this flu you speak of. I am a businessman. I have no connection to any flu or terrorist cell. You have the wrong person, Mr. Crowley."

The interrogation continued for the rest of the morning and after a quick break, Terry and Marty resumed the questioning. By five o'clock, Sutwa was beginning to give a little information. Marty had promised him that the British government would intervene on his behalf with the United States if he would only cooperate and reveal the location of the cells. Maybe he could avoid the death penalty, which would be a certainty if he did not cooperate.

Steadfastly defiant, the prisoner was taken back to the holding center at six o'clock and Terry and Marty headed over to Georgetown for a light dinner.

"Marty, I don't know if we're going to get anything out of this guy. He has about twelve hours to think about it and we'll go back at him again. What do you think? Can we break him?"

"Terry, you never know with these guys. Death to some of them is the final honor. They get to see Allah and they do not fear ending their lives. I suspect Mr. Sutwa is not one of those, however, but I believe he may come around if we keep up the pressure regarding the death penalty."

CHRISTMAS DAY

Terry and Marty had spent the better part of the past seventy-two hours interrogating Sutwa. The progress had been extremely slow. The terrorist had requested an attorney and had retained a noted, black Muslim defense lawyer who insisted no questioning take place unless he was present. The FBI could care less if this particular terrorist had an attorney present or not. In the mind of the FBI, this was a state of war and they were going to interrogate Sutwa with or without an attorney present.

Terry recognized that they were close to making a deal. Sutwa had admitted that he was a member of a breakaway terrorist organization. He had also told agents that there were cells not only in Malaysia, but in the United States, too. The only name he revealed after almost four days of questioning, though, was his accomplice in Dubai. He agreed to provide additional names and places, but first he wanted assurance that he would not receive a jail sentence. Terry thought that such an arrangement was lunacy, but the FBI had been known to strike stranger deals. Marty Harrington presupposed the possibility that the British Government could attempt to have Sutwa released on the premise that he was a British citizen.

Today, however, both agents preferred to share the day with their families. It was Christmas morning, and Mr. Sutwa could wait another day. Perhaps he would be more cooperative given more time to think about his situation.

Terry Crowley and his family, together with Marty Harrington and his wife, who had accompanied her husband to the States from London, were sitting down to a Christmas turkey when the phone rang. Terry handed the carving knife to Marty and said, "I'll be right back, folks." He walked into the kitchen and picked up the portable phone.

"Terry, speaking. Merry Christmas." Two minutes later, Terry re-entered the dining room with an ashen look on his face, as if he had just witnessed a beheading.   Marty knew something was drastically wrong. "What is it, Terry?"

Terry almost stuttered as he answered Marty. "Sorry to tell you, friend, but we have lost our number one captive. They found him about an hour ago hanging in his cell. There was a note pinned to his jumpsuit that read 'Death to the Infidels.'

"Why would he hang himself when we were so close to a deal?"

"Marty, the holding center does not think that he hung himself. They believe somebody did it for him."

 Terry's wife, Diane Crowley, said, "Gentlemen, I'm very sorry you've had a setback, but it's Christmas. The turkey is getting cold and the kids are anxious to open presents. Can we leave the FBI and terrorism for later, just once?"

Terry sat down at his place and said, "Honey, you're right. Let's say grace and get this show on the road." They all joined hands and thanked God for his gifts and asked his guidance in ending this terrible fight.

*   *   *

Back at the White House, President Doyle and the First Lady were finishing dinner with their family when a Secret Service agent entered the dining room. He bent to whisper something in the President's ear, and Sean abruptly left the room to take a phone call, returning within a minute, solemnity on his face.

"It seems we continue to receive bad news. Our terrorist captive, Muhammad Sutwa, was found hanging in his cell."

Brendan Doyle asked, "Dad, what does that do to your investigation of this guy? Wasn't he the key to finding the terrorist cells?"

"Yes, Brendan he was, and we were close to getting from him the locations and names that we need so desperately. Someone had to know how close we were, because he didn't hang himself. That someone got to him and killed him before he could tell us any more."

Maggie reached for her husband's hand and said, "Sean, we just need another break. You watch; it will come soon." "Maggie, you are so positive all the time. I hope you're right. We definitely need a break, and a huge one."

At that moment, a Secret Service agent entered the dining room and said, "Mr. President, there is a call for you from Mr. Roche. He says it's urgent."

Sean once more got up from the table, leaving his already cold cup of coffee and stepping out into the hallway. "Bob, what do we have now?"

"Mr. President, this could be a tremendous break for us after the news about Sutwa."

"This better be good, Bob. Right now I'm desperate for a good break."

"Mr. President, we have apprehended Mr. Sutwa's co-terrorist, Dr. Farah Zayed, the doctor with whom he worked in Dubai. We believe that she is the one who developed the weaponized version of the Spanish flu. She was taken into custody by the same Japanese officers who stopped Muhammad Sutwa from boarding his plane at New Tokyo International Airport."

"Bob, you've made my Christmas. A few minutes ago, I was ready to throw in the towel. This is wonderful news. Keep me informed."

"I will, Mr. President. Merry Christmas."

"Merry Christmas to you and your family. See you in the morning."

Sean walked back into the dining room and turned to his family, a smile on his face. "Maggie, you were right. You said something would happen and give us that break and it has. I don't know how it happened so quickly, but once more, you were right. Honey, you sure do have a positive outlook. U.S. agents have arrested Mr. Sutwa's partner in crime at the same Tokyo airport where we apprehended him."

The entire table of Doyle's, accompanied by the Harrington's, erupted into applause as everyone stood up and cheered. They all surrounded the President and shook his hand as if he himself had single-handedly caught the terrorist.

"Okay, everyone! I appreciate your enthusiasm, but it was our FBI that did the work, not me. Let's hope that this detainee will tell us what we need to know. Now it's time to go in and enjoy our Christmas."

TAMPA BAY

Situated across the bay from Tampa is the city of St. Petersburg and beautiful St. Petersburg Beach. Long known by the nickname the "Wrinkle City" because of its elderly population, St. Pete's has long been a favorite tourist spot during the cold winter months. From late November until late April, "the snowbirds," as the northerners are affectionately called by the Florida seniors, flock to the warmer climate to escape the frigid temperatures. This winter season, however, was a disaster; people simply were not traveling due to the flu pandemic. Florida tourism was suffering along with the rest of the economy.

Three days before Christmas, the first cases of anthrax were diagnosed in Tampa and now on Christmas Day, the emergency room at Pasadena Hospital was filled with seniors complaining of flu-like symptoms. The medical staff was frantically trying to determine whether patients were presenting with Spanish flu symptoms or anthrax. Anthrax spores had been discovered in the air ducts of a local theater-in-the-round, which the senior citizen population of St. Petersburg and neighboring communities frequented. Within the past forty-eight hours, the hospital had admitted twenty diagnosed cases of inhalation anthrax, its deadliest form, as spores are inhaled directly into the lungs. Highly communicable, the anthrax spores thrive on the internal organs, where the lungs are attacked with a vengeance if patients are not treated with antibiotics. Most seniors, because of their lowered resistance and often compromised immune systems, are very susceptible to anthrax attack.

The area around Tampa Bay had not been as affected by the flu pandemic as some other Florida communities, possibly because of the climatic conditions and perhaps partly due to the fact that the population was older than most communities, and the flu seemed to be attacking the young population. Anthrax, however, was attacking at a startling rate.

The local Publix and Albertson's grocery chains, as well as Eckerd's Drugs, had completely sold out of HEPA masks. Some seniors were wearing handkerchiefs over their faces. The lines at most of the emergency rooms were made up of people in their seventies, eighties, and some in their nineties, and all with their faces completely covered.

The luxurious senior complex at Boca Ciega Bay was immediately put under quarantine. Boca Ciega's twin tower residences, each comprising twenty stories of independent and/or assisted-living communities and a long-term nursing facility, was also home to ten of the initial twenty patients diagnosed with inhalation anthrax. They had been on an outing together to the theater where the anthrax attack had occurred.

Inhalation anthrax is extremely communicable from one person to another. The spores, if left alone, could have a lifespan of over seventy years. Quarantine was the best solution for the facility with so many seniors in residence. This scenario was probably going to be played out at many other facilities and not only in Florida. The same strain had now been discovered on the west coast in Seattle.

WHITE HOUSE PRESS ROOM

Sherry Katz, the White House Press Secretary, stepped to the podium in the press room and the room fell silent. "Ladies and gentlemen of the press, I do believe this is the most quiet and orderly gathering you've ever assembled. Thank you for not calling out questions prior to my delivering my statement."

Sherry checked her notes and continued. "Yesterday afternoon, the President received both positive and negative news on the fight against the Spanish flu epidemic. Before you ask, I will give you the bad news first. The terrorist suspect, Muhammad Sutwa, who the FBI had been interrogating for the past five days, was found hanging in his cell at the holding center. At this time, we do not believe that he acted alone; that is, he did not hang himself. It appears that someone murdered him, and obviously to keep him quiet. The FBI has informed us that they were very close to having a list of names from Sutwa and expected him to divulge his co-conspirators sometime today. Unfortunately, we will not have that list of suspects to go after."

"Sherry, what do we know about the murder and do you have a suspect?" asked reporter Kim Carney.

"I would prefer to hold questions until I finish my statement. Thank you for being patient. I promise I will take questions at that time. Let me continue.

"That was the bad news. Here is the good news. Shortly after we discovered Sutwa's body, we received a call from our contacts in Japan informing us that they had apprehended a woman who was Sutwa's alleged accomplice in his Dubai operation. The captive has been positively identified as Dr. Farah Zayed; the doctor's area of expertise is microbiology. The FBI and the CIA suspect that she is probably the person who developed and directed the weaponized flu strain with which we are dealing."

The press room erupted with questions, so many at once that no one could be heard. Sherry raised her hand, and the room immediately quieted.

"Ladies and gentlemen, one question at a time. Bill, go ahead."

"Thanks, Sherry. Bill Marshall from Reuters. Can you tell us anymore about the person arrested in Tokyo? Do FBI agents believe they can get the same information from her that they expected to get out of Sutwa and if so, when do we expect to have her back here in Washington?"

Sherry smiled at the reporter and said, "Very nice, Bill. Three questions in one. First of all, what I can tell you is that we have positively identified Dr. Zayed and we do know that she spent the last year in the United Arab Emirates, and mostly in Dubai. We have placed her at the scene of the crime. We also know that she was frequently seen in the company of Muhammad Sutwa and that they both left Dubai together just before the FBI and CIA raided their warehouse. Secondly, the FBI intends to interrogate her shortly and hopefully, she will be as cooperative as her late co-conspirator. As for the third part of your question, Dr. Zayed is en route and should

179

be landing in Washington as we speak. Next question. Dan, go ahead."

"Sherry, what is the administration doing about the current crisis regarding the anthrax attacks? We have reports that there are currently at least seven cities that have anthrax situations, including the most serious presentation of the illness, inhalation anthrax."

"Dan, I can tell you that the CDC is on top of the anthrax crisis and that most of the cases that have been identified are quarantined and are being treated with Cipro. The CDC believes that we have the situation under control and that the anthrax threat has also been brought under control."

"Sherry, Bill Johns from the Seneca Nation. How confident is the President that we can finally bring this situation into focus, and what is the administration doing to find these terrorist cells?"

"Mr. Johns, I can tell you that the President has initiated a directive that calls for all available resources of Homeland Security to bring these criminals to justice as soon as possible. That's all at this time. Thank you, ladies and gentlemen. We will continue to bring you up to date."

DOCTOR ZAYED

Agents Terry Crowley and Marty Harrington were back in the Washington, D.C. interrogation room where they had previously spent five days questioning the late Muhammad Sutwa. Seated across the table from them was an attractive, dark-haired woman with almond-shaped, green eyes and olive skin. With her fine features and slim figure, the suspect could have been a model. The only thing missing that could make her even more alluring was a smile. Her face was frozen in a look of disdain and disgust for her two interrogators.

Terry leaned across the table. "Dr. Farah Zayed," he began, "we have a lot of questions to ask you and it would be much easier for all of us if you would cooperate by being honest with us."

The microbiologist almost spat in Terry's face as she answered, "I have no intention of cooperating with you, Agent Crowley, or anyone else for that matter! I am a Malaysian citizen who has been done a grave disservice by your country and your friends. I am not guilty; I have not done anything to be dragged halfway around the world to this disgusting city and country."

This time it was Marty Harrington who spoke. "With that attitude, Dr. Zayed, I suspect that my American friends will simply put you in a jail somewhere, possibly Guantanamo Bay, with your terrorist friends and just forget about you."

"You cannot do that to me!" Dr. Zayed hissed. "I told you; I have done nothing wrong. I am a Malaysian citizen. The United States has an excellent relationship with my country. It would never do what you are suggesting."

"Doctor, I am afraid that you are sadly mistaken. Yes, my American friends do have a good relationship with Malaysia, but your country, as you call it, is cooperating fully with us to arrest all of your fellow terrorists." "How dare you call me a terrorist!" Dr. Zayed roared. Terry interjected, "Dr. Zayed, let's stop playing games here. We know who you are, what you are, and what you've been doing for the past year in Dubai. Do you think we actually believe your cry of innocence? Your friend, Muhammad Sutwa, the now deceased Muhammad Sutwa, provided us with a lot of information before he left us to join Allah. We know that you were the person responsible for creating this deadly flu strain that is killing hundreds of thousands of people across the globe. Now let's start back at the beginning and stop the false cries of innocence."

Dr. Zayed glared at Terry Crowley, and refused to speak. Further questioning eventually ceased after twenty minutes of complete silence on the part of the doctor. Terry finally said, "Dr. Zayed, it appears that you prefer to stay silent, so we have no choice but to put you in a cell at the holding center until you agree to speak with us. Let's hope you do not meet the same demise as your late friend, Muhammad Sutwa.

Terry and Marty rose from the table, prepared to leave the room, when Dr. Zayed stammered, "Wait! Don't go!" Terry turned. "Well, it looks like you've regained your voice. Can we sit back down now and have a discussion?"

Taking a deep breath and leaning forward, Dr. Zayed said, "Yes, but I would like someone from my embassy to be here."

"I believe we can arrange that. We'll be right back." After exiting the room, Marty stopped Terry in the hallway. "I have a good feeling that she may be willing to talk. It would help if we implied that we already know a lot from interrogating Sutwa, more than we actually got out of him, obviously."

"Yeah, Marty, I agree. Let's get a hold of the Malaysian Embassy and get on with this."

Forty-five minutes later, the diplomat from the Malaysian Embassy arrived, and Marty and Terry led him down the hallway to the interrogation room. As they entered the room, introductions were made and Dr. Zayed immediately seemed to be more relaxed than one hour before. The presence of a representative from her homeland was obviously a calming influence.

The questioning began and continued for four hours. It was apparent to both Terry and Marty that this cold-blooded woman, who was responsible for thousands of deaths, was actually scared to death herself. She continued to answer their questions and also pleaded for her life. She would provide information, but she did not want to be executed. At one point during the interrogation, she broke down completely, crying uncontrollably and expressing sorrow for what she had done.

Marty and Terry agreed that "Dr. Death," as they had nicknamed her, was exhausted. The interrogation would continue in the morning. Dr. Zayed was led back to the holding center and the order was given that she be guarded on a twenty-four hour basis. The agents did not want a repeat of what had taken place with their first captive.

Once she was gone, the two agents compared notes and listened to the tape recording of Dr. Zayed's interrogation. She had revealed that there were cells throughout Malaysia and the United States. These were cells that were largely silent. In other words, they existed, but had not been activated for any specific mission. Only the cells that were involved in the distribution of the St. Gustaf's flu had been active. The remaining cells were only beginning their missions, such as the cells responsible for the recent anthrax attacks and the suicide bombings.

The information did not include names, except for Dr. Zayed's contact in Malaysia, a Mr. Sulanni. She confirmed that he was the person who had brought her the flu strain to be weaponized. She also confirmed that the strain had come from below the permafrost in Norway. She knew that there was a higher ranking person in the organization to whom Sulanni reported, but did not know his name. She predicted that there would be more attacks against the U.S. with biological agents and also dirty bombs that would spread radiological material. This was an all-out, full-scale attack against the United States with all available weapons of mass destruction.

Terry Crowley called the Director of the FBI, Ted Graham, and asked for a meeting to report on the interrogation of Dr. Zayed. The director instructed Terry and Marty to come right over.

Upon reporting their findings on the interrogation of Dr. Zayed, the director replied, "The evidence against Dr. Farah Zayed will keep her incarcerated for a long time. It will be at least three years before she ever comes to trial. Good work, men."

The meeting with Director Graham completed, Terry and Marty headed home for dinner; they were to be ready for a full briefing to the FBI and CIA agents at eight o'clock that evening. "Time is of the essence," Director Graham had said, "if we're going to get to these cells before they can attack again."

MALAYSIA

Sulanni entered the Marriott Hotel and immediately stepped into an elevator, taking it to the eighteenth floor. Four doors down to the left, he knocked three times in rapid succession. A voice from behind the door said, "Hello."

Sulanni answered, "Praise Allah."

The door opened and Kemal pulled Sulanni into the room, gave him a bear hug, and then kissed him on each cheek. "My good friend, you have surpassed what I could possibly have hoped for. The infidels are dying by the thousands because of your work. Allah will reward you to the highest degree possible. Thank you, my friend, for a job well done."

"Kemal, I appreciate your praise, but we are faced with a threat about which I am not sure you are aware." "And what could be so bad, my friend? Our flu strain is rampaging our enemy and our suicide bombers and our anthrax attacks are causing total panic in the country of Satan."

"Kemal, this news is not good. The Americans have Dr. Zayed and my intelligence tells me that she is giving them information

185

on our cell network not only here in Malaysia, but also our cells throughout the United States."

"Mr. Sulanni, how could this happen? I thought we took care of the situation by disposing of Sutwa. How did the infidels find Dr. Zayed?"

"She was captured on her way here while boarding a plane at New Tokyo International Airport."

Kemal sat down on the divan and exhaled an audible groan. "Sulanni, this is not good. We must alert our network immediately. Prepare the safe houses here and in the infidel's homeland."

"Yes, sir, I will do that, but let's hope it is not too late. We cannot be sure how much information the Americans already have."

"We have no time to waste, Sulanni. Get on it right now and report back to me by tomorrow evening."

HOOVER BUILDING

Over fifty FBI and CIA agents had gathered in the auditorium of the Hoover FBI Headquarters Building. Director Graham walked to the podium and began the meeting with the introduction of Ambassador Mahamood of Malaysia. "Good morning. I have asked Ambassador Mahamood to attend the first part of our meeting, as he will be coordinating our effort to detect and break these cells in his country. With the information that has been developed by our interrogation of Dr. Farah Zayed by Agent Crowley and Mr. Harrington, we have supplied the Ambassador with a list of the cells and their locations throughout Malaysia. We hope that we are not too late. Our intelligence tells us that this terrorist group has excellent intelligence sources of its own. That was proven by the murder of our former captive, Muhammad Sutwa. We are sure that they were responsible for his death."

Director Graham cleared his throat before continuing. "Let me begin our briefing by saying that we have a very tight time frame here. This operation has to be launched within the next few hours; it must be lightning fast. Otherwise, we stand the chance of not accomplishing our objectives. Ambassador Mahamood has assured me that we have the complete cooperation of his security forces in Malaysia. Our agents will work in concert with Malysian agents to break up these cells and apprehend the terrorists. At the top of our list is a Mr. Sulanni. You see his photo here on the screen. As you will notice, this man does not look like your average terrorist. He could be German, Italian, French, or even American. We do not know of his whereabouts at the present time; we do, however, know that he is not the top man in this organization, but that he reports directly to that person. We do not have a name of the leader of this group, but hope to soon, once we have these cell members in custody. I will now turn the meeting over to Agent Crowley, who will be heading up the operation here in the States and to Marty Harrington, the British Director of Intelligence for the United Kingdom, who has been so helpful in our investigation to date."

Terry Crowley walked to the podium looking very tired, with black shadows under his eyes, and said, "Friends, this will be the biggest counter-terrorism operation since we infiltrated the Taliban in Afghanistan. We have a list of cells operating stateside, but we also know that this list is not complete.

"This operation covers cells in seventeen states from coast to coast, mostly in the Northeast, Midwest, and the West, with a few cells in the states of Florida and Georgia. All FBI and CIA agents will be working directly with state and local law enforcement agencies to break up these cells and apprehend the alleged terrorists.

"An operation of this magnitude needs to have full cooperation, and at all three levels of government. Our agents are pressed thin as it is; they will need every available resource the locals can give us. We will begin at seven o'clock tomorrow morning by hitting thirty-five individual cells in seventeen states. That gives us about ten hours to get to our assigned locations. We leave here in forty-five minutes. Your individual assignments are being handed out as I speak. Marty and I will be coordinating from here in D.C.

"Good luck, and may God be with you all. Tomorrow is the first battle of this new war and we intend to win it."

OPERATION ROUNDUP

At exactly seven o'clock in the morning Eastern Standard Time, Operation Roundup began in thirty-five locations across the United States. It was only four o'clock on the west coast, but the operation was in perfect synchronization with the time zones. Law enforcement agents from the FBI, CIA, DEA, and ATF, as well as state police, county sheriff's, and city and town police agencies converged on the locations that had been identified. The various cells ranged from business establishments, such as a dry cleaning store and convenience markets in three states, as well as a Florida mosque and numerous private residences.

The reports began returning to Terry Crowley within one hour after Operation Roundup commenced. By eight o'clock, officials had uncovered ten locations that had already been completely emptied when agents arrived at the scene. The terrorist intelligence network had obviously reached these locations and told them to get out and get out fast.

By nine o'clock, the news was much better. Fourteen locations had been raided, and suspects and materials had been apprehended, including bomb-making stockpiles for building suicide bomb vests. Five of the locations also had anthrax, ricin, and a variant of a nerve gas.

By ten o'clock that morning, all thirty-five locations had reported back. Two more of the locations had been empty, bringing that total to twelve, but twenty-three were successful busts. A total of ninety-six suspects had been apprehended and were in custody. Future interrogations furthered the possibility of more arrests to be made.

The news from Malaysia was not quite as encouraging. The network had reported U.S. events very quickly there, and only nine locations out of forty-eight identified sites were successful raids. The remaining thirty-nine locations revealed no sign of terrorist cells. Suspects had fled and were probably in safe houses throughout Malaysia. Ambassador Mahamood was very apologetic to Terry Crowley when he received word from his Director of Security that the raids were only minimally successful.

Terry tried to make the Ambassador feel better by saying, "Sir, we don't always get the bad guy on our first try, but you can be sure that the FBI eventually does get its man. There will be another time and another place. You have helped us enormously and there are now forty-eight locations that are no longer useable for these guys, and we have twenty-five arrests out of the nine sites that your people did bust."

Ambassador Mahamood, in his very humble manner said, "Thank you, Agent Crowley. I appreciate your optimism. We will do better the next time."

Marty Harrington walked in with a grin from ear to ear.

"Hey, Marty! Good job we did today, huh?"

"Yes, Terry, it was most successful, and I just got some more good news: our agency has raided an additional thirteen cells in the United Kingdom. We have broken up their networks and have made arrests in England, Scotland, and Wales. The Irish have raided two cells in Dublin, as well. It certainly has been a good day around the globe."

"Marty, that is outstanding news! President Doyle will be very pleased with this operation. Now if we could get this flu under control, maybe he could get back to running the country again."

*   *   *

FBI Director Graham put a call in to Bob Roche, National Security Advisor to the President.

"Bob Roche here."

"Good morning, Bob, Ted Graham calling. I have good news for the President and I figured you would want to give it to him. We have completed Operation Roundup and we raided thirty-five suspected terrorist cells, twelve of which were empty. In other words, no arrests there, but the balance has resulted in ninety-six arrests and the confiscation of a lot of bomb-making materials and biological agents. Our friends across the pond in the United Kingdom also had a good day, breaking up thirteen cells and arresting a few dozen suspects, including two in Dublin. Our operation in Malaysia did not go as well, but we were successful in breaking up nine cells. Our top targets have still not been found, but we continue to pursue them."

"Ted, that is fantastic! I will go in and brief the President immediately. Thanks for the call."

Bob Roche could not contain his excitement as he reported to Sean Doyle. When he finished, the President looked like he was about to cry tears of happiness.

"Bob, this is the best news we have had in months. Are we finally beginning to win this war?"

"Mr. President, we certainly have won an immense battle today in removing a lot of scum off the streets and from our backyards. Now we need to beat this flu."

The President looked out the window of the Oval Office and said, "Amen, amen."

CNN ATLANTA

"Dan Quigley reporting from Atlanta. The Department of Homeland Security is reporting that the FBI, CIA, and other overseas foreign agencies have conducted a massive, worldwide raid on suspected terrorist cells and safe houses.

"Here in the U.S. there have been early morning raids from coast to coast and ninety-six suspects have been arrested and arraigned. The operation here in the U.S. began at seven o'clock this morning and thirty-five locations were targeted. Of those, we are told that twelve revealed no suspects and were literally empty when Federal agents arrived. Suspicion is that those locations were tipped off to the impending raid. Of the other twenty-three locations, there were, again, a total of ninety-six suspects apprehended. We now have a report from Josh Zimmerman in Seattle. Josh, go ahead."

"Thanks, Dan. Here in Seattle two safe houses were raided and seven suspects arrested. We know from an informed source that there were weapons of mass destruction also discovered in these two locations. Materials for constructing a dirty bomb and vials of what officials are referring to as a 'suspected nerve gas' were recovered. "Dan, as you know there has been suspicion of terrorist activity in the Seattle area for several years now, dating back to the 2000 New Year's celebration when suspected terrorists crossed the border, were detained, and then arrested. We now have proof that cells actually existed right here in the city. The havoc that these terrorists could have caused to the population has been eliminated with this successful operation. Dan, back to you."

"Thanks, Josh, for that report. We go now to Washington for a live interview with Special Agent Crowley from the FBI, who coordinated the massive raid conducted earlier today. Agent Crowley, this is Dan Quigley."

"Good morning, Dan."

"Good morning to you, sir, and congratulations on a tremendous effort to rid the nation of these terrorist cells. You must be elated at the success of this mission." "Yes, Dan, we are pleased with the way things went this morning. We realized at the same time, though, that this is only the beginning, one battle won in this war on terrorism. There is still a lot to be accomplished. We hope that the interrogation of the detainees will prove fruitful in finding the persons responsible for the flu epidemic, and also for the anthrax and suicide bombings we have experienced. As the CDC works feverishly to find a vaccine for the Spanish flu, our mission is to seek out and capture the perpetrators of these attacks."

"Agent Crowley, can you tell us of any progress made in identifying the individuals responsible for the flu attack?"

"All I can tell you, Dan, is that we have credible leads and information that have led us to Malaysia and that we are hot on the trail, but this morning's raids did not result in the capture of the leaders of this terrorist group that have put the entire world into turmoil."

"Agent Crowley, once again, congratulations on your success today. Best of luck in hunting down these culprits. We will be looking forward to further good news from you. Thank you for being with us today."

"Thank you, Dan, for having me."

"We will continue to follow this breaking story as it develops, but now we go to Angela Morrison at the Center for Disease Control here in Atlanta. Angela, what can you tell us about the progress in developing the vaccine for the flu strain?"

"Well, Dan, I just spoke to Dr. John Doyle, Director of the CDC, and he gave me a brief update. It has now been four months since the virus first appeared and it has been only two months since they were able to isolate the original strain from a body recovered in Norway. Dr. Doyle tells us today that they are making rapid progress in developing the vaccine. Although not quite there yet, Dr. Doyle is confident that they may be able to have it ready for testing by the end of the fourth month, rather than the original estimate of six months. Meanwhile, the CDC is concerned with the continual spread of the flu. Dr. Doyle emphasized once more during our interview that people absolutely must wear their HEPA masks everywhere they go. It is of the utmost importance, and I quote Dr. Doyle, 'that all citizens maintain caution and protection.' The death toll continues to rise, and mostly in that twenty-to-forty-year-old age group."

"Angela, did Dr. Doyle give you any estimate on when they could begin vaccinating the general public?"

"No, Dan, but what he did say is that the emergency responders would be inoculated first. That would include all firefighters, police, EMS, healthcare workers, hospital personnel, and public works folks. The general population would probably be vaccinated within two months following that."

"Angela, why the two month delay?"

"Dan, Dr. Doyle said the production of the vaccine cannot be completed quickly enough in order to take care of everybody at once. The two month lag is what it will take to produce the balance of the vaccine."

"Angela, thank you for that report."

"Thanks, Dan. This is Angela Morrison reporting from the CDC."

"Well, folks, you heard it. It sounds like a good news, bad news day. We are closing in on the trail of these suspects and in one day, ninety-six suspects have been arrested in our country with countless more arrested around the world. We still have quite a battle ahead of us, however, and it is going to be a very tough period over the next few months until we can get the vaccine developed and out to the general population. Stay tuned for further developments in this ongoing story about today's raids. We will bring you immediate coverage of any breaking news. This is Dan Quigley at CNN, Atlanta."

SUNDAY MORNING

"Good morning. I'm Tim Clark and welcome to *Meet the People*. My guests this morning are Dr. John Doyle, Director of the Center for Disease Control in Atlanta, Georgia, and Mr. Ted Graham, Director of the FBI. Dr. Doyle is the man responsible for locating the Spanish flu strain; he is currently heading up the project to develop a vaccine. Director Graham helped organize the recent and highly successful Operation Roundup.

"Director Graham, let me begin with you. First of all, congratulations to you and your agent, Terry Crowley, whom I understand lead Operation Roundup, a very well- coordinated attack, if I may, on the terrorist organization. Director Graham, the operation took place almost a week ago now. Can you tell us what has developed since then? Are we any closer to finding the leaders of this organization and to facilitating their eventual capture?"

"Tim, thank you for your kind remarks. Agent Crowley coordinated the operation superbly and is being recommended for a special commendation from the President for his efforts. However, I need to point out that this was a total team effort involving several Federal agencies under the Department of Homeland Security. Our partners at the CIA, the DEA, the ATF, and hundreds of state and local agencies were involved in Operation Roundup and they are all to be commended for a successful operation. We, of course, did not succeed in rounding up all of the suspects. It is apparent to us that the intelligence network of this particular terrorist organization is very deep and they were able to alert some of the locations before we arrived."

"Director Graham, are you saying that we still have an unknown number of terrorists throughout the country right now?"

"Tim, we are not certain of the actual number out there, but one thing we do know is that we have disrupted the organization and although no suspects were apprehended at twelve locations, we did uncover these individual cells. We have found caches of weapons of mass destruction that will no longer be useful to them; these suspects cannot go back to their safe houses. They will have to burrow underground to avoid capture and they have suffered a tremendous defeat. The war, however, is far from being over."

"Director Graham, it is obvious that the country is much safer now that these cells have been eliminated, but do we know if there are additional cells that we do not have information on?"

"Tim, it is quite possible that we have only scratched the surface, but I am confident that we have put a large chink in their armor. Our intelligence will continue to ferret out these cells if they exist and we will win this war."

"Thank you, Director Graham, for your candid comments. I am sure, as always, that the FBI will get its man. Now Dr. Doyle, let me turn to you now.

"Recently, you gave an interview regarding the process and progress of developing the vaccine so badly needed to combat the Spanish flu. Is it accurate to say that although you are making progress, we are looking at months before the vaccine will be ready?"

"Tim, I'm afraid that is the situation we face. We are proceeding as quickly as possible and much faster than I could ever have imagined, but we are still quite a way from having the vaccine available."

"Dr. Doyle, current estimates are that over 300,000 deaths have occurred so far and that seventy percent of those are fairly young people in the twenty-to-forty-year-old age group. We are losing our youngest, most vibrant, and healthiest citizens to this horrible virus. What kind of encouragement can we give to the citizens of our country?"

"Tim, as I said a week ago, everybody in this nation has to be extra cautious and extremely well-prepared when they go out in public. I cannot be more emphatic in directing that all citizens must wear a HEPA mask at all times to avoid infection. We must remember that the Spanish flu was very strong the first time it appeared almost eighty years ago, and now it is worse because it has been weaponized."

"Dr. Doyle, as you know there is panic in the streets. Peoples' lives have been turned upside down. Funeral homes are overloaded preparing the deceased for burial and are operating day and night to keep up in some localities. Families are torn apart and those not affected are afraid to even venture outside. Where and when does this all end? How long can we survive before we get back to some semblance of normal life again?"

"Tim, I wish I had the answers you are looking for and I would give anything to say that I have the magic bullet to end this horrible disease, but I don't. All I can tell you is that I am confident that we will prevail and we will have a vaccine within a few months and will be able to vaccinate the general public a few months after that. In the interim, we can all pray that although we are fighting a weaponized version of the Spanish flu, maybe it will follow the route of the first strain."

"Dr. Doyle, excuse me but could you please elaborate on that statement? Are you saying that we could be looking at a turnaround here?"

"What I'm saying, Tim, and please don't take this as the miracle that we are hoping for, but the original strain of the Spanish flu left as quickly as it appeared with no warning. It faded away and was gone before we were ever able to develop a vaccine. We must keep in perspective that this current flu has been altered or weaponized to make it stronger, so it is very possible that it will continue until we can control it on our own. The possibility, although remote, still remains that it could just go away."

"Dr. Doyle, that sounds encouraging if you believe in miracles, but it doesn't sound practical. I believe that prayer might be our best option right now."

"Tim, I could not agree more with you. In the interim, we are going to lose a lot of family and friends unless we practice caution and preparedness. I am not saying we will all survive under those recommendations, but we will certainly reduce the death toll, which is rising every day."

"Dr. Doyle, thank you for appearing on our program this morning and thank you, too, for your candidness. You certainly don't pull any punches and I appreciate that. Thank you for being straight with us and with our audience."

"Thank you, Tim."

"Director Graham, thank you again for visiting with us this morning. We will be following your investigation closely and hope that you are able to eliminate all of the cells in this country and bring these people to justice." "Thank you, Tim. We will do our best to accomplish exactly that."

"Our guests this morning have been Dr. John Doyle, Director of the Center for Disease Control in Atlanta, and Director Ted Graham of the FBI. Until next Sunday, this is Tim Clark on *Meet the People.* Have a super Sunday."

PRESIDENTIAL QUARTERS

Maggie Doyle was busily setting out some shrimp when Sean entered their comfortable den in the Presidential quarters.

"Well, Mr. President, how did it go today?"

"Maggie, I think each and every day just gets more and more stressful. It seems like as the weeks go by, we have a constant 'good news, bad news' scenario. I would give anything to have this nation go back to a normal life and regular routine."

"But Sean, isn't John making strides in getting the vaccine to a finished product?"

"Yes, Maggie, but it has been four months now and look at what has happened to our country. They are calling for my head. I even received calls today from three foreign leaders and you would swear they thought I was responsible for this round of terrorism. The countries around the world are having a worse bout with this enemy than we are here, even though we have more deaths and have been targeted by the terrorists with numerous weapons of mass destruction."

"Oh, Sean, I wish I could make it all go away for you. I feel so bad that you are going through all this, but let's look at the good side of the situation."

"What might that be, luv?"

"Sean, there is no one better to lead the country though this crisis than the guy sitting in the Oval Office and that is you, luv. You are doing a superb job under the circumstances."

"Maggie, the problem is I don't know how much longer I can continue to deal with this. We need a miracle and a lot of help in rounding up what is left of these terrorist cells. This panic in the streets cannot continue. People are panicking; they're looting, destroying property, and rioting on a daily basis. This cannot continue or I am going to have to enact martial law. I absolutely do not want to have to do that, Maggie."

"Sean, we need time. That is what we need. How long before you figure the inoculations will begin?"

"If we are lucky, John might have the vaccine ready by next month, but that will only take care of the responders. It would be a couple more months before the general population would be able to get the vaccine."

"Sean, does John believe that the vaccine will eradicate the flu? Do you think he is confident that there will not be a reoccurrence?"

"I believe in John more than he believes in himself. I really think he can do it, but time will tell."

"Mr. President, how about a Manhattan and some of your favorite shrimp?"

"First Lady, I thought you would never ask. Bring it on."

"I'll pour. Why don't you take off your shoes and relax and turn on the evening news?"

Sean sat down, removed his loafers, picked up the remote, and tuned to CNN. As the channel came in, Sean immediately recognized the familiar streamer at the bottom of the screen that read 'Breaking News.' *Oh my God, what now?'*

He adjusted the volume and heard the reporter saying, "As reported earlier, we have received word that three of the top airlines in the country filed for Chapter 11 this afternoon. This move will allow the airlines to operate on a limited basis while they cope with the downslide in the economy brought on by the flu pandemic."

Oh damn, Sean thought. *Not only are airlines filing for bankruptcy protection, but the media is now referring to the crisis as a pandemic.*

He quickly switched the channel to the FOX network and saw the same events being covered. The co-anchor was reporting, "With over three hundred thousand of our citizens killed by this horrible flu and hundreds of thousands more fighting for their lives, the economy is at its worst point since the stock market almost crashed back in the eighties. The three airlines that filed for protection today have seen declining fares since the day the flu epidemic was identified and have suffered losses for four months in a row. At their current rate of loss, without the action taken today, they would be out of business completely by year end. People are just not flying anywhere unless absolutely necessary. Oil prices are at an all-time high, almost double what they were back in 2004. The Middle East, and especially the oil-producing countries, has been hit very hard by the flu epidemic. Their economies are very brittle at this point; to compensate, they have raised oil prices each month since the crisis began."

Sean picked up the remote to change the channel again as Maggie entered with his drink in one hand and a dish of shrimp cocktail in the other. "So what are we hearing tonight on the old tube?"

"Maggie, it's not good. Three airlines have filed for Chapter 11 protection and the stock market is in the pits. Oil prices went up again this afternoon. People are not flying and they can't afford to put gas in their cars. Maybe the best solution is for everyone to simply stay home, protect themselves, and wait out this flu until John can get them inoculated. Meanwhile, I'm sure we are going to hear from Congress soon, because they have to appease their constituents. People want answers and they want that magic bullet and they want it yesterday."

Sean could not have been more prophetic in his statement. As he bit into the shrimp, his Chief of Staff, Ken Sitarek, knocked on the door to his quarters.

"Come on in, Ken. You're just in time for a cocktail."

"Mr. President, I would like nothing better. Unfortunately, I'm here with some news you probably don't want to hear."

"Ken, I've been listening to bad news for the past fifteen minutes from the news media, so let me have it. I'm ready for whatever you throw at me."

"Mr. President, you know we now have over three hundred thousand deaths here in the States. The European Union is reporting over five hundred thousand deaths throughout its twenty-one countries. I received a call from the Speaker of the House and he informed me that Congress will be convening tomorrow; they are most likely going to ask you to declare a state of martial law."

The President leaned back in his chair and sighed. "Ken, I was afraid that this was coming. I just said to Maggie before you came in that this was a possibility. I guess we'll wait and hear the debate tomorrow on the Hill and then take it from there."

"Good. Mr. President, I'll inform Bob Roche and George White. Do you want to call Secretary Roberts, sir?" "Yeah, Ken, I'll get a hold of Arnie and alert him. He's over in Moscow attempting to reassure the Russians that they'll get the vaccine as quickly as we can develop it. The Russian government hasn't released any figures on their death toll from the flu, but we suspect that it is probably triple what the European Union is experiencing."

Ken frowned as he looked at his boss and said, "Sir, the CIA is attempting to get an accurate death toll worldwide. The best estimate they can come up with right now is somewhere between ten million and fifteen million. We don't have figures on the Chinese or the Russians, so it could be much higher than that."

Sean stood up and said, "Ken, thanks for coming over so quickly. If you need anything further tonight, please call me."

"Yes, Mr. President. Sorry to be the bearer of bad news all the time, but hopefully by next year, we'll look back on this as just a bad experience and will have put it behind us."

"That's what I like about you, Ken. Always the optimist. Good night."

"Good night, Mr. President."

CAPITOL HILL

The following morning, all three major networks led their morning newscasts with the breaking story that the House of Representatives would be meeting in a special session to discuss the pandemic crisis and what steps might be taken to stop the nationwide rioting.

Speaker of the House John Quinn was interviewed on two of the three networks, but refused to confirm that Congress would recommend to the President that he declare a state of martial law. When asked, Speaker Quinn would only say that whatever the House decided on, Representatives would then refer it to the Senate and ask for the Senators' support in any recommendation that would be made to the President.

On the third network, the morning news anchor interviewed Senator Harold Atkins, Chairman of the Health Care Committee. When asked about the special session being held in the House, Senator Atkins took the position that it would be improper to speculate what, if anything, the House might recommend. Senator Atkins instead switched the subject to the current health crisis and what his committee was doing to speed up the process at the Center for Disease Control.

The Senator said, "It is of the utmost urgency that a vaccine is developed posthaste and that the entire population is inoculated against this horrendous scourge that terrorists have inflicted upon our great nation. We support President Doyle in whatever steps he takes to eradicate this virus and we give him one hundred percent backing on fighting this terrorist organization. Whatever it takes to defeat these barbarians, the Senate will support the President."

CNN reported that the House of Representatives would call for the President to declare martial law and claimed they had gathered this information from very reliable sources. All calls to the congressmen were either unreturned or were met with "No comment" or statements such as, "I was not aware what the Speaker of the House wanted on the agenda."

The special session of Congress convened at eleven that morning, later than usual, but many members had to fly back into Washington from points nationwide. As Speaker Quinn banged his gavel to bring the session to order, a loud explosion shook the chamber. Plaster affixed to the walls and ceiling came crashing down upon the Congress members. Within seconds of the explosion, sirens and fire alarms throughout the Capital began to blare. Speaker Quinn asked for order and calm as he banged his gavel over and over.

"Ladies and gentlemen! I'm not sure what we've experienced, but you all know the evacuation procedures, so let's do this as orderly as possible!"

Looking down the aisle, the Speaker saw that while some members had been injured by falling debris, everyone else appeared okay, incurring only bruises and scratches. The exit was orderly, and the security guards led the members of Congress down a hallway and out the rear of the building. The urgency at the moment was to get the Congress members to safety as soon as possible in case there was a second explosion or other incendiary device.

As they exited the building, the captain of the security force explained that a late model SUV had driven right up the front steps of the Capitol and exploded, killing the occupants and four security personnel. No other fatalities occurred because the Capitol Building had been off limits to tourists and the media for the past month. The building itself, however, did not fare so well. The two columns at the top of the stairs and entire façade of the front of the building were in shambles.

Back at the White House, the President had been notified within minutes after the bombing. Ten minutes later he received a call from the FBI that the same terrorist organization that had taken credit for all of the events since the flu virus was now taking credit in the name of Allah for the car bombing. The caller declared that this was not intended to kill the Congressmen or women, but to give the President a warning that they would strike again and again until the infidels were brought to their knees.

The President slammed the phone down and swung his chair around to see black smoke drifting toward the sky from the Capitol. He reached again for the phone and said, "Aggie, ask Bob Roche and Ken Sitarek to come in, please." "Yes sir, Mr. President, right away."

Within thirty seconds both men entered the Oval Office together.

"Come on in, guys, and sit down. Would anyone like coffee or a Coke?" Both men declined anything to drink.

"Bob, what is your take on this bombing? How in the hell did it ever happen, a vehicle blowing up on the top steps of the Capitol? Where the hell was security? Are we leaving ourselves that vulnerable that some God damn terrorist can reach the entrance to our Capitol Building and blow up a car bomb?"

"Mr. President, this could not have happened normally, but because of the urgency to get the entire House together, they took down the Jersey barriers at the bottom of the stairs and had not yet replaced them when the SUV came speeding up the stairs. Capitol Security Police began shooting immediately at the SUV, but to no avail; when the vehicle exploded, they were all killed."

"This never, ever should have happened, Bob! Someone is going to be held responsible for this act and for the deaths of those four officers."

"I understand how angry you are, Mr. President, and believe me, someone will be held accountable. The FBI also has a good lead on where this vehicle came from and has already confirmed the identity of two of the men in the SUV, despite the fact that there is not much left to identify."

"Ken, we need to get the names of the officers who were killed and their family's names so I may call them personally and express my condolences to their wives and children."

"Yes, Mr. President, that information is being collected as we speak. One of those officers was a young woman who leaves a husband and two young children. The other three were men, and all have wives and families. I'll get the numbers to you this morning, sir."

"Thanks, Ken. Anything else to report, let me know as soon as you can. Call Director Graham at the FBI and tell him I want leads and I want them yesterday. This situation has gone too far and it is time we caught these bastards." "I will get a hold of Ted Graham as soon as I leave your office, Mr. President. Is there anything else, sir?" "No, Ken. That's all for now. Bob, I apologize for taking my anger out on you, but I'm sure you know how it was intended."

"I do, sir. Thank you."

Both men rose, shook hands with the President, and left the Oval Office.

TWO DAYS LATER

After the debris was cleared from the façade of the Capitol Building and the entire property was checked and re-checked, the building inspectors from the District of Columbia declared that although there was extensive damage, the building was safe to enter. All entries, however, would be made from the rear entrance. Almost forty-eight hours to the minute from the time of the explosion, the House of Representatives reconvened their meeting at the sound of Speaker Quinn's gavel.

There were five hours of discussion on what to do regarding the worldwide crisis. The opposing party was critical of the way the President was handling the situation thus far. They suggested that maybe he was not up to the job of the highest office held in the entire world. These comments were made by a Freshman Congressman who had lost two siblings to the flu. There was yelling and screaming from across the aisle, and abusive language was spewed in the direction of the young Congressman. The Speaker banged his gavel for order, and slowly the noise subsided and decorum was restored.

Although the issue had been debated regarding how the President could restore order in the streets, the motion was not put forward until six hours into the closed door session. The vote to recommend that President Doyle declare martial law was not unanimous, but clearly had enough votes, putting the majority in favor. The motion passed, and was sent to the Senate for their approval.

Two days later, the Senate met and voted to approve the recommendation, with only three dissenting votes.

The President was informed of the vote before it was released to the media, and he and Maggie immediately prepared to leave the White House for Camp David. This would be a monumental decision for Sean and he wanted absolute solitude to think it through. What better place than the Presidential retreat.

Meanwhile, the streets were getting worse, with looting and gangs roaming and robbing anyone and anything in sight. The local police forces were overworked, undermanned, and at the point of total exhaustion. The thought of declaring martial law and having Federal troops patrolling the streets of America sickened President Sean Doyle, but if something did not change drastically, the country would be on the verge of anarchy.

Sean and Maggie hurried across the White House lawn to the awaiting Marine One Presidential helicopter and were quickly helped up the steps and into the aircraft. As the helicopter lifted off the lawn at the White House, Maggie looked down at the beautiful city and saw that repairs were already being made to the Capitol. There was scaffolding everywhere around the front of the building. She thought to herself, *In a small way, this shows our country's resolve to deal with this crisis as quickly as possible. Here we are at the biggest crisis in our history, and we begin rebuilding within only a few days of the terrorists' attempt to destroy one of our most visible symbols of democracy.*

Sean leaned over to Maggie and said, "A penny for your thoughts."

"Oh, Sean, I was just thinking about the resiliency of our nation. I know you have a very difficult decision to make, but I am praying it will be the right one and will help to restore our country's way of life."

"Maggie, I am confident that whatever decision I make, it will be the right one. We cannot continue to let terrorists run our lives. We are going to win this war, Maggie. You just wait and see. Besides, I have confidence because I am married to the ultimate optimist. Remember, you're the one that always keeps my head on straight. Let's relax this weekend and I promise that things will look better on Monday morning when we go back to Washington."

*   *   *

Saturday morning, the talking heads for all three television networks speculated on the President's decision. They interviewed anyone they could find that knew anything about martial law and what impact it would have on the nation. This included General Frank Spencer, who was on the teaching staff at the United States War College. "General Spencer, can you define martial law for us?" The General leaned into the camera and said, "The term martial law, in its simplest terms, means military law. When martial law is declared, as we suspect that the President may do this weekend, the nation will be then governed by the army. This is implemented by the President of the United States declaring a State of Emergency throughout the country. The U.S. Army would then send troops to whatever areas are in need of them so that order may be restored."

The anchorman asked, "General, why so drastic a measure as martial law?"

The General frowned and replied, "There are times when drastic measures must be taken. We not only have a major health crisis to deal with, as thousands of our citizens are dying from this horrible flu, but we have total chaos in the streets of our cities and towns. We cannot let this situation continue. The local responders are unable to cope with the magnitude of the lawlessness that is taking place and until we can get it under control, martial law would seem the most logical step."

"Thank you, General Spencer, for such a direct explanation. If the decision is made, let's hope that order can be restored."

CAMP DAVID

The flight to Camp David, the Presidential retreat, was only thirty minutes long and as Marine One dropped down in altitude on its approach, Maggie said, "Oh Sean, it is so beautiful down there. Why don't we come here more often to simply relax, rather than to make monumental decisions?" "That sounds good to me, luv, once we get back to normal," Sean said before adding, "if we ever see normal again."

Located in the Catoctin Mountains in Maryland, the Presidential retreat was established in 1942 for then President Franklin Delano Roosevelt as a private retreat for the leader of the country to relax, and to entertain foreign dignitaries far from the press and stress of Washington.

Turning to Maggie, Sean said, "President Roosevelt called this camp "Shangri-la," after the imaginary land of the same name in James Hilton's novel, Lost Horizon. It was known by that name until President Eisenhower re-named it Camp David ten years later after his grandson. Almost seems appropriate for today's events: our country seems to have lost its horizon, but damn, we will get it back."

Sean leaned across Maggie to look down on the left side of the aircraft. He said, "You know, Maggie, a lot of history was made down there. The Normandy Invasion back in World War II was planned at this location. President Carter invited the leaders of Egypt and Israel here and the result was the Camp David Accord, making peace between the two countries. It is humbling every time I return to this retreat to think about how much of our world history has been shaped here at Camp David."

Marine One began its descent to the landing pad not far from the Aspen Lodge, the Presidential cabin. The President and First Lady stepped off the helicopter and were chilled by the biting wind of late winter. They walked along the short path to the cabin, where they were greeted at the door to the lodge by Marcus, the White House chef.

"Welcome, Mr. President and Mrs. Doyle."

The President turned to look at Marcus and said, "Marcus, it amazes me how you get here long before us. How do you do it?"

Marcus smiled and said, "Well, sir, I have friends in high places. Please come in out of the cold. Dinner will be served in one hour. One of your favorites, Mr. President, but it's a surprise."

"Marcus, you always surprise me. I can't wait for dinner."

Sean and Maggie entered the cabin and immediately felt the warmth of the fire blazing thirty feet away. They took off their coats and handed them to Marcus and headed straight for the hearth and the inviting fire.

Seated across from each other in matching Queen Anne chairs, Maggie smiled and said, "Mr. President, it doesn't get any more relaxing than this."

"It is wonderful here, Maggie. I pray that I can relax, though, after I meet with my inner circle and make my decision."

Ten minutes prior to dinner, the invited attendees arrived at Aspen Lodge. Secretary of State Arnie Roberts, National Security Advisor Bob Roche, White House Council George White, and Chief of Staff Ken Sitarek all came in together and gathered around the fire. The President was just returning from the library.

"Welcome, gentlemen. Please have a seat. Dinner will be ready shortly. How was your flight?"

"Very smooth, Mr. President," Arnie Roberts answered for the group. Arnie had returned that afternoon from Moscow, where he had met with the Russian leader, President Putin, in an attempt to calm Putin's fears of not getting the vaccine when it was available.

"So Arnie, how did you and our Russian friend make out in your discussions?"

"Mr. President, I believe he is still a little skeptical, but I assured him that he had your solid promise to get the vaccine to Moscow and St. Petersburg, where they have their distribution center for Russia, as quickly as it is available. From our discussion, I have ascertained that the Russian death toll is approaching close to four million victims."

"How is the general mood over there? Are they experiencing the same unrest we are here?"

"Yes, sir, they are, and all of the borders with the former Soviet Union countries have been sealed and no one is allowed in or out of the country. President Putin is about to impose martial law there until order can be restored."

"Arnie, that's what we're here to discuss. Let's go in to dinner and see what Marcus has for us tonight. I hope it's something of substance, because we certainly need it with the decisions we have to make."

As they entered the dining room, the aroma told Sean what dinner would be. He could recognize that smell anywhere and Marcus was the best at preparing one of the President's favorite meals.

Once the group was seated, Maggie took Sean's hand and said, "Gentlemen, I believe that grace is in order. May we ask God to direct all of you in making the right decisions tonight." George White offered to say the grace and he was very eloquent as he thanked God for the meal and for all of the blessings that had been bestowed on our great nation. He also asked for guidance as the group moved forward in the battle against the evil forces of terrorism.

As grace ended, the waiter entered the dining room with Caesar salad for everyone. Marcus followed right behind him with garlic breadsticks and an alfredo sauce. "Marcus, would I be correct in guessing that we are having chicken tettrazini for dinner tonight?"

"Yes, Mr. President, that is a correct assumption. Bon appetit, everyone."

Marcus left the room and Ken Sitarek said, "Mr. President, I hope you pay this guy well. You don't ever want to lose him as the White House chef."

"Are you kidding, Ken? The man absolutely loves his job. He would work for peanuts, he loves it so much. We're lucky to have him. However, at times I feel the need to exercise more after the sumptuous meals he puts in front of us."

Dinner was the usual five stars and after coffee and spumante, the group retired to the library where the discussion was to begin.

Bob Roche was first to speak and he was blunt. "Mr. President, I know this is your decision to make and God knows it is extremely difficult for you and for the nation, but I firmly believe that we have no other course of action, sir, than to impose a state of martial law. Without martial law, we could be looking at complete anarchy. The patriot groups in the Northwest and in many of the Midwest states have never been stronger. We have so many of our resources fighting this terrorist war that these maniacs who have advocated a new form of government for years are now gaining strength every day."

The President looked over at George White and said, "George, do you agree with Ken? Do you believe that martial law is the only solution?"

"Mr. President, I don't believe it's the only solution that we have here, but with the country nearly out of control, I think that it is the most logical decision to be made. The local resources plainly cannot cope with what is going on in the streets of mainstream America. They need help, and I believe our only option is the United States Army. We will be criticized, and in some areas we will be condemned for making such an extreme decision, but as we all know, extreme conditions call for extreme measures. We cannot let our country fall into chaos and face the challenge of anarchy."

The President turned to Arnie Roberts and nodded. "Mr. President, I concur with both George and Ken. I have just returned from Russia, as well as Italy, France, Germany, and Spain. I can tell you that these countries are convinced that we are losing control of our nation. We need to do something drastic to turn this around while we wait for John Doyle to come through with the vaccine."

"Gentlemen, I appreciate your input on this. George, can you put together the legal ramifications of martial law? I have read most of the material sent to me by the Attorney General, but I don't feel it's enough."

"Yes, sir. Mr. President, I have some excellent legal opinions that I have brought with me."

"Arnie, assuming we go this route, I would like you to prepare a statement for all of the countries we have diplomatic relations with and then a separate statement for the rest of the world. Give it to Sherry Katz to review, with a copy to me. Bob, I need you to call together all of the Homeland Security people, including the FBI and the CIA, so that everyone is on the same page. Also, call a joint meeting of the Homeland Security folks and the Joint Chiefs of Staff to go over the military plan that has been in place, but never used. You can make that meeting for Monday morning. If I decide against martial law, we can always cancel.

"Gentlemen, it has been a very long and demanding day. Let's get together at eight tomorrow morning and discuss this further."

As everyone stood, ready to depart, the President put his hand on George White's shoulder and said, "George, I will review those legal opinions tonight and will be prepared to discuss them at breakfast."

George said, "Thank you, Mr. President."

The President said, "Good night, everyone. Have a good rest, and I'll see you all in the morning."

In unison, the group said, "Good night, Mr. President."

With that, they all retired to their guest cabins, and Sean headed to the master bedroom to be with Maggie and to await the legal opinions.

KUALA LUMPUR

Over fifty percent of the residents of Malaysia are Malays and the majority of them are Muslim. The city of Kuala Lumpur, with over one and a half million residents, is the center of commerce for the nation of Malaysia. Until the Chinese built their skyscraper in Singapore, Kuala Lumpur was proud to have the two tallest buildings in the world, the Petronas Towers. The towers are as identifiable to the people of Malaysia as the Twin Towers of the World Trade Center were to Americans prior to 9/11.

It was on the thirty-seventh floor of the west tower where Kemal, a Muslim Malay and avowed terrorist leader, had his office. He was a bitter man, full of hatred for anything American and the United States. It sickened him that his own country had patterned its country's flag to imitate the American flag. *The red and white stripes, and the blue background up in the corner with the moon and sun of Islam are an injustice to my people*, Kemal thought. *The founders of the democracy in Malaysia are fools to imitate the homeland of the infidels. I will fight them to my death and take as many of the fools with me as I am able.*

As Kemal looked out toward the Central Market of Kuala Lumpur, his daydreaming was interrupted by a faint knock on his office door. "Come in! Come in, please."

Sulanni entered Kemal's office and Kemal stood to greet him. There was no hug this time and no kisses on the cheek, as when they had last met at the hotel.

"Mr. Sulanni, you were to get back to me the next day. Where have you been?"

"My fearless leader, you know that we have received a very serious blow to our network of cells."

"Yes, of course I know. Do you take me as a fool, Sulanni?"

"No sir, not at all, sir. It is just that I have been working day and night to determine the damage done to our network. It is heavy, sir, very heavy indeed. We have lost many cells and almost one hundred of our soldiers have been detained. The Americans and their allies have dealt us a severe setback; I don't know how we are going to recover."

"I will tell you, Mr. Sulanni, how we will recover. We will hit them again and again, as they die now by the millions across the world from our St. Gustaf's flu. We know that it is only a matter of time before their medical people stop the flu with a vaccine, but in the meantime, we will declare a tremendous victory. The idiot President Doyle is about to declare martial law in his homeland. Our actions have brought him to his knees, but we are not finished with him yet. Do you understand me, Mr. Sulanni?" "Oh, yes sir, Kemal, I understand completely. Tell me what you want done and I will get it accomplished for you." "Sulanni, it is time to activate our most secret sleeper cells all across the infidel's homeland. Now is the time to attack before they send their army to try and restore order in their streets. I want you to contact all of the sleepers and tell them the hour of Allah is at hand. We attack on Sunday morning and the country of Satan will never be the same. Do you know what to do, Sulanni?"

"Yes, Kemal, I will follow your orders completely.   Praise Allah."

Sulanni left the office with his head bowed and Kemal sat back down in his executive chair and looked out over the city of Kuala Lumpur with a satisfied smile on his face. He thought to himself, *Mr. Doyle, you are about to go down into the depths of despair.*

Sulanni headed back to his hotel in downtown Kuala Lumpur. Once in his room, he lifted his laptop computer from its case and plugged it into the internet connection provided in each room. He went to the secure site he had been using for over two years and prepared an e-mail to be sent to all of the sleeper cells in the United States. As he typed, he thought, *those American fools think that they have located all of the cells in our network. They are in for a big surprise on Sunday morning, their day of worship. The pigs will never forget the day, and martial law will be needed more than ever. There will be total destruction of their favorite places.*

He completed the e-mail and sent it out to sixty-five recipients as priority mail with the return receipt request. This would insure that all of the cells were ready to strike.

Sulanni clicked off the internet site. "Praise Allah," he said.

ASPEN LODGE

"Good morning, gentlemen. Hope you all had a restful night."

"Good morning, Mr. President," the men replied together. They all looked at each other and smiled with a look that said, *Okay, who goes first?*

Ken Sitarek was the first to speak. "Mr. President, no matter what the circumstances of the moment, I always seem to sleep well here at Camp David. My cabin is very comfortable and once again, I slept well. Thank you for asking." The rest of the men, except for Bob Roche, said they, too, had slept well. Arnie had jet lag and said he could have used another four hours, but said he would get over it.

Breakfast arrived and everyone dug into bacon and eggs, home fries, and toast. All of the men drank black coffee, a standard with most of the White House staff. Maggie chose to have breakfast in the master bedroom, as she knew the men would want to discuss the situation at the breakfast table.

As they were into their second cups of coffee, the President said, "Guys, I know you'll support me in whatever I decide, but this is the most difficult decision I have ever had to make in my life; I will probably never make a decision this difficult again, no matter how long I live. George, I reviewed all of the legal opinions until almost midnight last night. I have read them over and over and they certainly make sense. The situation we are faced with almost demands that I declare martial law. The nation is deteriorating more each day. Although I am extremely reluctant, I have decided that I will go before the American public on Monday and ask for their patience once more and for their prayers for our nation as we fight this war on terrorism. I will then declare martial law for a period of ninety days, after which time it could be extended or lifted, if circumstances improve, and we are able to seriously damage the operations of this terrorist organization. We cannot, and I will not let this nation fall into anarchy, and I cannot, in good judgment, expect the local responders who are at the point of exhaustion, to continue to try and defuse the out-of-control situation in many of our towns and cities. The military will take over responsibility from the local authorities, but will work with them to attain law and order in every city, town, and village in this nation."

Arnie Roberts spoke first. "Mr. President, you are making the right decision. We support you one hundred percent."

"Thank you, Arnie. May God be with us."

Bob Roche said, "Mr. President, I sent out an e-mail this morning to the parties you requested to be at the meeting on Monday morning, and they have all replied. The meeting is set for 8:30. Do you want me to invite anyone else?"

"Yes, Bob. After thinking about it, I would like to have the rest of the Cabinet at the meeting as well."

"Consider it done, sir."

Ken Sitarek set down his coffee and said, "Mr. President, how do you want to handle the announcement of your decision?"

"Have Sherry set up a press conference for noon on Monday and alert all of the networks that this is a major announcement in the war on terror. They will speculate until noon on Monday, but no leaks, please, as to what I intend to say."

"Yes, sir. I will emphasize, Mr. President, that you do not want anyone talking to the press until you have had your press conference."

"Thanks, Ken. You can all go on back to Washington and to your families. Maggie and I are going to spend the rest of the weekend here and fly back tomorrow evening." As he rose from his chair, he added, "Have a good weekend, gentlemen, and thank you for your counsel and your friendship."

Sean left the room and the rest of the staff left for their cabins to retrieve their overnight bags and head for the helicopter.

SLEEPERS RESPOND

By Saturday afternoon, a total of fifty-two of the sixty-five sleeper cells had responded to Sulanni's e-mail. All had indicated they were ready, willing, and able to carry out their deadly mission. Thirteen did not respond; Sulanni suspected that they had either backed out on their commitment, or had been discovered by the authorities. Another possibility was that they had contracted the St. Gustaf's flu and were unable to respond either because they were too ill, or they were deceased. All of the sleeper cells had been dedicated to dying in the name of Allah. Sulanni would not make himself believe that any of them had simply backed out of their mission.

Of the fifty-two that confirmed their availability, there were five from New York State. The balance of forty-seven was located in thirty-nine states. That meant that out of the fifty states in the country, all but ten would be spared an attack by the sleeper cells. New York would be hit the hardest.

In Manhattan that Saturday night, two fair-skinned and light-haired men who looked like they could be from Germany or perhaps Scandinavia, met in a coffee house in Greenwich Village. Neither would ever be suspected of being a terrorist. They did not fit the usual profile that people were used to seeing, but they were indeed part of the sleeper cell network across the country. They had been activated and were ready to carry out their mission.

As they entered the coffee house, both men wore HEPA masks over their faces to protect them from the flu strain. Once in the shop, they took a booth at the rear of the coffee house and removed their masks. One said to the other, "There really isn't much need for these anymore, is there? After tomorrow we will be with Allah and who needs a mask then?"

The second man nodded in agreement and said, "You certainly are right about that, but until now, we needed to stay healthy until we could carry out our mission. Are you all set for tomorrow morning?"

"Yes. Did you have any problem getting the clothing?" "No, not at all. Our Malaysian friend at the dry cleaning establishment came through, as he said he would. I did have trouble finding the sash, however. He didn't have one. I had to go out and buy one."

"Isn't that taking a chance of being discovered?" "What difference will it make twelve hours from now? I'll be gone. The sash will be gone and all they will know is that someone bought a black sash at the Goodwill store." "Do you have any regrets about what you are about to do tomorrow?"

"None at all. I have been waiting four years for this day to carry out my mission. I have stashed away enough money for my wife and children to live comfortably for the rest of their lives. They will not suffer, except emotionally, but that will pass in time. Hopefully, they will look at their father as a hero who died for Allah." "Since I have no family, there will be no one to grieve or wonder if what I did was right or wrong. I'm ready. I must go now. Be well until tomorrow, my friend. I will see you together with Allah."

The two men embraced and left the coffee house separately, and each went back to his apartment to wait for morning.

MANHATTAN

Sunday morning in New York City dawned brilliantly sunny and the temperature was predicted to be in the high forties by late morning. A front page article in *The New York Times* speculated what the President might announce at his press conference on Monday. Speculation was high that he might declare martial law. The networks actively debated the merits of martial law should it be declared.

Meet the People had just ended an interview with Army General James Glass, the Chairman of the Joint Chiefs of Staff. He had expounded on what previous guests had said about martial law and gave a layman's view of what would happen or not, assuming martial law was declared.

Churchgoers, including tourists who took the chance of visiting New York in spite of the flu restrictions, were streaming into St. Patrick's Cathedral for ten o'clock mass. Cardinal Schultz entered from the side door to the main altar to begin mass, with two deacons, and four altar boys and girls; two extraordinary ministers followed closely behind. The Cardinal bowed to the altar with his hands clasped, then turned to face the congregation. As he looked up the center aisle and began to speak, he noticed a slightly overweight priest dressed in a black cassock with a black sash around his waist that hung down in front. He assumed this was a visiting priest who had come to hear mass and he bowed his head to begin the opening prayer. At that moment, the visiting priest drowned out the Cardinal's voice as he yelled, "Praise Allah!" Pulling on his sash, he blew himself up, killing everyone within thirty-five feet of him and causing severe damage to the cathedral. The Cardinal was hit with shrapnel and fell to the floor at the altar. There was panic everywhere; people screamed and tried to escape the carnage. In the name of Allah, one of fifty-two suicide bombers had just attacked the most famous cathedral in the United States.

Across the country, between the hours of 7 and 10 a.m. depending on the time zone, and at precisely the same moment as the attack on St. Patrick's Cathedral, fifty-one other churches and cathedrals were attacked by suicide bombers dressed as priests and ministers. The National Cathedral in Washington was hit, as was St. Joseph's Cathedral in Buffalo, the President's hometown. The terrorists had carried out their promise to bring death and destruction across the homeland.

The fatalities numbered in the thousands; the property damage would take days to even estimate. The death toll was sure to surpass the 2001 attack on the World Trade Center and the Pentagon.

At Camp David, Sean and Maggie were preparing to go for a walk after they finished watching *Meet the People* when breaking news was aired to report the bombings. A local reporter was standing outside the National Cathedral where the front of the church was in a shambles.

"Reports are coming in from all over the country that churches and cathedrals were the targets of suicide bombers this morning. Only the Jewish synagogues were spared, as their Sabbath is observed on Saturday, and the buildings were empty."

Sean turned to Maggie and said, "Get our bags and let's get back to Washington."

His military aide walked in and said, "Mr. President, Marine One is preparing for take off. We assumed that with the news, you would want to head back to the White House." "You assumed right, young man. Mrs. Doyle and I will be right out to the helipad."

Forty minutes later, the President and the First Lady landed on the White House lawn and were met by Ken Sitarek and Bob Roche. As the President stepped off Marine One, he said, "Ken, Bob, this changes things. Call a press conference immediately."

MARTIAL LAW

It was five o'clock Sunday afternoon, and all networks were tuned to the White House Oval Office for the Presidential address. The announcer said, "Ladies and gentlemen, the President of the United States."

Sean Doyle stared directly into the camera. "Good afternoon, my fellow Americans. I probably should rephrase that. It certainly is not a good afternoon for thousands of our citizens. This morning, we were hit with the worst terrorist attack this country has ever experienced. Our war on terror has made tremendous strides, as evidenced by our recent breakup of terrorist cells across the world. "Today's attacks took the lives of thousands of our fellow Americans whose only wish at ten o'clock Eastern Standard Time this morning was to visit God in his house of worship and to pray that this horrible war on terrorism would be won once and for all. Instead, they were met with more death and destruction. Our hearts and prayers go out to all of the victims of this tragedy and to their families. We are Americans, and we never give up the fight. I will promise you now and forever that we will track down these terrorist cells and eliminate them completely. It will not happen overnight—it will take months and possibly years—but God help us, we will do it. Let these barbarians beware. We are coming for you and we are going to eliminate every last one of you.

"My fellow citizens, as you know we have a pandemic eating at the hearts and souls of our countrymen. There is panic in the streets and there is destruction of property. Our local authorities are struggling to maintain control to protect the lives of all our citizens. This lawlessness cannot continue to destroy the very structure and the democratic way of life that we have held in the highest regard for over two hundred twenty-five years. I had originally intended to address the nation tomorrow, but after the devastating events of this morning, I have decided to make that address to you today.

"Effective at six p.m. Eastern Standard Time today, I am declaring martial law in the United States of America. This declaration will be in effect for ninety days, and could go longer if order cannot be restored by that time. I realize that the average American citizen may not be aware of what martial law is, so let me give you a brief explanation of what is involved. I am declaring this measure under Executive Order 12656, which reads as follows:

'**ASSIGNMENT OF EMERGENCY PREPAREDNESS RESPONSIBILITIES:** 'A national emergency is any occurrence, including natural disaster, military attack, technological emergency, or other emergency that seriously degrades or seriously threatens the national security of the United States. Policy for national security emergency preparedness shall be established by the President.' This order includes federal takeover of all local law enforcement agencies, and wage and price controls. It prohibits anyone from moving assets in or out of the United States; creates a draft; controls all travel in and out of the United States; and much more.

"I sincerely regret that this action has to be taken. However, it is in the nation's best interest at this time, and I am asking all of our citizens to cooperate fully with the military in helping them to maintain calm and order throughout our great nation. God bless America."

WALL STREET

That Monday morning, the day after martial law was enacted, the Stock Market opened with a very bleak outlook. The foreign markets, already open for hours, were taking a dive after hearing the news of martial law in the United States. The market continued to decline throughout the day and by close on Monday, it was down five hundred points. Wall Street could not take much more, or the market would be on its way to a crash.

Late in the afternoon, three more airlines declared bankruptcy and filed for chapter eleven protection, just as their competitors had done a month before. Air traffic was practically at a standstill; no one was flying anywhere. Those citizens who had not been out in the streets looting or protesting were holed up in their homes trying to avoid the flu. The death toll continued to rise, with over one hundred thousand deaths in New York City alone and another seventy-five thousand deaths in San Francisco.

Tuesday brought more bad news from Wall Street. The Far East markets had taken a devastating plunge after Monday's performance of the New York Stock Exchange. Standard and Poor's continued to dive on Tuesday; it seemed like everyone was selling. The cost of shares was plummeting, and by the end of the day the market was down another five hundred and twenty points. This could not continue.

On Wednesday morning the market opened tentatively. Most analysts were saying this would be the day to climb out of the depths. Not one of them was correct. At twelve noon the crash occurred, and Wall Street closed down. The American economy was in dire straits and the number of potential bankruptcies might be astronomical. The next day there was a run on the banks, and it took the army to hold off people at bank branches and tell them that they were not allowed to go into the banks. The Cabinet was running the economy now under martial law and the Federal Government had control of business. The banks would be directed what to do by the Cabinet.

Panic escalated to rioting; the country was in total chaos. Good news was something that viewers never saw on the television anymore. In the minds of its citizens, the United States was falling apart at the seams.

The polls showed that President Doyle was experiencing the worst Presidential approval rating in the history of the country. People in the streets were calling for him to resign or for Congress to impeach him. The people of the United States wanted answers and solutions, not martial law. They were depressed and desperate. The war against terrorism was destroying their nation.

Sean Doyle called a special meeting of his Cabinet and his advisors. As he entered the room, he looked at least ten years older than when the crisis had begun back in the fall. Everyone at the table knew he was doing the best he possibly could to end this crisis, but no one at the table had a clue about how to help him to solve it.

"Ladies and gentlemen, we need to reassess our situation. Firstly, we need to hit this terrorist organization strong and soon. The recent killings in our places of worship were carried out by sleeper cells throughout this country. Intelligence tells us that the terrorist organization may have exhausted their capabilities here in the U.S. after this recent attack. I hope to God that this is correct. If it is correct, now that we are under martial law, there should be no more terrorists running around freely if the army does its job well.

"Secondly, we need to get the economy back in gear. We need the confidence of our business community restored or we are going into financial oblivion. We need answers, people.

"Thirdly, we need that vaccine as soon as we can possibly get it out to the public. John Doyle tells me that he is very close to releasing the 'first batch,' as he calls it. That supply will be given to all responders and the military. God knows we need all of them to keep order during this chaos.

"Going back to our first priority—getting these terrorists—I keep thinking about when I was a kid and went to see all of those cowboy and Indian movies. The cavalry was always instructed to try and kill the chief of the Indian tribe because without their leader, the tribe would fall apart and the cavalry would rule the day."

Secretary of State Arnie Roberts leaned forward and said, "Excuse me, Mr. President, but with all due respect, could you tell us what Indians have to do with terrorists?" "I certainly can, Arnie. I firmly believe that we are dealing with one very strong, individual leader of this terrorist group. I also believe that without him, they will fall apart. We need to identify this bastard and we need to find him quickly before he destroys our country." "Mr. President, that is a very real possibility. Not the destruction of our country, of course, but the fact that without him, these terrorists may be ineffective." "Arnie, you can almost bet money on it. It worked in the movies all the time and it has worked throughout history. Take out the head of the organization and the rest of the body caves in. I would like you, Arnie, to get a hold of our friend from Malaysia, Ambassador Mahamood, and ask him to come and see me. Both suspects were on their way to Malaysia when they were apprehended in Tokyo. There has to be a connection there."

"I'll set it up for tomorrow morning, sir."

"Okay, Arnie. Thanks." Turning to his left, the President said, "Okay, General Glass. How is the army taking to running the local governments?"

General Glass, the Chairman of the Joint Chiefs, sat straighter in his chair and said, "Mr. President, overall I believe martial law is working the way it is supposed to. Our soldiers have been welcomed in most localities and most of them are reservists, so they are from the community and know most of the people. The rioting has basically stopped. With the army patrolling the streets, the looters are too afraid to come out for fear of being shot. I think within a week or so, everything should be back to some sort of normalcy. Of course, the general public is not going to want the army running their government for any length of time, but I think people understand your decision. I also believe that the citizens are more concerned with the development of the vaccine than anything else. The flu pandemic is breaking communities apart and families are suffering devastating losses."

"Thank you, General Glass. I have absolute faith in the American citizens. Together, we will make it through. Meanwhile everyone, let's work on these three goals and get them accomplished as soon as possible. I will begin tomorrow morning by speaking to Ambassador Mahamood and asking for his help in locating the leader of this terrorist organization. Thank you all for coming."

THE OVAL OFFICE

At eight-thirty the next morning, Ambassador Mahamood of Malaysia entered the Oval Office for his meeting with President Doyle.

"Ambassador, how good of you to come on such short notice."

As he extended his hand to shake the President's hand, the Ambassador said, "No, no, not at all, Mr. President. I am honored to be asked here at any time. I also bring greetings from my Prime Minister. He is a great admirer of you and the United States."

Sean smiled and said, "Yes, sir, I'm an admirer of him as well. He has done a superb job in your country. If only we could rid your country and ours of these terrorists. This is why I have asked to see you, Ambassador. Please take a seat."

The Ambassador sat back in one of the large armchairs in front of the President's desk. He waited for the President to take his seat before continuing. "As I have said many times, whatever we may do for you, Mr. President, we will be more than willing to do."

Bob Roche entered the room and Sean said, "Mr. Ambassador, you know Bob Roche, our National Security Advisor?"

Ambassador Mahamood stood to greet Bob and said, "Yes, I do. How are you, Mr. Roche?"

Bob shook hands with the Ambassador and said, "Just fine, sir, and I expect you are well? How is your family?" "Oh, my wife misses home, but my children love living in Virginia. They will miss it very much if I am ever transferred to another country. Everyone is well and happy; thank you for asking. Now what is it I can do for you, Mr. President?"

"Ambassador Mahamood, you know that we apprehended two of the key figures in this terrorist organization, one of whom was killed while in our jail. The other is awaiting trial on mass murder charges in the case of the weaponized flu attack."

"Yes, sir, I am very aware of both of these people." "Well, Ambassador, both of those individuals were arrested at Tokyo International Airport and both of them were on their way to Kuala Lumpur in your country."

"Lucky for us that they did not make it to Malaysia, sir. It is wonderful that you were able to apprehend them and bring them back here. How does this connect to Kuala Lumpur, Mr. President?"

"Mr. Ambassador, we believe that they may have been traveling to meet with the leader of this terrorist organization; we suspect that he is probably still there. In fact, he could possibly be a Malay, since the majority of Malaysian citizens are Muslims, and you have terrorism problems as well."

"I understand where you are going with this conversation, Mr. President. Are you about to ask me to have our government search for this individual?"

"I would be most grateful for any help your country can give us, Mr. Ambassador, but the problem is that we do not have any leads on who this person might be. We believe that he is their leader. Other than the likelihood that their leader is a Malay and a Muslim, we have no other information available on him. Our detainee awaiting trial claims that she was never allowed to know his name. The only contact she had was a Mr. Sulanni, and she only saw him while in Dubai."

"Mr. President, we will do whatever we can to help you. After all, your country is the leader of the world and these terrorists are destroying your homeland piece by piece. Thank God you declared martial law in order to return calm to your communities. As a democratic nation patterned after your own, we believe, as you do, that these terrorists must be eradicated. There is no room for this type of barbarism in the Muslim faith. We have preached that for longer than you and I have lived."

"Ambassador, I would like to request that your intelligence experts work side by side with our FBI and CIA in Kuala Lumpur and other cities in Malaysia if the leads take them there. Do you think your Prime Minister would agree to that? We need your assistance in identifying this individual and bringing him to justice."

"I cannot speak for my Prime Minister, of course, but I will take the message back to him. As you know, we are a very independent people and believe that most times we do not need assistance in handling such things as this, but I also know that this is a special situation. I will encourage my Prime Minister to agree to your request. If he says yes, I would think the first approach would be to try and locate this Mr. Sulanni. Would you agree?"

"Absolutely, Mr. Ambassador. I will have the Director of the FBI send our best agents over to Malaysia to assist your intelligence agents. We will anxiously await your Prime Minister's response."

Sean stood up and extended his hand to the Ambassador and Mr. Mahamood took his hand in both of his and said, "Mr. President, it is always an honor. Hopefully, I will be back to you with good news."

Once the Ambassador had left the Oval Office, Bob Roche said, "Mr. President, I have a good feeling about this. I think we just might track down this scumbag."

"I hope you're right, Bob. Nothing would please me more."

GOOD NEWS

Three days later Sean received a phone call from the Prime Minister of Malaysia informing him that whatever assistance he needed, his country was willing to help. The FBI and CIA would be most welcome to participate in any investigation as long as they understood that the sovereign nation of Malaysia would be in charge of any intelligence operations. Sean was ecstatic at the news and called Ken Sitarek and Bob Roche into the Oval Office to tell them the news.

After informing them of the decision reached by their friends from Malaysia, the telephone rang on the President's desk. "Yes, Aggie, what is it? I have Bob and Ken here for a briefing."

Aggie coughed and said, "Mr. President, it is Dr. Doyle on the phone and I think you are going to want to talk to him, sir."

"I'm sorry, Aggie. I know you wouldn't interrupt me unless it was important. Put John through, please."

Sean pushed the speaker button. There was a slight pause and then John Doyle came on the line. "Mr. President, are you there?"

"Yes, John. What do you have?"

"Well, Mr. President, would you like some encouraging news?"

"I certainly would, John. Are you about to tell me that the vaccine is ready for distribution?"

"No, cousin Sean. I wish that were the case, but I need at least another three to four weeks. I think this is very encouraging, though, and if I'm right, we may be turning the corner."

"John, you have my attention. What exactly are you talking about?"

"Well, if you recall, I reported earlier this month that the original Spanish flu spread quickly and that it was a very stubborn strain. That is the reason we were unable to develop a vaccine back then, but it wasn't even necessary as the Spanish flu disappeared as quickly as it came. One day we had a pandemic, and the next day it started to disappear."

The President took a deep breath and said, "John, what are you trying to say? Is history possibly repeating itself?"

"It looks that way, Mr. President, though very slowly. It does appear to be following the same path as back in 1919."

"John, I have a ton of questions, but let me ask first: how do we know this? Do we have any proof that the Spanish flu is 'going away' so to speak?"

"Mr. President, the only way we can gauge this is to monitor the reduction in the number of new cases. Let me give you some statistics. We are experiencing a sharp decrease in new cases of the flu in Toronto, Buffalo, Cleveland, and Tokyo. We have been unable to determine any perceptible change in New York City, but in the smaller cities, the percentage of new cases is down dramatically. We don't have an explanation for Tokyo other than the Japanese must have a better, more effective way of keeping track than we do. In any event, it appears on the surface that the number of new flu cases is declining. I hope this makes your day, even though I cannot provide the vaccine yet."

"John, it's been a good day since the start. I still have one question for you, though. If the current strain of flu is weaponized, how could it follow the same path as the original and begin to disappear as quickly as it came? After all, it was strengthened and introduced into the population. I would think it would be more powerful than the original and so would be more difficult to not only combat, but eradicate."

"Mr. President, I'm afraid I don't have an answer for you on that one, but we're working on it."

"I am sure you are, John. Keep up the good work and let me know at any time, day or night, when you have more good news."

Sean put the phone back in the cradle and said, "Can you believe that, guys? Did you get all that? This is fantastic news! The flu seems to be disappearing. There is a dramatic decrease in new cases. We could be on the road to recovery!"

Bob Roche stood and said, "Mr. President, this is the most positive I have seen you look in months. This was exactly the kind of news you needed. It is fantastic. Now if you will excuse me, I am off to make arrangements for our people to get on a flight to Kuala Lumpur, Malaysia."

"Thank you, Bob. Thank you, Ken. I think I will take a walk over to my quarters and tell Maggie the good news myself."

OPERATION HEADHUNTER

Director Graham of the FBI selected Special Agent Terry Crowley as the agent in charge of the Malaysia mission, code named "Operation Headhunter." Crowley would lead a group of twelve of the best agents available, along with ten CIA operatives. The CIA had acquiesced to the FBI running the operation, even though it was an overseas mission. After Agent Crowley's recent success, no one was going to second guess his capabilities of running this type of operation. The Director of Homeland Security had made it explicitly clear in his remarks that the President had requested the operation be run in this manner.

The flight to Kuala Lumpur, Malaysia, was long and tiring. Most of the agents on board, however, were used to such travel and the majority of them slept on the flight across the Pacific. Eighteen hours after leaving Washington, Operation Headhunter arrived at Kuala Lumpur International Airport. They were met by the Malaysian Director of Intelligence and were ushered through a private lounge, bypassing customs, and out through a side door of the terminal to awaiting vans.

The Director explained that their baggage would be in their hotel rooms when they arrived in downtown Kuala Lumpur. It was four o'clock in the afternoon in Malaysia; the agents who did not get much sleep on the overseas flight were exhausted. The Director suggested that they all consider putting off any meeting until the next morning, and simply relax or sleep until the next day. Agent Crowley, although anxious to get on with the operation, agreed that this made sense, because he wanted everyone in the group to be sharp when they began the mission.

At precisely eight o'clock the following morning, four vans pulled into the circular drive in front of the Kuala Lumpur Marriott, and the group of twenty men and women climbed into the vehicles for the ten block drive to the Ministry Building and the offices of the Malaysian Intelligence Service. As they drove through the streets of downtown, most of the agents who had never been to Malaysia were in awe of its modern city, with skyscrapers everywhere, and especially the Petronas Towers in the distance, once the tallest structures in the world. Even though these buildings had lost that claim to the building in China, the ongoing construction back home at ground zero in New York City, where buildings were being erected to honor the fallen victims of 9/11, would be the tallest when completed. Target date for completion was 2008.

The center of commerce in Malaysia, Kuala Lumpur at eight o'clock in the morning was already bustling, and traffic was almost at a standstill. The ten block drive to the Ministry required a nearly twenty minute trip. Upon arrival, the Operation Headhunter group followed the Director into the building and took the elevator to the twelfth floor, where the Malaysian Intelligence Service had its headquarters.

Once inside the offices, Terry Crowley could not help being impressed by the surroundings. The latest in computer technology was evident everywhere he looked. The communications center was state of the art and it was obvious to Terry that the Malaysian government had spared no expense in outfitting its intelligence service with the best tools available. The Director led them into the most expansive conference room Terry had ever seen. The conference table appeared capable of seating at least fifty people.

The agents took their seats and via intercom, the Director requested his staff to come to the conference room. Within seconds, the table was filled as the Malaysian agents filed into the room and took their seats.

Standing at the head of the table, the Director welcomed everyone to the first meeting of Operation Headhunter. He introduced the Special Agent in Charge, Terry Crowley of the FBI, and suggested that everyone introduce themselves and explain to the group their individual responsibilities and areas of expertise.

After background information on what the FBI and CIA had developed to date, Terry suggested that they form four- person teams for the operation. Each team would have an FBI agent, a CIA agent, and two Malaysian agents; each team would also have similar specialties. Investigative assignments would highlight each team's specific operative specialty. Terry further suggested that all teams would meet each morning at eight o'clock, giving reports of the previous day's progress and outlining the agenda for the day. The number one priority for all agents was to find any information that might lead them to this terrorist by the name of Sulanni. From there, assuming the investigation led them to the suspect, the next step would be to find the mysterious terrorist.

Two of the teams were assigned to interrogate the terrorists captured in the recent raid of cells throughout Malaysia. With diligence and pressure put on the detainees, the teams were determined to obtain the identity of Mr. Sulanni.

*   *   *

After two weeks of investigation, Operation Headhunter was not much further along than when they began the mission. Terry Crowley was reading the interrogation reports from the previous day when he received a call from Director Graham back in Washington.

"Terry, this is Ted Graham calling. I have some information that should help in your investigation."

"That certainly sounds encouraging, sir. What exactly do you have for us?"

"It seems that Dr. Zayed has had a memory gain. She is still negotiating with us on the death penalty, and she's been giving us little bits of information in her attempt to be spared. She seems to remember seeing a photo of this Mr. Sulanni; she told us that we are looking for the wrong person."

"What does she mean 'the wrong person'? We have good intelligence that Sulanni is the right guy."

"Yeah, I know Terry, but what she really means is that without knowing what he looks like, we probably all made the assumption that he is of Middle Eastern or Arabic descent. It appears that isn't the case and Dr. Zayed has described Sulanni's appearance in detail. We have an FBI artist doing a sketch as we speak and we will fax it over to you as soon as we confirm the likeness with Dr. Zayed."
"That is positive news, Director Graham. What exactly does this guy look like?"

"Terry, you're going to be quite surprised. He looks nothing like a Muslim terrorist. More English, or Irish, or even German. Wait until you see the sketch. We'll fax it as soon as we can. Good luck, Agent Crowley."

"Thank you, sir. I look forward to your fax."

ST. PATRICK'S DAY

March 17 dawned bitter cold in Washington, D.C. Weather forecasters had predicted scattered flurries for the morning, with heavier snow for the afternoon. In New York City, the weather was a little better, but temperatures were still close to the freezing mark. A special order was given to the military to allow the St. Patrick's Day Parade to proceed as scheduled down Fifth Avenue. One stipulation was that anyone not wearing a HEPA mask would be arrested and quarantined. An orderly crowd had already gathered along the parade route, and all of the citizens lining Fifth Avenue wore their masks. The parade began promptly at one o'clock and the long green line proceeded down the avenue with bagpipe bands, school marching bands, and of course, every Irish organization in New York.

Back in Washington, President Doyle had just returned from his annual luncheon at the Irish Club, where he dined on the traditional corned beef and cabbage. Upon entering the Oval Office, he noticed the television coverage of the St. Patrick's Day Parade in the Big Apple. He was impressed at how orderly the crowd appeared, and also noticed that there were soldiers everywhere the camera panned. His attention was broken by the sound of the telephone.

"Yes, Aggie, what can I do for you?"

"Mr. President, Dr. Doyle is on the line and needs to speak with you."

"Thank you, Aggie. Put him through."

"Mr. President, this is John. How are you feeling today?"

"Like a contented cow, John. I'm just back from the Irish Club and you know that means I'm sitting here with a very full stomach."

"Wish I could have been there. The corned beef and cabbage is the best there, except for maybe in Buffalo at their Irish Center."

"So, John, I know you didn't call me to discuss St. Patrick's Day food. What do you have for me?"

"Mr. President, we are ready to release the first vaccine batch for the military and the first responders. I wanted to know how you want to announce this to the country, and to the world for that matter."

Sean Doyle could not contain his excitement as he almost shot out of his chair and said, "John, this is wonderful news! We'll schedule a press conference right away and make the announcement. When can we expect the vaccine to arrive?"

"Well, Mr. President, we will distribute the vaccine the same way we would for the National Pharmaceutical Stockpile: all shipments will be air-freighted to the localities and then taken to the PODS."

"Whoa, John—you lost me. What are PODS?"

"Points of Distribution. We call them PODS for short and they are pre-designated. Believe me, this is a plan that has been in place for years. Each locality knows exactly what to do in getting the vaccine out to the recipients."

"John, when will we be able to start the vaccination process?"

"Three days time. We have enough vaccine for all of the military and the first responders. We are talking hundreds of thousands of doses. The balance will be ready in about six weeks and then we can do the rest of the population, beginning with the twenty-to-forty-year-old age group."

"John, I don't know how to thank you; this is the best news. You are to be congratulated."

"Mr. President, I didn't do this on my own. It took hundreds of people down here at the CDC to develop this and to get to where we are. I'm just sorry that we couldn't do it in less than six months."

"Please don't apologize, John. We both know that our original estimate was six months and you have accomplished that. No one is going to blame you or your staff for delay. I'll set up a press conference for late this afternoon, so the media can then play excerpts on their nightly news programs. John, thank you again."

"You're welcome, Mr. President. And, oh, by the way? The new cases of flu have diminished drastically. We have reports in from health departments all over the country that newly diagnosed cases of the Spanish flu are down fifty percent from last month at this time. I really believe that the flu is on the wane. With the vaccine, we should now be able to turn this situation around."

"John, you are full of positive news! Can I give this information out at the press conference, or do you think it might stir false hopes?"

"No, Mr. President. Our stats show that there is a definite turn in the road here and we are headed back to normalcy sooner than we had projected. I would say that you can tell the nation that there is a definite downward trend in the number of new cases and that it has been that way for the past month with fewer and fewer newly diagnosed cases."

"Thanks again, John. If I have any questions or need any statistical information, can I have my staff give you a call back?"

"Absolutely, Mr. President. I'll be available all day."

"Wonderful, John. Take care and we'll talk soon." "Goodbye, Mr. President. Good luck with your conference."

THE EAST ROOM

The White House press corps was assembled in the East Room of the White House along with every major news service throughout the world. It was standing room only as Sherry Katz made her way to the podium to welcome everyone to this very important news conference. None of the reporters had been informed what would be covered and there was wide speculation that it could have something to do with the recent suicide bombings of the churches and cathedrals. The entire nation was still reeling from the terrorist attacks and funerals were still taking place three weeks after the bombings.

Sherry had to quiet the group of news people, because everyone was trying to speak at once.

"Ladies and gentlemen of the press, we are here today to make a major announcement that will have an impact around the world. Please welcome the President of the United States, Sean Doyle."

The entire assemblage rose to its feet in shock, applauding the President. Everyone had assumed that Sherry Katz would be holding the news conference. Now they were going to hear from the President himself.

Sean Doyle stepped up to the podium and thanked Sherry Katz and then the press corps for their warm reception. Once the room was quiet again, Sean said, "Today, for the first time in months, I am able to bring you good news. In fact, I have two announcements to make and they are both positive. We have suffered for six months now since the first attack by the terrorists, when they spread the weaponized flu strain throughout our country and the rest of the world. Our nation is under martial law, but our citizens are accepting this measure to keep order in our cities and towns. They are accepting it because they are Americans and they are resilient. They have faith in God that this situation we are in will also pass and that we will be victorious in this battle with the barbarians who have wreaked havoc on our nation.

"I am very happy to announce today that the vaccine is ready to be delivered to the military and the first responders; within three days, the vaccinations will begin. Six weeks from now, the rest of the population will be vaccinated as well, and the vaccine will be shipped to all designated countries around the world for global production."

The East Room erupted with a torrent of questions, but the President held up his hand to stop the rush of inquiries.

"Please, ladies and gentlemen. I will take questions, but I have only given you the first announcement. I did say that I had two very positive developments to announce to you. The second one is that we have statistical proof that over the past month, there has been a steady decline of newly diagnosed cases of the flu. The CDC had advised us a month ago that in certain areas the flu seemed to be on the downtrend. Since that time, the number of new cases has dropped by fifty percent. We are all hopeful that this means that the flu may leave abruptly as it did back in 1919. Meanwhile, the distribution of the vaccine will take place over the next few days. Now I will take your questions."

The press conference went on for another twenty-five minutes, and ended just in time for the nightly news programs to open their shows with the lead story about the vaccine being ready for distribution. The cable network channels gave full coverage to the story and two of them had continuing coverage of the flu pandemic and a rehashing of what the last six months had wrought upon the country. The coverage included the initial appearance of the flu, and how it had been spread and become a worldwide pandemic. More coverage was given to the anthrax attacks, the suicide bombingsers, the arrest of the two terrorists, and of course, the death of the first terrorist, Muhammad Sutwa, in his jail cell.

Nothing was reported about the top secret mission named Operation Headhunter because the press did not have any information that it was even taking place. Homeland Security had kept a very tight lid on the mission so as to obtain the utmost security and insure that the operation would be successful. The one thing they did not want was the media following them everywhere they went in Malaysia. The news channels had plenty to talk about that St. Patrick's Day night. Coverage, too, was given to the parade down Fifth Avenue. As it passed by St. Patrick's Cathedral, the scaffolding was visible, as the church was already under reconstruction. It was a great day for the Irish and a great day for America.

KUALA LUMPUR

Agent Terry Crowley was watching the CNN coverage of President Doyle's press conference when one of the Malaysian agents walked in and handed him a fax. Terry thanked the agent and looked down at the face on the fax. He was amazed at the photo he was holding. This man would never have been suspected as a terrorist on appearance alone. The typical FBI profile would show a slightly dark-skinned individual with a Middle Eastern ethnicity about him. Looking up at Terry was a sketch of a light-skinned young man with a somewhat handsome face; he could be Eastern European or from the British Isles. He definitely did not look Middle Eastern or look like any terrorist Terry Crowley was used to seeing.

Immediately, Terry picked up his portable radio and called for his Interrogation Team Leader. When he answered, Terry asked him to get right over to the Ministry.

Thirty minutes later, the Team Leader arrived and Terry said, "I want you to copy this fax and have your agents show it to every one of the terrorist suspects you have interrogated. Ask them if they know this guy or if they have ever seen him. If you can make a deal for information, you know what to do. Make sure that the Malaysian agents are with you on every interview and if possible, have them put whatever pressure they can on the suspects. There has to be one of them that will recognize Sulanni and be willing to inform and make a deal."

"Will do, Agent Crowley. We may have to fax that to other locations because we have some agents up north doing interviews right now. Will that be okay with you?"

"You can fax it, but make sure it is marked 'Law Enforcement Sensitive' and for 'Intelligence Agents only.'"

After the Team Leader left, Terry called the Director and asked how they could get to the Security Agents at the airport. He wanted to give this sketch to every agent on a confidential basis; it was not to be distributed to anyone else.

"If Mr. Sulanni has the urge to take a trip somewhere, I want him stopped at the airport."

"Agent Crowley, consider it done. My brother-in-law is head of security at Kuala Lumpur Airport. I will call him immediately."

"Great. Thank you so much."

Terry Crowley was beginning to feel the fatigue of the last two weeks and the frustration at the lack of leads coming in from the teams. Now that he had an artist's sketch of the Sulanni suspect, he was experiencing that adrenaline rush he always got when a new development took place in an investigation. Terry stared out the window to see the Petronas Towers in the distance and thought to himself, *I just have a good feeling about this. This is the break that we have been hoping and praying for. I am certain we are about to finally get it.*

The fax was circulated quickly and the interrogation of the numerous detainees throughout the country began at various locations.

The next morning, Terry was stepping out of the shower in his hotel when the phone rang. Wrapping a towel around himself, Terry ran to the phone and picked it up on the fourth ring.

"Crowley, here."

"Agent Crowley, this is Agent Schultz of Interrogation Team B. I didn't wake you, did I?"

"No, Schultz, I was just getting out of the shower when the phone rang."

"I didn't want to call you too early, but we are an hour ahead of you, so I knew it would be early in Kuala Lumpur."

"That's okay, Agent Schultz. If you have news for me, you can call me at any time, day or night."

"Well, sir, we have been interrogating one of the suspected terrorists for about two days now and when we received your fax yesterday afternoon, we decided to show it to him. At first, he did not even make the slightest sign of recognition, but as we talked again early this morning, we casually mentioned that there could possibly be some arrangement in return for information."

"Where exactly are you, Agent Schultz?"

"We're in the city of Kelantan, on the east coast of Malaysia, where there was a big sleeper cell until the raid last month."

"So what kind of reaction did you get from this guy?" "After we agreed to broker a deal for him, he finally admitted that he had seen this Sulanni guy. He also told us that he is in Kuala Lumpur often. He does not know the head man, but he is convinced that Sulanni goes to Kuala Lumpur to meet with the top guy. He further revealed that Sulanni has stayed in one of the downtown hotels, but he does not know which one."

"This is good news, Schultz. We need to get that photo to every hotel registration desk in Kuala Lumpur immediately. I'll get one of the teams on it. Meanwhile, keep up the interrogation and let me know as soon as you have anything further."

"Yes, sir, I'll do that. Have a good day."

"Thanks, Schultz. You've made my day."

Within two hours, every desk clerk at every downtown hotel in Kuala Lumpur had received the photo of Sulanni. As of noon, not one of them had identified the photo. By 3:30 in the afternoon, Terry Crowley felt the frustration creeping back into his body.

It was 3:45 when the radio crackled and he picked up the portable to hear Team Leader E calling for him. "This is Crowley. Go ahead."

"Agent Crowley, this is Team Leader E and we have a possible ID on our suspect. Can you come down to the Mandarin Oriental? It's only about two miles from the Ministry."

Terry jumped out of his chair and said, "I'm on my way." As he burst out of the office he ran right into the Director. "Sir, I just got a call. They have a lead at one of the hotels. I'm on my way over there. Do you want to come with me?"

"Absolutely, Agent Crowley. I'm right behind you."

Ten minutes later, Terry and the Director were ushered into the General Manager's office at the Mandarin Oriental. Sitting in a chair was a pretty, young Malaysian woman, age about twenty-five. The young woman, who introduced herself as Anna and who spoke perfect English, said that she recognized the photograph that had been shown to her when she came on duty at 3:30 that afternoon. When asked by Terry if she was sure she knew this man, her answer was that she never forgot a face, but often names. She definitely knew this man to be a guest at the hotel on two occasions recently. She did not remember his name, but she was certain that it was not Sulanni. When asked what she could remember about him, she said that she remembered his room number from the last visit and the fact that he always wanted a room on a higher floor.

Terry asked the General Manager to get the guest register for that date and to look up the room number that Anna had given them. He was back in two minutes with the information. Mr. Sulanni had used the name Donald Frost and had given his home address as Glasgow, Scotland. That would make sense, since the man did not look like a Sulanni, but rather more like an Englishman or a German.

Terry Crowley turned to his Team Leader and said, "We need to get all of the phone records for Mr. Frost during both of his stays. I don't expect them to reveal much. He probably used his cell phone, but maybe we'll catch another break. Also, get a hold of Team Leader C and tell him to have his team check every hotel in town to see if they have a Mr. Donald Frost as a current guest."

KEMAL KABIGTING

Kemal Huang Kabigting was born in the city of Penang, on an island of the same name off the west coast of Malaysia and connected to the peninsula by the Penang Bridge. Once known as the Pearl of the Orient, Penang is steeped in Malay tradition and is one of the most beautiful areas in the peninsula nation of Malaysia. In addition to Malay inhabitants, the population is also a melting pot of nationalities. In the early sixties, many visitors traveling to Malaysia found the South China Sea area so inviting that they remained there and started a new and more relaxing way of life. One of those touring the country was Kemal's mother, who was from Samsun, Turkey, and on holiday in Penang when she met her husband, Muhamood Kabigting, a Malay and a devout Muslim. Two years later, the Kabigting's had a son, Kemal. Kemal's name was his mother's choice, in honor of the father of democracy in Turkey, Kemal Ataturk. Kemal was also given the surname of his paternal grandmother, Huang, who was of Chinese descent.

Kemal was an intelligent child, and growing up in Penang was an opportunity to learn all about the old cultures of centuries past. Through his school years, though, Kemal became rebellious not only to his parents, but to his teachers and to his given religion. After graduating from the university with a degree in business, he left Penang for Kuala Lumpur.

Within three years he had gone from an account clerk in an import/export firm to chief of the import department. As Kemal rose the corporate ladder, his politics and religious beliefs began to interfere with his performance. When Kemal was twenty-six and at the end of the fourth year at the firm, he was given an ultimatum: leave politics and religion where they belonged, or leave the firm. Kemal chose to leave his employer and traveled to the Middle East to visit the birthplace of Mohammad the Prophet.

While in Saudi Arabia, Kemal was introduced to a man that his compatriots referred to as "the chosen one to rid the world of the infidels from the land of Satan." His hatred for America was unparalleled, and he was recruiting all young Muslim believers who shared the same hatred for America. Kemal signed up immediately and traveled to Afghanistan, where he underwent rigorous training in terrorism. Kemal would not be directly involved in bombings, but his excellent accounting skills and ability of persuasiveness in recruitment of new members to the terrorists cells were invaluable to the organization.

Kemal also hated his Malaysian government for imitating the United States with their democracy and their allegiance to Christianity. His government needed to change and that would be his goal in life.

After two years of training with the al-Qaida organization, Kemal returned to Kuala Lumpur with enough financing and experience to open his own import/export business. Kemal's marketing talent enabled him to quickly become a successful competitor in the Southeast Asia markets. Within a few years, with his business running smoothly, Kemal was able to turn to the recruitment of young Malaysian Muslims to join the terrorist organization, sending them over to the camps in Afghanistan for training and then returning to Malaysia to set up sleeper cells waiting for their assignments.

He rejoiced in the actions of his brothers-in-arms when they first attacked the World Trade Center in February of 1993, the Khobar Towers barracks in Saudi Arabia in June of 1996, and the USS Cole in October of 2000. It was not until the destruction of the World Trade Center Towers in 2001 that Kemal became disillusioned with his leader, who was by then running through the hills and hiding in caves in Afghanistan, trying to elude the American forces. Kemal decided it was time to break ties with his former idol. The ideological differences between the two were growing wider every month. Kemal had a plan that would bring the land of Satan to its knees and it didn't involve crashing planes into buildings or even blowing up buildings with car bombs. Kemal's plan was something the world had never before experienced, at least not in the form of terrorism. He would show the world that he was the most ingenious fighter for Allah that it had ever encountered.

Over the next year, Kemal continued to build his network of cells throughout his home country of Malaysia, and in the United States and its ally countries. He also researched his plan and the possibilities that it could produce. He recruited brilliant scientists and former al-Qaida operatives who believed that a true Muslim was one who gave his life for Allah in the name of Allah, sending all infidels to the burning fires of hell where they belonged.

The plan had worked better than Kemal could have believed. The entire world of infidels was in total chaos, with millions of them dead and gone to wherever infidels go when they have been eliminated. In the war he had begun through his recruitment techniques five years earlier, Kemal had known the fight would not always be simple. He had expected to lose some of the battles, but never the war. The attack on the cathedrals and churches was in retaliation for the raid on his sleeper cells. Fortunately, the infidels had not found all of the cells and Kemal's brothers were able to wreak havoc on the religious sites throughout the land of Satan. Because of the suicidal nature of the attacks, a high percentage of recruits and sleeper cells throughout the United States were now depleted.

He would not be deterred. He would continue to recruit and to plan for the future. It could take years; it had taken five years to unleash the St. Gustaf's flu pandemic. The Americans and their allies were so stupid, though, that they could always be caught by surprise, no matter how much they prepared with their stupid Homeland Security.

PETRONAS TOWERS

The luxurious offices and suites of the Petronas Towers told any visitor that this must be where the most successful and profitable companies in Kuala Lumpur were located. In the thirty-seventh floor suite occupied by Kemal Kabigting, the opulence confirmed that his was the elite business location in Malaysia.

The sun was beginning to slip slowly down to the horizon as Kemal turned his chair to view the always spectacular sunset. His reverie was rudely interrupted by the ringing of his desk phone.

"Good afternoon, Penang Enterprises. How can I help you?"

"My brother and mentor, it is Sulanni. I must talk to you."

Kemal lurched forward in his chair and screamed into the phone, "You fool! I told you never to call me on my direct business line! Hang up, and call back on my cell phone! You idiot!"

With that, Kemal slammed down the telephone and picked up his cell phone from his briefcase. He thought to himself, *that man is making too many mistakes. It may be time for Mr. Sulanni to meet Allah, if he does not learn better how to operate.*

The cell phone rang once and Kemal picked it up. "Sulanni, it had better be you. How could you be so stupid?"

"I am sorry, my brother and mentor. I am so upset that I just never gave it a thought. It was stupid of me, but it will not happen again."

"You can be sure, Mr. Sulanni, that it will never happen again because if it does, I will have no more use for you. Do you understand me?"

"Oh yes, sir, I understand fully. I promise on my mother's memory, it will not happen again. I must see you, though. Can I come there?"

"I don't think that would be wise right now. Why don't you meet me at the Istana Hotel in about thirty minutes? I will meet you in the Bali Bar on the first floor."

"Thank you, Kemal. I will be there in half an hour."

Kemal again turned to the massive window looking out on Kuala Lumpur and the beautiful sunset about to take place. The more he thought about Sulanni, the more nervous he became. Something was definitely wrong. The man sounded terrified on the phone. He thought to himself, *I am not sure how useful this man is to me any more, but I will hear him out and then make my decision.*

Kemal left his suite and headed for the elevator. As he entered the elevator, he found there were two men already in the car. He recognized one of them as an old schoolmate from the university, but he did not acknowledge him and did not have any intention to do so, but the man said, "Kemal, is that you?"

"Yes, I am Kemal. Do I know you?"

"Come on, Kemal. Have I aged that much since school? I was in your economics classes and your business administration classes as well. I'm Henry Chin."

"Oh, yes. Henry. How could I not have recognized you? A little bit less hair, but still that silly grin. How are you and what are you doing now?"

"Great, Kemal. I work for the government."

The elevator stopped at the first floor and the door opened to the lobby. "Gee, Henry, who would have thought you would be working for the government? Let's get together for a drink sometime and you can tell me all about it."

Kemal swiftly exited the elevator and was halfway across the lobby before Henry could even say, Okay, let's do that sometime.

Henry Chin turned to Terry Crowley and said, "That guy has not changed one bit in twenty some years. He was always abrupt. Wonder what he's doing now?"

Terry smiled and said, "You know, I knew a lot of guys like that in college. Most of them turned out to be real introverts. He probably doesn't have too many friends and he is more than likely the kind of guy who is successful, but so wrapped up in his own success that he doesn't take time to make any friends. I wouldn't hold my breath waiting for him to have a drink with you. He didn't even ask for your card or give you his."

"Yeah, you're right, Terry. I wouldn't have told him that I was in the intelligence branch of the government, but I wonder what he does? Working in the Petronas Towers, he must be with a big firm or maybe he even has his own, but I doubt it. This place is the Ritz when it comes to office space. It's very expensive."

Terry Crowley pushed the revolving door and said, "Maybe your old schoolmate was just paying a call on one of the companies in the Towers."

As Terry and Henry were getting into their van in front of the Petronas Towers, a black Mercedes exited the ramp of the underground parking garage. The windows were tinted, but the driver was able to observe the government van pulling away. *I wonder just what department Henry works for,* Kemal thought, *and why he was in the Petronas Towers. There are no government agencies in the building that I am aware of . . .*

ISTANA HOTEL

The black Mercedes swung into the circular drive of the Istana Hotel and stopped at the front entrance of the hotel. Kemal exited the vehicle and the valet handed him a ticket stub. He thanked the driver politely and smiled as he walked toward the door. The Istana Hotel was a favorite of tourists and was the perfect place for a meeting in the Bali Bar, because it was a bustling establishment eighteen hours a day. One could easily go unnoticed; the bar was standing room only most of the time, and especially at the end of the business day.

Kemal entered the lounge and spotted Sulanni at the end of the horseshoe-shaped bar. As he approached his number one operative, he was amazed by Sulanni's transformation since he had seen him last. The man was disheveled, his color, pale. His entire demeanor was that of someone who was on the run, or had something to hide. He frequently looked over his shoulder, as if in fear that someone was watching him.

Kemal noticed one small table for two available at the far corner of the lounge and he motioned for Sulanni to follow him. As he sat down at the round cocktail table, Sulanni approached and bowed as he took his seat. Kemal ordered a drink from the waitress and Sulanni placed his drink in front of him. With very shaky hands, he reached for some peanuts in the small dish sitting in the middle of the table.

Kemal observed him for a few seconds and then said, "Sulanni, what in the hell has happened to you? You're acting like that character in *Casablanca* played by the late actor, Peter Lorre, who was running from the police and looking to Rick for help."

"Kemal, I'm looking for help from you. The government people, with the help of the Americans, are closing in on me, and I am afraid to be out in public. I need to get out of the country. You have to help me. I don't know where to go or how to escape."

"What do you mean *escape*? Escape from what and from whom? Who knows who you are, Sulanni?"

"Kemal, it is horrible. They have my picture. Well, not exactly a photo, but a very good artist's drawing or interpretation of a photo and they are passing it around all over Malaysia. I must get out and get out now, Kemal. I will be hunted down if I don't leave the country now." "Whoa, wait a minute, Sulanni. How do you know this? And what is this about your picture being everywhere?"

"It is true, Kemal. An old friend who survived being caught in one of our sleeper cells works the afternoon shift at the airport and he saw my photo being shown by one of the security people to another employee. He passed the word along to our network and I have discovered that the sketch has not only been given out to all of the airports throughout the country, but also to all the hotels in every city in an attempt to identify me. It is not me that they want so badly, however. It is you, Kemal. They somehow believe that if they capture me, that I will give them you."

"And will you, Mr. Sulanni? Would you betray me? Do I have reason to fear that you would give me up, Mr. Sulanni?"

"No, no, sir. I would never do that. I would die first; believe me, I would never give you up to the infidels."

Kemal stared at his chief operative who had done such a superb job in accomplishing the most devastating terrorist campaign in the history of the world. Sulanni, however, did not look like he would last one more hour without cracking and possibly revealing who his leader was. He was quickly becoming a broken man and to Kemal, no longer a valuable asset; Sulanni was now a liability. "Sulanni, you must pull yourself together. We will get you a disguise and somehow find a way for you to leave the country. We have a worldwide network that you have helped put together. You must remember that we can do anything once we put a plan into place. Now try to relax, and tell me everything that you have learned and why you think the government is closing in on you."

"My leader, have you been hearing what I say? My picture is all over the country! I am scared to death to walk the streets or to go into public places! I should not even be in this hotel! I will guarantee you that they have my photo at the front desk! I cannot go anywhere or I will be recognized! I say again, I need to get out and get out now!"

Kemal removed a post-it note from his pocket and wrote down an address and handed it to Sulanni. "My friend, take this and go to this address. It is one of our most secure safe houses. I will call ahead and they will be expecting you. Go directly there and make sure that you are not being followed. I know you are excellent at that, but in your condition, you must be extra careful. Stay at the house until you hear from me and relax. We will find a way to get you out of the country and to safety."

"Kemal, how can I thank you? You are my most trusted friend. I cannot thank you enough. I knew you would have a way out for me."

They left the Bali Bar separately and as Kemal walked through the main lobby of the hotel, Sulanni walked toward the ballroom and meeting rooms and out to the side entrance. Kemal handed his valet ticket stub to the young man at the booth and thought, *What a shame that I must dispose of my most trusted and most loyal member of our brotherhood, but Sulanni has definitely become a liability and must be eliminated.*

The black Mercedes stopped in front of Kemal and the driver hopped out. Kemal tipped him generously and eased himself behind the wheel. He drove quickly out to the main street and pushed an automatic dial button on his cell phone. The number rang once and then was answered by a female voice.

"This is Kemal calling. I have a mission for you. Please see me at my villa in two hours. Bring your equipment with you and be prepared to wine and dine." Kemal reached over and touched the end button and the line was closed. He drove out of the city and toward his private residence. As he drove, a sad feeling came over him for what he was about to do. He thought to himself, *It must be done. I have no other choice.*

MALAYSIAN DEFENSE MINISTRY

Terry Crowley and Henry Chin arrived back at the Intelligence Headquarters to find the Director waiting for them. As they entered the office, the receptionist said, "The Director wants to see you immediately."

Terry knocked gently on the Director's office door and he said, "Come in, Terry. You too, Henry. I have news for you."

Both agents took chairs opposite the Director's desk and waited for the Director to begin. "Gentlemen, we have a very good lead on our number one suspect, Mr. Sulanni, a.k.a. Mr. Frost. One of our teams has been circulating the sketch of Sulanni to an underground organization that is known to be opposed to the terrorism network responsible for our current crisis. This organization would like nothing better than to put Mr. Sulanni and his friends out of business. They are, let us say, 'bad business' for the financial dealings of this underground organization. I need to say no more other than the fact that they have identified Mr. Sulanni as the chief operative of the terrorist group and they know where he is in Malaysia and what hotels he has frequented over the past year. This information, together with the identification of the sketch, will bring us to him very soon. This afternoon, one of the operatives of our informants believes he saw Mr. Sulanni in the Bali Bar at the Istana Hotel right here in Kuala Lumpur."

Terry Crowley could not contain his enthusiasm at this news. "Director, we must call in the other teams and concentrate our efforts here in the city! If this information is correct, and I have no reason not to believe so, then we can close off the city and any transportation routes out of it to prevent Mr. Sulanni from escaping the net we can throw around him."

"Terry, I believe this also. I have already given the order for all the teams to return to Kuala Lumpur." "Excellent, Mr. Director. Finally, we are getting close. Once we find Sulanni, it will simply be a matter of time before we get the big guy and Operation Headhunter will be a success. We must bring these barbarians to justice. By the way, this informant who gave us the information . . . Did he describe who Sulanni was meeting with in the Bali Bar?"

"Yes he did, Terry, and we have him speaking to one of our artists as we meet to come up with a sketch of that person."

"That is exciting news, Mr. Director. I'm looking forward to seeing that sketch. Henry and I will set up a meeting of the entire operation for first thing tomorrow morning and begin to tighten the net around our Mr. Sulanni."

"Thanks, Terry. We have already placed patrols at strategic exits out of the city to stop any suspicious vehicles, and all officers have the sketch of Sulanni. If he tries to leave the city on one of the main highways, we will get him."

Terry and Henry left the Director's office and headed to the conference room to plan the morning meeting and design the manhunt to take place the next day.

Two floors down, the police artist from the Malaysian Intelligence Service was interviewing a Malay who was giving details of the person he saw meeting with Sulanni. The artist said, "Can you give me more facial details? We have the hair and the profile pretty good, but the image is too fuzzy with the details you have given me so far."

"It was not well-lighted in the Bali Bar and they were sitting in a corner that was even more poorly lit. The man meeting with Sulanni kept his hand up around his face most of the time they were talking. I only caught glimpses of his face head on; from the side is what I saw the most." "Just do the best you can, and if we have to do it over and over again until we get the best image for you, then we will repeat the process."

*   *   *

Ninety minutes later, the Director walked into the conference room and handed a sketch to Terry and Henry. "Gentlemen, this is the best our artist could do with the sketch. The informant says that he did not get that good of a look of the man from straight on, but rather a profile view; he said the man seemed to shielding his face the entire time he was sitting at the table. Even as they left the bar, Sulanni and his friend had their backs to where the informant was sitting, so he only saw the back of their heads."

"Director, did he give you any information like what he thought about the age or the nationality of the man?" "Oh, yes. He said the man looked Malay, with maybe some other nationality mixed in, about forty-years-old, very well-dressed, and not bad looking. He said the man could be taken as a wealthy businessman and that his clothes were definitely expensive."

With that description, the Director handed the sketch over to Terry, while Henry looked over Terry's shoulder at the image laid on the table.

Terry looked up at Henry and said, "What do you think, Mr. Chin?"

Henry looked intently at the sketch and then picked it up and gave it a closer look. "Terry, I can't say for sure, but the sketch looks vaguely familiar, like maybe someone I have seen before. But you know in our business, that we look at so many mug shots, it's difficult to say." He threw the sketch on the table and became very pensive as he sat back down.

Terry looked at him and said, "What is it, Henry? Do you think you know this guy?"

"I'm not sure, Terry. There is something about him that makes me think I have seen him before, but I can't place it. The profile looks so familiar, but the sketch from straight on does not look that familiar. I just don't know."

Terry stared at the sketch once more and said, "Henry, just keep thinking about it and study it some more. If there's a familiarity about it, you'll eventually figure it out."

The Director said, "Gentlemen, I am sorry that the sketch is not perfect, but we must go with it. See you in the morning."

"Thank you, and sir? This is the first clue we've had to this guy since the initial flu attack," Terry said. "We'll find him and this sketch will be instrumental, mark my words."

ST. VINCENT'S HOSPITAL

The New York City hospital where the first flu victims had been taken with a then unknown ailment seemed to be the most logical place to hold a major announcement in the battle against the St. Gustaf flu strain. Dr. George Simpson walked to the podium in the main auditorium of the hospital and welcomed the members of the press. He paid special recognition to his staff, which had worked for over six months to fight the deadly virus.

"Good afternoon. It has been a very long and very exhausting six months since that day back in the fall when our emergency room treated patients with the flu-like symptoms of an illness that was eventually diagnosed as the return of the Spanish Flu of 1918-1919. The medical community has known for eighty-seven years following the disappearance of the Spanish flu that someday that flu might reappear, but none of us expected it to return with such a vengeance: as a weaponized version created by a terrorist organization.

"We have lost millions of lives here in the United States and millions more across the globe. The war on terrorism has told us that life will never be the same for any of us again. We must constantly be on guard. We are, however, winning that war on terrorism and thanks to the Center for Disease Control in Atlanta we now have a viable vaccine which has been distributed to our military and first responders. Two months from now, the rest of the country will be inoculated and people will once more be able to go about their daily lives without masks on their faces and without the constant fear of falling victim to this horrible weapon, the St. Gustaf flu.

"I am not here today, though, to talk about the war or the politics or even about terrorism. I am here today to confirm that even though we have had over one million deaths in the five New York boroughs alone, the death rate has declined drastically over the past thirty days. The diagnosis of new flu cases has dwindled to only a few dozen cases over the past week. In addition, tests conducted on the latest victims show that the strain of flu they are experiencing is much weaker than the original and most, if not all, of the newly diagnosed cases will recover from their bout with the flu. We have sent samples to the CDC and we have received confirmation that the strain has weakened dramatically, following a pattern similar to the Spanish Flu of 1918-19. What this means is that during that period, medical personnel were left without answers; the flu elusively disappeared as quickly as it had appeared eighteen months earlier. Ladies and gentlemen, we have been in contact with every major medical facility in the country and all are reporting similar findings at their locations. The flu definitely is on the wane."

The auditorium erupted in applause at the news Dr. Simpson had delivered. Half of the reporters could not wait to report back to their news services and rushed to call in the story. The rest waited patiently to ask questions of Dr. Simpson and the press conference continued, but only after the entire medical staff of St. Vincent's Hospital was asked by Dr. Simpson to stand and accept his heartfelt thanks for the wonderful job they had done over the past six months.

President Doyle and the First Lady watched the press conference from the White House with Bob Roche and Ken Sitarek. As he heard the news, the President let out a huge sigh of relief and stood and hugged his wife. Just then the phone rang and Sean Doyle picked it up on the second ring. "Yes, Aggie, who's calling?"

"Mr. President, the Chairman of the New York Stock Exchange is on the line." Aggie put the call through and the President heard the best news in weeks.

"Mr. President, the market is going crazy upon hearing the news announced by Dr. Simpson in New York! It looks like we are going to have one hell of a rally, sir. Sorry for the language."

Sean was grinning from ear to ear. "No need for apologies. That is fantastic! Keep me informed and thank you for calling."

The President turned to his wife and staff and said, "Well, how about that, folks? We are turning the corner."

CNN HEADQUARTERS

"This is Dan Quigley reporting and what a story we have for you tonight! Dr. George Simpson has just held a press conference in New York to announce that incidences of the St. Gustaf flu are diminishing; newly reported cases have dwindled to only a few dozen over the past couple of weeks. We hear more now from our correspondent, Mark Gibbs, in New York. Mark, what can you tell us about this breaking story?"

"Dan, people here at St. Vincent's Hospital are ecstatic over this news. It appears that the flu, although having been weaponized, is taking the same course that the Spanish flu did back in 1919. If you recall, the flu at that time actually disappeared as quickly as it arrived eighteen months before. This new strain, after wreaking havoc throughout the world, is leaving as the former flu did. Fortunately, we now have a vaccine, which was not the case when the Spanish flu hit eighty some years ago. This is Mark Gibbs reporting from New York."

"Folks, we should also note that hospitals all over the country are reporting similar declines in their numbers of newly diagnosed cases of the flu. The number of new patients being admitted for treatment has fallen drastically.

"In other late breaking news, the Chairman of the New York Stock Exchange reported this afternoon that the market has experienced the greatest rebound he has seen in all of his years on Wall Street. The report from Dr. Simpson at St. Vincent's Hospital is the impetus for this rally.

"Now let's go to Washington where Donna Weir has the latest on the distribution of the flu vaccine. What can you tell us, Donna, about the CDC's progress of getting the vaccine out to the first responders and the military?"

"Dan, the vaccine distribution procedures have been in place for years, as you know. Ever since the attack on the World Trade Center, local municipalities have been trained and readied for any type of biological attack. The national stockpile of pharmaceuticals is prepared for distribution and a plan has been in place since that time. Points of distribution, or PODS, have been designated and it is there where the responders and their families will go to be vaccinated by specialized medical assistance response teams. These SMART teams have been organized throughout the country and are key to making this whole operation work effectively."

"Donna, you said 'the responders and their families.' Why are the families being inoculated as well?"

"Dan, this has been part of the plan since the procedures were put in place back in 2002. The responders, the military personnel, and their immediate families will be given the vaccine first and then within two months, the rest of the population will be getting the vaccine as it becomes available. This is Donna Weir reporting from Washington."

"Donna, thank you for that report. In other news on the terrorism front today, four more cells were discovered and eighteen suspects were rounded up in Chicago. These cells were allegedly part of the unit that was responsible for the bombings of the bridges in Buffalo,

Detroit, and San Francisco. The Special Agent in Charge for the FBI in Chicago stated today that these cells were also planning to bomb the Sears Tower in downtown Chicago. U.S. agents have foiled the terrorists one more time. Another battle won in this war on terrorism. This is Dan Quigley in Atlanta. Have a good night."

SAFE HOUSE

Kemal was mixing himself a cosmopolitan straight up when the door chime sounded. He put his drink down and walked across the parquet floor to the main entrance. He opened the door, where his number one female operative, Sonia Wong, was about to ring once more, but dropped her hand back to her side and gave Kemal a little smile and then a kiss on the cheek. Dressed in a burgundy dress with a slit up the right side almost to the top of her thigh, her perfect body was enhanced by the tightness of the dress. Of Chinese descent, she was one of the most beautiful creatures that Kemal had ever laid eyes on.

"Come in, my beautiful lady. I was just having a cosmo. Would you like one?"

"No thank you, Kemal. If you have work for me tonight, then I will just have an iced tea with lemon, please."

Kemal poured the iced tea and handed it to Sonia. He then lifted his cosmopolitan and clinked the glass to hers and said, "Here's to success in your mission tonight." Sonia sipped the tea and then said, "And what might that mission be, Mr. Kabigting?"

285

"Here is an address that I would like you to visit to help out a friend of mine. When you are finished doing whatever he would like, you can perform your usual disposal service for me. Your standard fee will be deposited in your account first thing in the morning."

"Kemal, you are so good to me. How can I possibly thank you?"

"No thanks are necessary. Do a good job and that will be enough."

Sonia picked up the note paper with the address on it, finished her tea, and leaned over and kissed Kemal on the cheek.

"I will be going now. I will call you when my mission is accomplished."

She turned and walked out of the room. Kemal listened to the clicking of her high heels on the wood floor and smiled as he heard the door open and then close almost silently.

*   *   *

Sulanni found the safe house on the outskirts of Kuala Lumpur and was happy to see that it was well-hidden. The entrance had a gate that led up a long, winding drive that was completely covered with trees; from the road, one might never realize that there was even a driveway beyond the gate. He pushed the button on the side of the gate, identified himself, and the gate swung open. He drove up the winding drive to a brick, Tudor-style house that sat at the top, surrounded by large trees and shrubberies. A four car garage was off to the left and one of the doors opened as he pulled in front of the entrance. He assumed the empty bay was for him, so he drove into the garage and the door immediately closed.

An elderly Malay entered the garage from a side door and said, "Mr. Sulanni, I presume?"

"Yes, that's me. And you are . . .?"

"My name is Mamood. I am in the employ of Mr. Kabigting and I am here to serve you. I will show you to your room and after you freshen up, I will give you a tour of the house. Please come this way."

Sulanni followed the valet into the side door of the Tudor and up to the second floor, where he was led into a large bedroom with a king-size bed. Off to the left was the bath, with a whirlpool bathtub and walk-in shower. The room was almost as large as Sulanni's bedroom back in London.

Mamood said, "Mr. Sulanni, take your time unpacking and getting settled in. I will meet you in the living room at the bottom of the stairs when you are ready."

The valet turned and left the room. Sulanni put his bag on the bed and looked at the whirlpool and thought, *that is going to feel so good later. The perfect cure for the stress I have been under these past two days.* He proceeded to unpack and although the bed looked inviting, he decided that sleep could wait until later. What he needed right now was a drink. Maybe that would relax him. He headed for the stairway and as he descended, he saw that Mamood was waiting for him in the hall. Sulanni wondered how the valet could have known he was coming down at that precise moment. He thought, *this valet is somewhat scary.*

"Ah, Mr. Sulanni, right this way. Let me give you the grand tour." For the next ten minutes, Sulanni was led through numerous rooms: the living room; the dining room; the library; the entertainment center, with the latest in HDF and movie theatre seats and surround-sound speakers on all four walls; the kitchen; and the solarium.

Down at the basement level there was a bar, a game room, and a high-definition television, just as he had seen in the entertainment center. The tour ended back in the library where Mamood offered to make Sulanni a drink. Sulanni said, "I will have scotch neat."

As Sulanni put the drink to his lips, the door chimed, and Mamood left to answer the same. He returned to the library with the most beautiful Chinese woman that Sulanni had ever seen.

"Mr. Sulanni, let me introduce an associate of Mr. Kabigting's, Ms. Sonia Wong."

Sulanni gulped his scotch and took a few seconds to find his voice. He finally said, "It is a pleasure to meet you, Ms. Wong."

"Call me Sonia, Mr. Sulanni. Mr. Kabigting thought you might like some company for dinner this evening. Do you mind if I join you?"

Sulanni was so taken with the beauty of this creature that he almost stuttered as he said, "No, not at all. You're more than welcome. Please join us."

Mamood said, "It will not be us, Mr. Sulanni. After I serve dinner, I will be leaving. I have an appointment in town this evening. It will be you and Ms. Wong for dinner."

Sulanni tried to hide his surprise, and said, "Well, I am sorry you cannot join us, Mamood. I am sure that Ms. Wong and I will get along fine. Can I make you a drink, Ms. Wong?"

"Yes, but please call me Sonia."

"Okay, Sonia it is. What will you have?"

"How about a cosmopolitan?"

Sulanni grinned at her and said, "Coming right up."

"Dinner will be served in forty-five minutes," Mamood said. "I will ring the bell when I am ready and you can meet me in the dining room." He then turned and headed for the kitchen.

Sulanni turned to Sonia and said, "So what is it you do for my dear friend Kemal?"

"Oh, I cannot tell you exactly what I do, but let's just say I am part of Mr. Kabigting's support group. I do many things for him and he pays me well. How about you, Mr. Sulanni? What is it you do for Mr. Kabigting?"

"I, too, am unable to say exactly what I do for Kemal, but I will say that I have been quite busy and the job has brought me tremendous stress over the past six months." Sonia smiled, her china doll face beaming, and she said, "Maybe we can relieve some of that stress after dinner. I have many ancient Chinese secrets that I can apply to ease your stress."

Sulanni could not believe what he was hearing. *Is it possible that she is talking about being intimate? Dinner cannot come too quickly*, he thought, as he poured himself another scotch.

Dinner was served exactly forty-five minutes after Mamood left for the kitchen. As he finished laying out the covered dishes on the table, he bowed and politely said, "Good evening, friends. I must leave now. When you are finished with dinner, please leave everything. I will take care of it when I return. If you desire coffee or tea, it is brewing in the kitchen. Help yourselves." He turned and left the dining room and ten seconds later, they heard the front door open and then close.

Sulanni lifted his drink and said, "Here is to a wonderful dinner."

Sonia smiled and said, "Here is to a wonderful night."

Dinner was exquisite. Mamood had outdone himself. Everything was perfectly prepared, from the soup, to the crisp salad, and the entrée of veal picata. Wild rice and fresh asparagus complemented the entrée. A bottle of red wine, Pinot Noir, was open and breathing for the diners. As Sonia finished her cosmopolitan, she poured a little wine for both of them and then tasted the Pinot, swirling it around on her tongue and breathing in the aromas. "Excellent choice of wine. That Mamood is the best, isn't he?"

Sulanni tasted the wine and said, "Here is to Mamood. He is a stupendous cook and wine expert."

While dining, the conversation never touched on terrorism or religion. Sonia was an avowed Buddhist and Sulanni was Muslim, but neither was extremely religious and rather westernized, even though they would never admit it. They both had an extreme hatred for the west and longed to see the demise of the United States and its allies.

The wine was finished and Sonia went looking for more. Mamood had once shown her where the wine cellar was, and she headed down to find it in search of another bottle.

Sulanni was feeling the influence of the alcohol and began to worry that he might not be able to perform if they got to that point later in the evening.

Sonia returned with another bottle of Pinot Noir and said, "Why don't you show me around? I would love to see the upstairs especially. I understand that the rooms are quite large. Is your's large, Mr. Sulanni?"

"Oh yes, it is, and it has a huge bathroom with a whirlpool bath in it."

"Oh, that sounds like fun! Show me the way."

They both picked up their wine glasses and Sonia uncorked the bottle of red wine and took it with her. Sulanni led her up the stairway and headed for his room. Sonia took in the expanse of the bedroom and said, "You were right; this is very large. A king size bed! How nice."

Sonia walked over and took Sulanni's glass and poured the Pinot for him and then one for herself. She put the bottle down on the nightstand and after sipping her wine, she also set her glass down. She walked over to Sulanni and said, "Why don't we get more comfortable?" She took his wine glass and set it down and then began to unbutton his shirt, pulling it off his shoulders and down his arms. She then unbuckled his belt while he kicked off his shoes. In one swift motion, she unbuttoned his pants and unzipped and removed the same for him.

"Oh, Mr. Sulanni! The bedroom is not the only thing that is large! Come lay on the bed for me. I have something for you. One of those ancient Chinese secrets." She pulled down the bedspread and had Sulanni lay down on the bed and then she left for the bathroom. Sulanni was shivering, he was so nervous. Two minutes later, Sonia returned, completely naked, and had a tube of oil in her hand.

"Please roll over on your stomach, Mr. Sulanni, if you can with that obstruction you have there."

Sulanni rolled over and Sonia began to spread oil over his body, from his neck all the way down to his feet, stopping at his buttocks, massaging every muscle in his body. When she finished with his backside, she had him roll over on his back and performed the same procedure on his front side. Sulanni was so relaxed and excited that he thought he was going to explode. He attempted to pull Sonia to him and she said, "No, not yet. Wait until we get in the whirlpool."

Finished with the oil, she grabbed his hand and led him into the bathroom where she had filled the tub slowly while she was massaging Sulanni. Dropping a little bubble bath in the water, she then turned on the jets and the whirlpool began.

"You get in. I will go get our wine."

Sulanni stepped into the tub and sat down in the swirling waters. All of the stress of the past months seemed to be melting away as he relaxed in the tub.

Sonia returned and handed Sulanni his glass and he took a gulp and reclined in the tub. Sonia stepped in and Sulanni said, "You are the most beautiful woman I have ever met. Thank you so much for that massage. What's next?" "Oh, you will see Mr. Sulanni. Have some more wine." He sipped on his wine and Sonia seemed to be swaying back and forth. He had trouble focusing on her face. He went to reach for her and fell face first into the water. Sonia leaned over and submerged his head deep into the tub and held it there for at least two minutes. When she released her hand, Sulanni's body floated to the surface. With eyes wide open, he had the look that all victims of drowning have, the blank look of a deer in the headlights as an automobile approaches at night.

"Mr. Sulanni, I am so sorry you had to leave us, but now maybe you will meet all of those virgins you Muslims are always talking about."

The very slight sedative that Sonia had put in the wine was not enough to kill Sulanni, but if his body was ever found, the cause of death would be drowning and the amount of alcohol in his system would be a contributing factor.

Sonia cleaned up the wine glasses, left the bottle, dressed quickly, and left the Tudor. Mamood would be back soon to clean up the rest and then dispose of the body. She got into her Lexus and hit the speed dial on her cell phone. The phone rang only once.

"Hello," Kemal said.

Sonia said, "Mission accomplished. I will expect a large deposit in my account in the morning."

"It will be there, my lovely beauty. Thank you for another job well done."

ONE WEEK LATER

Terry Crowley and Henry Chin had been to every hotel, big and small, in Kuala Lumpur and had turned up nothing except for the initial lead that helped produce the artist's sketch of Sulanni. The entire Operation Headhunter team had been called into the city to narrow the search for the terrorist. Absolutely nothing had developed. It almost seemed to Terry that Mr. Sulanni had disappeared into thin air. Without his arrest, the investigation would go nowhere because no one had a clue as to who the mastermind of the operation was. Terry thought, *if we ever needed a break in an investigation, we need it now.*

Henry walked into the office and said, "You know, Terry, I cannot get that image of the drawing out of my head."

"You mean Sulanni?"

"No, the other sketch of the guy he was having a drink with at the Bali Bar. I am sure that I have seen that guy somewhere before. It is driving me crazy that I can't figure out where."

"Maybe he just looks like someone you know. After all Henry, the sketch is only a profile. We really don't have a frontal view of the guy. It could be anybody."

"Yeah, I know that Terry, but I just have this nagging feeling that it is someone I have met before. I have stared and stared at the sketch and just cannot figure it out."

One of the Malaysian agents walked in and said, "Hey guys, the Director wants you in his office right away." Terry and Henry got up and headed for the Director's office. "You wanted to see us, sir?"

"Yes, Terry, Henry, pull up a chair. I have some news for you and you probably should be sitting when I tell you."

Henry leaned forward and said, "What is it, sir?"

"We have found Mr. Sulanni."

Terry jumped out of his chair and said, "That is fantastic news, sir! Where did we find him?"

"Terry, please sit back down. We found him dead in the Klang River about ten miles northeast of here."

"Shit! I did not want to hear that, not at all. There goes our investigation right down the river with Sulanni."

"Let's not give up yet, Terry. An autopsy will be performed later today to determine the cause of death, but there were no visible signs of trauma to the body. He could have died of natural causes."

"But sir, why would he end up in the Klang River?"

"That we will have to find out, but first things first. I will let you know as soon as I get the results of the autopsy. Meanwhile, if we don't develop any new leads by the end of the week, then I am afraid I will need to pull my agents off the operation. I wish I had better news for you, Terry. I know how hard you and your team have worked on getting this terrorist, but without any other solid leads, I will have no other choice but to withdraw."

"I understand, sir. We need a break, a big break. This is a major setback in our investigation. Call me as soon as you get the results of the autopsy. I need to call my Director and fill him in."

"I will do that, Terry. Good luck. I sincerely hope you will develop something within a week's time."

Terry and Henry, dejected and disgusted, shuffled out of the Director's office and headed back to their office. Terry thought, *Director Graham is not going to be happy with this news.*

*   *   *

A few hours later, the agents were called back to the Malaysian Director's office.

"Gentlemen, we have the results of the autopsy and it appears that the cause of death was drowning."

Terry and Henry could not hide their surprise in this analysis. "Sir, are you saying that Sulanni drowned in the river?"

"No, Terry, I don't know where he drowned, but I don't believe it was in the river. The autopsy showed that Sulanni had a very high content of alcohol in his system and there was a trace of a mild sedative, but not enough to kill him. The cause of death was definitely drowning, but there were traces of another chemical in his lungs."

Terry asked, "What kind of chemical are you talking about, sir?"

"Well, it is used for many things, but the most common use is to make bubble bath solution."

"That isn't something that you would find in the river. Too large an area. It would have diluted. You don't suppose he died in a bathtub and someone found him and dumped the body in the Klang?"

"My suspicion is that he was drowned by someone else and then the body was disposed of. The question is, where was the scene of the crime, assuming he was killed?"

Henry asked, "Do we have a time of death, sir?"

"The medical examiner estimates that Mr. Sulanni has been dead for about a week. I would like both of you to go over to the M.E.'s office and get an in-depth briefing from him. Maybe some information will come out of it to produce a lead."

Terry stood up and said, "Thank you, sir. We will get right on it."

Henry and Terry left the building and drove their SUV to the Medical Center, only a short drive away from downtown Kuala Lumpur. As they passed the Petronas Towers, Henry thought about his former schoolmate, Kemal Kabigting. *One of these days,* he thought, *I am going to have to find out what that asshole does for a living.*

Terry Crowley parked in the visitors parking lot of Kuala Lumpur Medical Center, and Henry and he took the elevator to the lower level where the morgue was located. There they were met by Dr. Williams, a young British physician from Liverpool, England. Introductions were made and Dr. Williams invited them to his office.

"Gentlemen, I understand that your Director has already filled you in on the cause of death and a few other findings. What else can I do for you?"

Terry spoke first. "Doc, we need a more in-depth description of the body and what else you might have found that was unusual or anything that you don't usually encounter with a drowning victim."

"I don't know where the man was drowned, Agent Crowley, but I don't believe it was in the Klang River."

Terry said, "We understand that, Doctor, and we have been told about the chemical found in his lungs, and the alcohol content in his system. What else can you tell us?" Dr. Williams opened his file and said, "First of all, the body was completely naked and no clothes have been found. If he had drowned in the river, he must have been taking a swim without his clothes on. Secondly, there was a residue all over his body of the type that comes from body oil, and not natural body oil, but the type used by a massage specialist. That, together with the bubble bath chemical found in his lungs and the high alcohol content, would suggest that he may have been to a brothel, but that is just a guess."

Henry said, "Doctor, I'd say that's a good guess. What about the alcohol? Can you tell us what kind of alcohol he was drinking?"

"Yes, Agent Chin, I can tell you that it was mostly wine and our analysis tells us that it was a red wine, and more than likely an expensive Pinot Noir."

Henry put his hand to his head and said, "Wow, that is impressive! You're able to actually tell us what kind of wine he drank?"

"Yes, our test equipment has become very sophisticated. I could probably make a guess as to the brand of wine. There are only three that would qualify based on our analysis and only two are sold in Kuala Lumpur."

Terry leaned forward and said, "Doc, is there any way that you could tell if the victim had sexual relations before he died and if so, would it be possible to get any DNA samples from the alleged killer?"

"Sir, I can tell you that there was no evidence to suggest that. I will also tell you that we did not find any bruises on the body that would have suggested foul play."

"Dr. Williams, thank you for your time. You've been very helpful. Before we go, could you write down the names of those two wine brands for us?"

"Sure. Here they are. I hope you don't want to taste them. They are over fifty dollars a bottle, quite expensive for my taste."

Henry and Terry shook hands with the doctor and headed for their SUV. Once inside the vehicle, Henry asked, "Terry, why did you want the names of those wine companies?"

"Henry, we are between what we call back in America 'a rock and a hard place,' and we need a break. I intend to follow any possible lead we can."

"But Terry, how is wine going to help us catch the bad guy?"

"Think about it for a minute, Henry. You don't think our Mr. Sulanni was going out and buying fifty dollar bottles of wine, do you? My guess is that someone fed him the wine and someone who could well afford it at that price. I am going to have our agents check all liquor outlets to find out how many sell the Pinot Noir in question and see if there any big spenders who order a lot of it. At this point, we have very little to go on, so I'm open to anything we can do that will develop a lead."

Upon returning to the Ministry Building, Terry Crowley called a meeting of his teams and filled them in on the developments. He gave each team leader the names of two wines and said he wanted every liquor seller in Kuala Lumpur contacted to see which sold each brand and which had consumers who bought the same if, in fact, they had that kind of information.

Two hours later, the teams returned to the Ministry Building and Terry was shocked they were back so soon. As they filed into the conference room he said, "You guys are done already? How could you have finished this fast?"

The leader of Team B said, "Terry, it was quite simple. We called the two wine companies and inquired if they had a list of customers in Kuala Lumpur and they faxed it over to us. From that point, it was easy to contact the dozen stores out of one hundred and twenty that sell the two brands."

Terry smiled and said, "That's great, team, but what did you find out?"

Team Leader A stepped forward and gave Terry a list of the establishments and the corresponding list of customers. "As you can see, Terry, five of the stores stock the wine, but hardly sell any at all. Over the past six months, they have each sold two bottles. The other seven have had greater sales, but only two sell the wines in any bulk. Those two sell to the luxury hotels who serve the wine in their restaurants and they also sell to the five star restaurants in the city. The five stores that sell the wines on a regular basis have given us their customer lists and they include five millionaires and an import/export company."

Terry looked at Henry and said, "Why would an import/export company be buying from a liquor outlet in the city? Wouldn't you think that they could just buy direct from the wine company?"

Henry said, "No, they would be unable to do that. The law says that alcohol, including wine, can only be sold to an authorized distributor and from them, to a retail outlet that is in the business of selling alcohol. If the import/export company wants the wine, the company has to go directly to the store."

Terry turned to Team Leader A and said, "Did the store which sells to this import/export company say why the company buys the wine or how much wine is purchased?"

"Yes, Terry. The manager said he has a standing order for a case every month and it is delivered to Petronas Towers where the company has its offices."

Henry said, "They probably give it out to their customers as a perk. I'm sure their customers would appreciate getting a fifty dollar bottle of wine."

Terry turned to Team Leader B and said, "Call that liquor store and see if the manager can tell us who the CEO is for the import/ export company. Team C, I want you to visit each of the hotels and restaurants that sells these two brands of wine and show Sulanni's picture or sketch to them. We need to find out if he had dinner at any of those places one week ago. The rest of you split up this list of customers and get together with our Malaysian agents and see what we can find out on each of the buyers of this wine. If anything develops, then we will pay them a visit, but not until we have background information on each of them. We will meet again in the morning to go over your results. Thanks for a good job, guys."

POINTS OF DISTRIBUTION

SMART Teams all over the country had been activated to distribute the new vaccine. POD's were set up in every community. Since the first responders and military were being vaccinated initially, most of the points of distribution were either in community fire halls or at local armories. Martial law was still in effect and would most likely stay until the ninety-day period had expired.

The CDC announced that it would begin shipping vaccine to countries that had the ability to culture it and produce it in mass quantities. Shipments were made to the United Kingdom, France, Germany, Italy, Russia, Japan, Greece, Spain, China, and Canada.

Newly diagnosed cases of the St. Gustaf flu had dropped to only a few a day. The flu was rapidly disappearing and the citizens were looking forward to brighter and better days ahead. Every one of the cities that had experienced bombings in its churches and cathedrals was rebuilding at a record pace. However, there were still facilities that could not reopen their doors because of deadly anthrax spores within the buildings. Without decontamination and removal of the spores, no one could enter the facilities. The spores would live for seventy or more years. The cost to thoroughly clean the buildings was in the millions for each facility. Some were being decontaminated because they were Federal Government buildings and the Environmental Protection Agency was doing the cleaning. Citizens of the private sector, however, were on their own, and most could not afford the cleanup.

In President Doyle's hometown of Buffalo, the Peace Bridge had been repaired after the suicide bomber incident and traffic was once more traveling across the bridge to Canada. The Golden Gate Bridge in San Francisco had also been repaired in record time, but the border crossing at Detroit was still closed due to reconstruction of that bridge.

On her weekly radio call-in show, noted psychologist Dr. Jane Becker was breaking all records for listening audiences. Her reassurance to callers stressed by the terrorist events seemed to calm people right down. Her audience was clearly receptive to her advice, which was given with caring and understanding. A longtime friend of the President and the First Lady, Dr. Becker was surprised and pleased during a broadcast when she heard the familiar voice of the President.

"Mr. President, how nice of you to call in!"

"Dr. Becker, I wanted to call and tell you what a tremendous job you are doing and what a positive and beneficial service you provide for our citizenry. Keep up the good work. Brighter days are ahead! Maggie thanks you, too."

"Thank you, Mr. President."

At the Washington end of the phone, President Doyle hung up the receiver and turned to Maggie, who said, "Sean Doyle, that was very nice of you to call Jane and tell her what a good job she's doing!"

"Thank you, Maggie. I think it's important to compliment people when they are providing a service such as Jane's. Now I have to get to my meeting with the Surgeon General. See you at dinner."

Maggie kissed her husband, and left the Oval Office. Dr. Richard Carey entered the room only seconds after Maggie left. "Good afternoon, Mr. President."

"Good afternoon to you, Doc. What do you have for me? Good news, I hope."

"Mr. President, the PODS are performing admirably and we have finished over eighty percent of the vaccinations that we had scheduled. That is beyond our expectations. Of course, the remainder of them should be completed by tomorrow. We had originally estimated a week-to-ten days to complete the process and it looks like we will do it in eight days. As far as the progress in Atlanta, Dr. Doyle tells me that his staff is estimating they will have the remainder of the vaccine ready in one month. That would be three weeks earlier than we announced to the nation."

"Dr. Carey, that would be fantastic. We need all the positive news we can get right now."

"Mr. President, we can still expect a lot of deaths from victims that have been diagnosed for a while now, but there are very few new cases and of course, the flu has weakened considerably. It is a shadow of what it was six months ago."

"Dr. Carey, thank you for your efforts. Keep me informed on future progress."

"I will, Mr. President. You can bet on that."

As Dr. Carey left the office, the telephone rang. "Yes, Aggie, what is it?"

"Mr. President, I have Director Graham from the FBI on the line and he said it is very urgent that he speak with you."

"Put him through, Aggie."

"Yeah, Ted, what do you have for me?"

Ted Graham cleared his throat and said, "Mr. President, I'm afraid that this is not good news. We have lost our number one enemy, Mr. Sulanni. He was found floating in the Klang River northeast of the city of Kuala Lumpur this morning. This is a tremendous setback; we were never able to identify his superior."

The President sighed heavily and said, "Damn it to hell! Ted, how could this have happened? I thought we were hot on his trail and now you tell me he's dead?"

"I am truly sorry, Mr. President. We wanted this guy just as badly as you did. We were so close. We had a sketch of him distributed throughout the country over there. It would have been almost impossible for him to leave Malaysia. Someone got to him before we did; we don't believe his death was accidental. Our analysis is that someone drowned him and then threw the body in the river. Problem is, we don't know who and have very little to go on at this point. I wanted you to know as soon as I got the word. Once again, I apologize that we did not get our man, but we are still working on finding the killer."

"Ted, I know your people are the best and I'm sorry I snapped at you. I also know that Terry Crowley is the finest agent you could have sent over there to run Operation Headhunter. If anything can be done to find the killer, then I am sure that Terry will be the one to do it. Keep me up to date, Ted."

"I will, Mr. President. As soon as I know anything, you will be contacted immediately. Goodbye, sir."

"Goodbye, Ted." Sean put down the phone and rubbed his temples, knowing another headache was coming on. He picked up the receiver and buzzed Aggie. "Aggie, do you have one of those Excedrin with you that you take for your migraines?"

"Yes, Mr. President. I'll bring one right in."

Sean put the phone back down and reached for his bottle of water. Aggie appeared in the doorway with the Excedrin and said, "Mr. President, you look very stressed. Maybe you should take two of these."

"No, Aggie, one is fine. You know me. I hardly ever get a headache, but when I do, then one of these will do it. If I need more, I'll buzz you. Thanks for your help." "Call me if you need me, Mr. President."

THE NEXT DAY

Terry Crowley walked into the conference room at precisely nine o'clock the next morning where his teams were already assembled. Henry Chin entered right after, and Terry began the meeting with a report that he had given to Director Ted Graham and informed the team that Director Graham had further informed the President of the current situation.

"Let's see what we have, folks. Who wants to begin?" Team Leader A spoke first. "Terry, we have checked out most of the buyers and have found that of the five millionaires, only two are in the country right now and both of them are in their eighties. Neither one is Muslim or has any connection to the Muslim faith or community. We believe that would put them low on our suspect list, or not on it at all. The other three order one to two cases a year and they are all delivered to their yachts, one of which is docked on the same river that Mr. Sulanni was dumped in. The owner of that yacht is Muslim and the other two are not. One is Chinese and the other is Indian."

Terry said, "It looks to me like we may have one suspect for our list. What about the rest of the list?" "One guy buys a bottle about every other month and he lives on an estate just outside of the city. He's semi-retired and living on his stocks and bonds. Another one is the head waiter at one of the restaurants which sells the wine in its establishment. He must have tasted it and liked it, so he splurges from time to time, but not on a regular basis. That's about it, Terry. Nothing further at this time."

Terry said, "Thanks. How about those restaurants and hotels? Which team was going to check those out?"

Team Leader C stood and said, "That was us, Terry. We've been to every one of the hotels and restaurants and showed the sketch to the head waiters who were on that night; only one recognized the sketch. He only knew the face because he said, 'This Sulanni was a regular customer, but he was not in last week and I have not seen him for about a month.' He also said that Sulanni never drank either of those brands of wine."

Terry frowned. "Shit! We're getting nowhere here! Team B, what do you have for us?"

"Terry, you asked us to find whatever information on the import/export company was available and believe me, it was tough to get. This is a closely held corporation and very little information is available on it. However, we do have some of the best hackers in the business working here at the Ministry and one of them was able to hack into the company's website and then into its intranet."

Terry smiled and said, "You mean 'internet,' right?" "No, Terry. An intranet is like your own internet within your company, and not available to outsiders, but our hacker was able to get into it."

"Okay, so what did you find?"

"Not a lot of information, but we did find the name of the CEO. He is the founder and sole stockholder of the corporation. He is Muslim, about forty-years-old, single, and somewhat of a recluse. He buys a case of the Pinot Noir every month, and he can well afford it: his company is the biggest import/export firm in all of Malaysia. His name is Kemal Kabigting."

Terry spun around and looked at Henry Chin as Henry jumped out of his chair. Henry looked at the Team Leader and said, "Did I hear you say Kemal Kabigting?"

"Yes, Henry, that's his name. His company is located in the Petronas Towers office building."

Henry turned to Terry. Simultaneously they shouted, "Holy shit!"

PENANG ENTERPRISES

Kemal had just finished an overseas call with his manager in Saudi Arabia, when his Information Technology manager entered his office.

"Sir, I am so sorry for the interruption, but I have urgent business to discuss."

Kemal looked up from his desk, almost scowling at his chief computer operator and said, "Yes, Chang, what is it that has you so upset?"

"Mr. Kabigting, there has been a breach in our computer fire wall, sir. Our secure intranet has been compromised by someone on the outside."

"Chang, how could this happen? You told me we had the most secure network in all of Kuala Lumpur."

"That is true, sir, but during the midnight shift, we discovered that there was an intruder who was able to break through our fire wall and somehow get into our intranet. It was only for a short time, but we have determined that this intruder was able to get into many of our files before our shift supervisor closed down the intranet and shut the hacker out."

"Chang, what files were hacked and how much have we been compromised?"

"We are still working on that, sir, and I expect we should know within the hour. We have installed a new version of the fire wall software and we are confident that this will not happen again."

"It damn sure better not, Mr. Chang, or you will be pushing a cart down at the farmers' market at the city port! Do we have any idea where this hacker came from and from where he was operating when he broke down our fire wall?"

"Mr. Kabigting, it is very difficult to trace the intrusion back to the hacker, but we do have information that it possibly came from a government network right here in the city."

"Mr. Chang, I want confirmation of that information and I want to know exactly who is intruding on our intranet and if you don't give me that information by this afternoon, you are out of a job! Do you understand me, Mr. Chang?"

"Yes, sir, absolutely Mr. Kabigting. I will have it for you by the earliest possible moment, sir."

"Good! Now get out of my office and get to work on that!"

Once the door to his office was closed, Kemal picked up an eight by ten photo from his desk and slammed it down on the mahogany desktop, smashing the glass into dozens of pieces. He was seething with anger. His business had been compromised and somehow the government agency or whomever was snooping around his intranet either knew about him and his operation, or was just checking into import/export companies.

Kemal would have to be extremely careful. He had contacts in the intelligence agency. Maybe he could find out what the local government was up to. If it had to do with Sulanni, he knew he was absolutely clean on that and there was no way they could trace Sulanni to his former operative. He had also covered his tracks from Dubai to Casablanca and back to Kuala Lumpur. The intelligence operatives had nothing on him. He had run a mistake-proof operation from day one. If there was a breach in his security, it was probably some hacker snooping around many intranets. To be sure, however, he would contact his friends in Malaysian intelligence.

The telephone rang on Kemal's desk, startling him out of his contemplation. "Hello, Penang Enterprises, how can I help you?"

"Kemal Kabigting, is that you?"

"Yes, it is. Who is calling, please?"

"Kemal, my old friend, it is Henry Chin from college. We ran into each other on the elevator the other day."

"Oh, yes. Henry, how are you?"

"Fine, Kemal. You mentioned we should get together for a drink, and I thought I would take you up on your offer. Are you free for lunch?"

The hair on the back of Kemal's neck stood up as he remembered the encounter on the elevator and Henry Chin mentioning that he worked for the government. *Could this have anything to do with this computer intranet intrusion? Only one way to find out,* he thought.

"Sure, Henry, as a matter of fact I am free for lunch. How about noon? Come to my office and we'll take my car from here. I assume that since you knew where to contact me, that you have also discovered that I am in the Petronas Towers. So no directions are needed, are they?"

"No, I know exactly where you are, Kemal. See you at noon. Looking forward to a nice chat and a delicious lunch."

"See you then, Henry." Kemal put down the phone and thought, *events are happening too close together. I will listen to Henry and then make my decision. Maybe my offices will have to be moved.*

Back at the Ministry Building, Henry Chin put the phone back in its cradle and turned to Terry Crowley. "Terry, you were listening. What do you think?"

"Henry, I think your friend is a very cool customer and if he is our man, we have to be very careful about how we handle him. At present, we have no proof of anything other than the gentleman has a liking for a certain Pinot Noir red wine and that he owns a successful import/export company. We have our people in Dubai and Casablanca working overtime to find a connection to Mr. Kabigting and his company and the recently departed Sulanni and Sutwa. Now we need to research everything on this guy since you last saw him in college. I have a gut feeling we are going to find a lot of interesting facts about our friend, Mr. Kabigting. Henry, you need to be careful when you meet your former schoolmate."

"Believe me, Terry, I will be extremely careful. Wish you could join me, but that would be somewhat obvious, especially if he has any suspicion about why, after twenty years, I want to meet for lunch."

Terry Crowley extended his hand to shake Henry's and said, "Good luck, my good friend."

Henry took Terry's hand and said, "Thank you, Terry. I think I'll need all the luck I can muster."

TWELVE NOON

Henry Chin entered the suite on the thirty-seventh floor of the Petronas Towers at exactly twelve o'clock noon. The receptionist, a beautiful Chinese woman, smiled and said, "May I help you, sir?"

"Henry Chin to see Mr. Kabigting."

"Of course, Mr. Chin. Mr. Kabigting is expecting you. Go right in, please."

Henry entered the spacious office with very expensive furnishings sitting on the biggest oriental carpet Henry had ever seen. French provincial sofas faced each other from either side of the carpet. An exquisite Chinese coffee table, with dragons carved out for the four legs that were holding up the one-inch thick glass table top, sat in the middle of the carpet. Beneath the carpet was a magnificent wood floor made from the best teak lumber produced in the Southeast. Kemal Kabigting stood as Henry walked through the office and extended his hand across the most exquisite mahogany desk Henry had ever seen.

"Henry, how nice to see you again! Twice in such a short space of time after twenty years. This is indeed an event. Should we get right to lunch and begin our reminiscing? I have a very busy schedule this afternoon."

"Sure, Kemal, let's get to it. Did you have a place in mind?"

"I have made a reservation at one of my favorite places: Ming's. Have you been there?"

"I certainly have. Ming's is one of the best Chinese restaurants in Southeast Asia. Unfortunately on my salary, I haven't been to Ming's often. I'm looking forward to lunch even more so now, though, than when I arrived."

Henry and Kemal left the office and took the elevator down to the sublevel, where the parking garage was located. Kemal directed Henry to his parking space and to his Mercedes.

"Nice car, Kemal. Looks like you have done very well for yourself."

Kemal smiled and said, "Being in business for yourself does have its advantages, as long as the bottom line stays in the black. We have been very fortunate, to say the least."

"I can't wait to hear all about your success," Henry said, as Kemal drove out of the parking ramp.

Five minutes later they pulled into the parking lot of Ming's Dynasty Restaurant, which specialized in excellent Chinese cooking, including szechuan, one of Henry's favorites.

The head waiter bowed and said, "Good afternoon, Mr. Kabigting. Your favorite table is waiting right by the window overlooking the waterfall."

"Thank you, John. This is Mr. Chin, an old friend, and we will want privacy, if you can keep our table somewhat isolated."

"Of course, Mr. Kabigting. As usual."

The waiter showed them to their table and asked if he could get them anything to drink. Before Henry could speak, Kemal said, "John, bring us a bottle of my favorite. Henry, here, works for the government, but one glass of wine will not interfere with his duties."

Henry was about to protest when John said, "The Pinot. Of course, Mr. Kabigting, coming right up."

"So, Henry, tell me: what exactly do you do for the government? Is it the city government of Kuala Lumpur or are you with the federal government of Malaysia?"

"Kemal, I am not with the city or the state. I work for the National Intelligence Service of Malaysia."

"Is that right? Does that mean, my friend, that you are a spy for the government?"

Henry laughed and at the same time thought, *it is best that I be truthful with him, because he probably has ways of finding out what I do with the government and that would end any form of trust I could hope to forge with my former college pal.*

"Kemal, it is nothing that exotic. I am sure the government has spies probably working within our department, but my job is not that intriguing. I am actually an investigator for the intelligence branch, not anything to do with spying." Henry hoped that Kemal would take that at face value, but knew that he would have numerous questions that might be difficult to answer now that Kemal knew he was intelligence.

John returned to the table with a bottle of Pinot Noir and removed the cork, handing it to Kemal. As Kemal smelled the cork, he smiled and said, "Always perfect. John. Let's have a sip." Kemal took the glass from John, who had poured a small portion for Kemal to sample. As Kemal sipped and rolled the wine around his tongue and then breathed in and swallowed, he smiled widely and nodded his head in agreement. This was a good Pinot. "John, you have done it again. Go ahead and pour."

As John poured the two glasses he said, "Thank you for the compliment, sir, but I cannot take credit for this incredible wine. All I do is uncork it and pour. The vineyard deserves all the credit."

John left the table and a young Chinese waitress arrived to take their order. "Good afternoon, Mr. Kabigting. What is to your liking today?"

"Mei Lei, I will have the special. This is my friend, Mr. Chin."

The waitress smiled and said, "Nice to meet you, Mr. Chin. What can I get for you today?"

"I have a desire for good szechuan. What would you recommend?"

Mei Lei smiled and said, "Our chef has an excellent chicken and beef dish that is as spicy and as hot as you can get it, Mr. Chin. It is one of the favorites on the menu."

Henry smiled and said, "Sold. Bring it on."

As Mei Lei left the table, Henry took the initiative while Kemal was sipping his wine and asked, "So Kemal, how did you get into the import/export business and manage to become so successful?"

"Well Henry, after I left school, I wasn't sure exactly what I wanted to do and I went to work for a firm that did import and export and worked my way up the corporate ladder. There came a time that I felt I could do as good a job on my own or even better. There were so many opportunities here in Malaysia that it made good sense for me to set up shop in my homeland, and especially with the tax advantages the country was giving to native Malaysians if they started their own businesses. Having made so many contacts with my former employer, once my customers realized that I was offering a better product with better pricing, many of them decided to do business with me and the rest, of course, is history. Penang Enterprises has become the most successful import/export business in Malaysia."

"You must be very proud of your accomplishments, Kemal! What a wonderful success story! Where is your former employer at now, or should I say, where was it located here in Malaysia?"

"No, actually the company was based in the Middle East and conducted most of its business there and in Europe. That company is not even a factor to me anymore. My firm has grown so large that we have overtaken my competitors in most markets."

"What about family? Are you married, any kids?" "Henry, I'm afraid I have been so locked into my career that I did not find time yet to get married or have a family. Maybe some day in the future, but not right now. How about you?"

"I stayed a bachelor for fifteen years, but then five years ago I met a wonderful girl back home in Penang and we were married six months later. My parents were very happy, as my wife is Chinese as well. We are expecting our first child, which makes them even happier."

The food was delivered and as Kemal took his first bite, he came to the meat of the discussion.

"So, Henry, I have told you about my career. How about yours? If you are not a spy for the government, then what exactly do you do in your investigations?"

Henry was caught off guard as he relished his first bite of the Chinese dish that his mother had prepared for him more than once at home in Penang.

"Kemal, it is usually very routine and boring. It could be anything from an investigation of government officials taking bribes, to someone smuggling goods into any of our ports. Sometimes it gets interesting, especially if there is an incident like a terrorist attack such as what happened on the island of Bali in that nightclub where the Australian tourists were killed."

"That must be fascinating, trying to track down those extremist Muslims that are so intent on wreaking havoc and terror on our population. They are a disgrace to my religion."

"Yes they are, Kemal. Fortunately we do not have the severe problem with terrorism that they have in America or Europe or the Middle East, but we must always be on guard for any eventuality."

Kemal lifted his wine glass and said, "Here is a toast to you, Henry, and to our National Intelligence Agency for keeping us all safe and sound."

"Thank you, Kemal. We try to do our best and believe me, even if it turned out that one of my friends was a terrorist, I would treat him no differently than any other terrorist. We must protect our homeland. That is our motto. This is excellent wine, by the way."

"Thank you, Henry. It is my favorite. I keep a private stock of it at my home. Come out to dinner sometime, and we will enjoy some more."

"I'll do that, Kemal. Thank you for the invitation."

As the coffee was delivered, Kemal threw a curve at his old friend, Henry. He leaned forward somewhat conspiratorially and said, "Henry, since you are in the intelligence service, maybe you can give me some input or should I say, 'advice.'"

"Sure, Kemal. What can I do for you?"

"In your line of work, you have probably run into computer hackers from time to time. Last night, we had a computer hacker break into our private intranet. Even though our fire wall was secure—at least we thought it was—someone was able to penetrate it and get into some of our files. Do you have suspects that you investigate for hacking into computers and if so, could you help me in my investigation?"

"Kemal, I'm sorry to hear about your intrusion, but unless it is a government break-in, I would not get involved. I can look into our hacker files, though, and see what has taken place over the past few weeks, and check whether any of our suspects might have made a similar intrusion."

"That would be helpful, Henry. My IT people are the best and they may have something for me by this afternoon, but anything additional you can do to help would be appreciated."

"You bet, Kemal. Anything for an old friend."

As Kemal reached for the check, Henry said, "Kemal, you don't have to do that, but thank you for a superb lunch."

Kemal smiled and said, "You are more than welcome. I am glad you enjoyed the lunch, and especially the wine."

HEADHUNTER UPDATE

At two o'clock, Terry Crowley convened a meeting of the entire Operation Headhunter team.

"Fellow agents, welcome to our update meeting. We have made some strides in the last twenty-four hours and I want everyone to be aware of our progress.

"First of all, our investigation into the red wine that was found in Mr. Sulanni's stomach is still continuing, but we have narrowed the number of buyers of this rare Pinot Noir to a small group of five. That does not include the hotels and restaurants that purchase the wine, but we do not, at this time, consider them to be suspects in our investigation. At the present time, we are concentrating on one of the buyers and we have stepped up our investigation to include assembling as much data as we can on this person's business dealings dating back twenty years, to before he began his current business.

"Our data analysts are scouring the internet and financial institutions here in Malaysia, and others across the world in Europe, Japan, South America, the United States, and the Caribbean. We are searching for any bit of information, big or small, related to our suspect's business dealings. Twelve hours ago, we were successful in hacking into the suspect's private company intranet and were able to access a number of files before the IT department of the company shut us out and resealed their system's fire wall. The information derived from those files is still being evaluated and we should know more later today. Through further investigation by our agent, Mr. Henry Chin, we have additional information that is being evaluated. Henry, can you give us an update of sorts as to what you have learned so far?"

"Thanks, Terry. First, let me tell you that our suspect comes from the same city in Malaysia that I do and I have known him since college. However, I had not seen him in over twenty years until a week or so ago.

"He is very successful, and owns an import/export business that he started about fifteen years ago. Prior to that, he worked for a corporation in the same type of business and was one of the chief financial people when he decided to leave and begin his own company. I can tell you that his former employer operated in the Middle East and Europe and from additional data that we obtained, it appears that most of the business conducted by his former employer was with primarily Muslim countries in the Middle East; they were suspected of doing extensive business with al-Qaida. However, nothing was ever proven.

"The period we are talking about was while our suspect was a key financial officer within his former organization. At this time, we do not have enough information to even approach this individual with any type of accusation, but as we develop our investigation, we feel confident that we will find evidence that may link him to the recently deceased suspects in Operation Headhunter. That is all I can tell you at this time."

Terry Crowley stood once more and said, "Thank you, Henry. I have a strong feeling that by this time tomorrow, we are going to have some solid leads. Thanks for your good work. Any questions?"

Team Leader B spoke up and said, "Terry, you have given us a lot of info, but no name. When do we find out who this guy is and where he is? Are you keeping something from us here or what?"

Terry cringed as he said, "Yes, I am, and I'm afraid that I can't reveal the name for at least another day. All I can tell you is that it is for security reasons. I know that sounds crazy to some of you, but I promise I will reveal the suspect at tomorrow's meeting."

The meeting broke up and Terry and Henry headed back to the office.

"Terry, what the hell was that all about? Why can't we tell the team who Kemal is? Do you know something you're not telling me?"

"Henry, come in and close the door, please." Henry entered the office, closed the door behind him, and sat down at the desk. "Henry, I did not mean to leave you out of the loop, but we had so little time once you returned from your lunch, that I didn't have an opportunity to fill you in. The fact is that while you were at lunch, we discovered that we have a leak here at the Ministry. We think we know who it is, but I did not want to tip him off during that meeting or we could blow the whole investigation."

"Are you telling me, Terry, that we have a traitor among us, right on our Operation Headhunter Team?"

"Henry, all I can tell you is that we have a mole somewhere in the Malaysian organization and until we know who it is, I am not taking any chances whether he is on our team or not. We hope to know by tomorrow morning and have him in custody, and then we can proceed with our investigation and inform all of the agents about Kemal Kabigting."

"Well, thanks for filling me in, Terry. I certainly would not have put Kemal's name out there if I knew we suspected a leak on the team. Our investigation would be down the tubes, and Kemal would be underground for sure. That is, assuming he *is* our man, and I'm getting very good vibes that he is. You know, I get the impression from him that he is too smooth, way too smooth. Of course, you know that our agents are totally stupid."

"What do you mean by that?"

"What I mean, Terry, is that remark both of us made the other day in front of one of the teams when we said, 'Holy shit!' together at the mention of Kemal's name."

"You're right, Henry. Let's hope our mole was not in that meeting."

TORONTO GENERAL

Dr. John Cooper stepped up to the podium in the auditorium at Toronto General Hospital and smiled into the camera.

"Ladies and gentlemen, welcome to our briefing and welcome to a new day. We have wonderful news for you today. First, let me tell you that we have not had a newly diagnosed case of the St. Gustaf flu in over ten days now and the majority of our patients have either been released or have been upgraded to fair or good condition. We still have six patients in our intensive care unit, but all are holding their own and we expect a full recovery.

"As you know, Toronto was the first city to report that fewer and fewer cases of the flu were showing up at our medical facilities and we suspected at the time that history might be repeating itself. The fear, of course, was that since the current strain was weaponized, that we would not see the flu leave as it did back in 1919. It has waned, however, and appears to be leaving as quickly as it came.

"I must caution our citizens, though, that we are still not 'out of the woods,' as we like to say in Canada. We have been working diligently with the Center for Disease Control in Atlanta and the vaccine they sent us is being reproduced as rapidly as possible. We intend to begin inoculations this weekend and a schedule will be issued soon. All citizens between the ages of twenty and forty will be vaccinated first, as they have been the most vulnerable age group. Ironically, to this day we still are not certain why that is, but it has followed the same pattern as the original Spanish Flu Pandemic of 1918-19. Within two months time, we hope to have every Canadian citizen vaccinated against this horrible infection. Now I will take questions."

"Dr. Cooper, Donna Weir from CNN. Why do you suppose that Canada has had fewer flu cases than other countries? Can this be explained?"

"Donna, we have not yet been able to determine why. As you know from your hometown of Buffalo, that city too, is experiencing fewer and fewer cases. Buffalo is only ninety miles from Toronto, so perhaps it is a regional recovery, but we really cannot answer that."

"Dr. Cooper, Patrick Kelly from the Irish Times. Sir, would you be telling us, now, that this region is somewhat immune, if you understand what I'm sayin,' sir, as opposed to my homeland, or are the people of Canada more careful in how they have handled the flu now?"

"Mr. Kelly, as I said to your colleague, Ms. Weir, we don't have a definitive answer for you at this time, but we do hope to soon."

The briefing by Dr. John Cooper ended and the talking heads on all television channels offered numerous opinions on what exactly caused the Canadian flu pandemic to subside before that of the rest of world. It was a mystery and not one of the experts on the cable channels really had an explanation.

President Doyle was watching the briefing and when it ended, he called Dr. Cooper to congratulate him on the Canadian progress.

As he hung up the phone, he noticed on the bottom of the television screen that CNN was reporting breaking news.

Sean turned up the volume to hear Dan Quigley saying, "We have this information from a very reliable source close to the White House that a major operation is being conducted somewhere in Southeast Asia to find and capture the terrorists that have been responsible for the spread of the St. Gustaf flu and for the horrible bombings of our places of worship. It is believed that the group is one and the same and that the bombings were in retaliation for the breakup of the terrorists' cells across America a few months ago. Just where the operation is taking place in Southeast Asia is not known at this time, but sources tell us that it is a joint operation between the United States and one of the nations in Southeast Asia. More as this late-breaking story develops."

Sean slammed his fist on the desk and said, "Damn that CNN and damn whomever is leaking information from my government! This is traitorous!" He picked up the phone and said, "Aggie, get me Bob Roche, Ken Sitarek, Henry Volner, and Ted Graham! Tell them I want them in my office in thirty minutes, if not sooner!"

"Yes, Mr. President, right away, Mr. President." Aggie made the phone calls and let each of the men know that the President did not sound happy at all.

Within fifteen minutes, all four men were assembled in the Oval Office and seated in a semicircle. Henry Volner thought to himself, *I cannot remember the President sounding this angry or looking this red in the face in all the time I have known him.*

"Gentlemen, I want answers and I want them now! I do not want to hear it from that damn Dan Quigley and his cable news network! What the hell is going on here? Who the hell is leaking information about Operation Headhunter?"

As National Security Advisor, Bob Roche felt responsible to speak first. "Mr. President, I can assure you that it did not come from the White House. I know that CNN said a reliable source close to the White House and Quigley is probably correct, but I can say categorically that it did not come from within the White House."

Ken Sitarek spoke up and said, "I agree with Bob, sir. Operation Headhunter has been kept 'top secret crypto'; there are only a handful of people on staff here that even knew there was an operation, and they did not know what it was about. I am sure the leak did not come from the White House."

The President turned his attention to his two directors, looking first at the FBI Chief, Ted Graham, and then at his CIA man, Henry Volner. "Who wants to go first, gentlemen? It sounds like someone has some explaining to do."

Ted spoke first. "Mr. President, we have no information that anyone from the FBI was involved in this leak and I don't believe that the CIA was either."

The President's face reddened even more. "Mr. Graham, do you now speak for both the FBI and the CIA?"

"No, sir, sorry sir. I meant that CNN probably got their information from someone not involved in the operation, and purposely said this person was close to the White House. It happens all the time, sir."

"I don't give a shit how it happens or how often it happens, but when it happens on my watch, I don't appreciate it at all! Mr. Volner, do you have anything to add, now that Mr. Graham has spoken for both of you?"

"Mr. President, I agree with Ted. Nobody from Operation Headhunter would have leaked this information. I also agree with your National Security Advisor. I don't believe it came from the

White House, either. We will give it our top priority to find out where the leak is, and get back to you immediately."

The President frowned and stood up. "Thank you, gentlemen. You have twenty-four hours to come up with that information or heads are going to roll. Believe me, none of you is irreplaceable."

The four men stood and left the Oval Office. Sean Doyle looked at the clock and thought, *well, it must be five o'clock somewhere,* before he realized it was actually five-thirty Eastern Standard Time. Sean left the office for his private quarters, where Maggie would have his evening drink ready for him before dinner.

TWENTY-FOUR HOURS LATER

After a telephone call from Director Graham at FBI headquarters, Terry Crowley and Henry Chin knew they had very little time to find their mole in Operation Headhunter.

The conversation with Ted Graham was intense to say the least. Terry learned that there was a leak at both ends, one there in Malaysia and another right in Washington, D.C. Terry went directly to the Malaysian Intelligence Service Director with his information and said, "Sir, we need to arrest our suspect as soon as possible. We cannot wait much longer or he is going to get to Kabigting and our operation will be compromised."

The Director nodded his head and said, "Terry, I agree with you. We have been monitoring the individual for the past two days and have followed him everywhere he has gone. His phone log has not shown any calls to Penang Enterprises, but he is too smart for that; he probably makes personal, face-to-face contact with Kabigting. We will bring him in this afternoon. We have a tail on him right now, waiting for him to attempt a contact."

"Thank you, sir," Terry replied. "We are looking forward to putting this person in a cell where he belongs, and I do mean a jail cell."

* * *

Kemal Kabigting logged onto his computer after he was assured by his IT manager that the system was completely secure. Kemal's technology specialists had determined that the fire wall intrusion had come from the Malaysian Intelligence Service headquarters. This news dismayed him so much that he had to assume that he was under suspicion. He could no longer convince himself that they knew anything concrete enough to even question him, never mind make an accusation.

As Kemal entered his password to retrieve his encrypted e-mail messages, he wondered how much time he would need to relocate his offices. The plan began to formulate in his mind as he looked through his e-mails. Four messages into his e-mail list, he saw the red priority flag and he clicked on it immediately. It was from his contact at the Intelligence Service. Kemal quickly read through the e-mail and found that he was indeed under investigation by the Intelligence Service, but his contact claimed that they did not have enough evidence of any kind to accuse him of wrongdoing.

Kemal took a deep breath and let out a slow sigh of relief. He thought, *no information to tie me to anything, but I'm still under investigation.* Although his friend sounded confident, Kemal was skeptical and was convinced that while they must have something on him, it had to be something that they just could not prove or tie him to at the present time.

It was time for Kemal to put his plan into action. He had worked too hard to this point to ruin everything now. Penang Enterprises might have to close down, but he would still continue his mission to rid the world of the Great Satan and the infidels. The St. Gustaf flu was on the wane, but other projects could be put into place and there were armies waiting to be recruited and cells waiting to be formed throughout the industrialized countries. It might take a few years, but he would come back with a vengeance. They would not be able, no matter how hard they tried, to completely put him out of business.

He was too smart for Mr. Henry Chin and his friends to be taken into custody for anything he had already done.

Kemal closed down his secure e-mail system and began to shut down his computer when his secure phone rang. He opened the drawer of his mahogany desk and picked up the receiver. "This is Kemal. Who is calling, please?""Kemal, it is Sonia. Darling, how are you?"

"I am doing just fine, my beautiful lady. To what do I owe this pleasure, you calling me in the middle of the day?"

"Kemal, I am calling to warn you about something. I know how secretive you are; you have not always told me what you do outside of Penang Enterprises, but you need to know that you are in danger."

"What kind of danger, Sonia?"

"A mutual friend of ours—and I don't have to mention his name—even though we are on a secure line, you will know to whom I refer. This mutual friend has just been apprehended by his employer and is being questioned while we speak by the Malaysian Intelligence Service."

"How do you know this, Sonia?"

Sonia Wong sighed and said, "Kemal, I have many friends in many places and one of them is our country's Intelligence agency. I was just informed five minutes ago that he was arrested and is being questioned about our late friend, Mr. Sulanni. I am not at all fearful that they can trace anything to me, but the name of your company also came up in the conversation that I had. The government is apparently questioning our friend about any connection he may have with Penang Enterprises."

"My dear Sonia, thank you so much for this information. I will owe you one very big favor. Please keep me informed if you hear anything further."

"I certainly will, darling. Stay safe, Kemal."

The line went dead and Kemal replaced the phone and sat back in his chair and thought, *it looks like my plan will commence much sooner than I had anticipated.*

*   *   *

At the Intelligence Ministry, Terry Crowley began the briefing that he had promised twenty-four hours earlier. "Team members, thank you for your patience over the past day. I hated to give you so much information and not be able to tell you the identity of our suspect. The reason for that was that we had a mole here at the Ministry and we needed to apprehend him before I could divulge the name of our terrorist suspect for fear that the mole might blow our investigation by contacting the man we've been investigating. That fear has been erased: our mole was apprehended one hour ago and is in custody here at the Ministry.

"Fortunately for Operation Headhunter, he was not on any of the teams, but he did have access to information that was being developed. His name is Chang, and he is the lead analyst in the IT department here at the Intelligence Agency. Apparently, he is the cousin of another Mr. Chang, who is the IT manager for our suspect in Operation Headhunter. I have been informed by my Director back in Washington that a third cousin has been identified as the leak at our Pentagon; he gave information to the United States media regarding our operation here. We are not sure yet how much of that information our Mr. Chang here has passed on to the suspect, but we have ordered a twenty-four hour surveillance of the suspect and believe me, when we have enough proof, we will make the arrest. Once again, thank you for being patient. Now let's move forward.

"On the screen you see a photo of the individual in question. His name is Kemal Kabigting, and he is the owner and Chief Executive Officer of Penang Enterprises, the largest import/export firm in all of Malaysia. He is located in the Petronas Towers and is one of the richest men in Malaysia. He conducts business worldwide and has had offices in the locations that were investigated early on in the investigation of the St. Gustaf flu. They included Dubai, Casablanca, and Oslo, Norway.

"As you know, we have been investigating the possible connection to our terrorist suspect of the very expensive wine found in the Sulanni suspect's stomach during the autopsy. We have determined that Mr. Kabigting is the largest buyer in Malaysia of this particular wine. That alone will not convict him of any crime, but we hope that with the interrogation of our mole, that we will come up with more information that will allow us to interrogate Mr. Kabigting.

"As we said yesterday, our suspect grew up in the same town as our Agent Henry Chin, and went to school with Henry. Agent Chin has met with Mr. Kabigting over lunch and was asked by the suspect if he could possibly help him in his own investigation of the intrusion into the fire wall of his company's computer network. Our concern right now is that the IT staff at Penang Enterprises may have already determined who broke into their system, and we will be compromised once they know it was the Malaysian Intelligence Service. For that reason, we need to fast track this entire investigation. We do not want the possibility of our suspect making a run for it."

Team Leader B raised his hand and Terry recognized him.

"Terry, other than the expensive taste in red wine, what else do we know about this guy?"

Terry advanced to the next slide in his presentation, which displayed a worldwide map with icons showing all of the locations that Penang Enterprises had offices. "Looking at this slide will give you the magnitude of this man's business. If you will notice, there is a heavy concentration throughout the Arab world. We know that Mr. Kabigting claims to be a devout Muslim, but we also know that he drinks alcohol, which contradicts that claim. Although he has never been accused of any terrorist involvement, we do know that while at his previous job, he did business with companies that had al-Qaida connections. We also have information that he personally knew Osama bin Laden and could have been trained by bin Laden himself before he began his business. We are still waiting for confirmation on that detail.

"At this time, Mr. Kabigting cannot be tied to any terrorist activity and the only connection between him and the late Sulanni is that every month, Mr. Kabigting buys a case of the same red wine found during the postmortem on Sulanni. I know that sounds very circumstantial, but I also believe that it is key in our investigation. We need more information and we need it yesterday, folks.

"This next slide has a photo depicting the opulence of our suspect. It is of his sprawling home outside of Kuala Lumpur. It is estimated to be worth about twenty million American dollars. He leases the most expensive office suite in the Petronas Towers, shown here. Agent Chin was able to click these next photos with the ring camera supplied to him by Malaysian Intelligence.

"The next few slides showed the office suite of Penang Enterprises, the Mercedes in the sub-basement parking lot, Ming's Dynasty Restaurant, and the bottle of Pinot Noir red wine sitting on the table." A close-up shot of Kemal Kabigting was next, showing both men shaking hands.

"Agents, we have a lot of work to do and the President is not being very patient on this. He wants Operation Headhunter to conclude this investigation and deliver him the person responsible for the killing of millions of people around the globe. The person responsible for the worst pandemic the world has ever seen must be brought to justice. If that person is Kemal Kabigting, we want him alive and we want him put on trial. Let's get to work and get this job done."

THE OVAL OFFICE

Sean Doyle leaned back in his swivel chair and looked very impatient, moving in his seat from side to side as he waited for one of the men to begin speaking.

Bob Roche, as usual, took the lead and said, "Mr. President, we have located and identified the source referred to by CNN on its late-breaking story yesterday. The person who contacted CNN is a computer operator in the Pentagon and knew nothing more than what was reported by CNN. He heard the name Operation Headhunter and knew that it was in place in Southeast Asia, but knew nothing more than that. We do not know how he got the information, as scant as it was, but he is being questioned as we speak. "The important part of this leak is that it was insignificant as far as information, but it has tipped off our suspect in Malaysia, and that is not good. CNN, meanwhile, has no information and we intend to keep it that way. The interrogation of the Pentagon employee will continue, and then he will be detained until Operation Headhunter has concluded its mission."

Sean leaned forward and said, "And what other information do we have, gentlemen, that CNN does not have? Where are we on this investigation?"

Ted Graham spoke up and advised the President on the progress made so far in Kuala Lumpur, emphasizing that agents had who they believed was a good suspect. Information was being gathered before any move was made to bring him in, and he was under twenty-four hour surveillance.

The President said, "Gentlemen, it sounds like we are finally making progress. You know how badly I want this bastard captured, and alive if at all possible. Keep me up to date as often as you can. I want to know every single detail, no matter how minute. Do I make myself clear, gentlemen?"

In unison, all four men said, "Yes, Mr. President." "Thank you. This meeting is over. Thank you for finding our leak so quickly. Now let's get to work."

*   *   *

One week later, Dr. John Doyle called the President in his residence as Sean and Maggie were about to sit down to dinner.

"Mr. President, am I disturbing your dinner?"

"No, not at all John. Always glad to hear from you. What do you have for me, cousin?"

"Mr. President, I am happy to inform you that the vaccine will begin shipping on Monday, only three days from now, to vaccinate the rest of the country."

"John, that is fantastic news! You can interrupt my dinner any time with this kind of news!"

"As planned, the vaccine will be shipped to the POD's. The first vaccine recipients will be the twenty-to-forty-year-old age group, and senior citizens. From our statistics, we have determined that of the nearly twenty million deaths, almost seventy percent have been in the former age group, our young, vibrant citizens. Just as we experienced back in 1918, this group bore the brunt of the virus but this time, it was much worse and the percentage was much higher."

"John, you have done a wonderful job. I don't know how to thank you or how our nation will ever be able to thank you enough for the monumental effort you have put forth on this project to get the vaccine developed and out to the nation."

"Mr. President, it was not me, but the people who work here at the CDC and all of our pharmaceutical subcontractors mass producing the vaccine. They are the ones that deserve the credit for doing this so much quicker than we ever could have imagined."

"John, thank you again. Can you get up here to make the announcement with me?"

"Well sure, I guess so. When do you want to do it?""As soon as possible. How about tomorrow?"

"Sure, I can do that."

"Fine. Then tomorrow it will be. I will have Sherry set up a press conference for early afternoon. See you then, John."

"Okay, Sean, will see you tomorrow."

Maggie walked over to Sean and said, "Can I assume that the good news John just delivered is that the rest of the country will be getting the flu vaccine?"

"Yes, luv, you can assume that. We are already ahead of schedule. Since the cherry blossoms are out, I think we should do the press conference outside in the Rose Garden. What do you think?"

"Mr. President, I think that is a wonderful idea." "You know, Maggie, every time I think about this whole mess we have been in for almost eight months, I cannot help to think back to Philadelphia when John and I went there to dedicate the monument to the flu victims of 1918-19. Who would have thought that we would lose twenty million of our citizens to the same flu just a few months later?"

"The country will be so happy to hear this news, Sean."

"Yes, Maggie, they will, and now we have to get the bastard that unleashed this horrific virus on us."

Marcus entered the living room and said, "Mr. President, First Lady, dinner is served."

*   *   *

The next day, at precisely one o'clock, the President and Dr. John Doyle entered the Rose Garden and held their news conference. Washington was ablaze with blossoms. A new day was about to begin in America, and a very bright one for all Americans.

BREAK IN THE CASE

Kemal Kabigting had been followed for over a week and he had not altered his routine one bit. He left his estate every morning at exactly seven o'clock and drove into Kuala Lumpur to his suite in the Petronas Towers. He left the Towers every day at noon for lunch and alternated between Ming's Dynasty and two other restaurants, one Italian, and the other a French place that specialized in continental cuisine. He was always back in his office by one o'clock, or one-thirty at the latest. His telephone was being bugged by the Malaysian Intelligence Service, but they had yet to uncover any incriminating evidence. Every night at five o'clock, Kemal left his office and headed back to his estate. The surveillance team would park just close enough to the estate so as not to not draw attention to themselves, and every evening at about ten o'clock, the lights in the mansion were switched off. Kemal had only left the estate once during the week and that was to attend a fundraiser for the orphan population of Malaysia, to which Kemal Kabigting donated twenty thousand dollars. He was back at his estate by ten o'clock that evening, and lights were out by eleven.

Operation Headhunter had uncovered information relating to Kemal's business and had found that he had thirty-five such locations around the world, most of them in the Middle East and in Southeast Asia. It was estimated that his net worth was somewhere around ten billion dollars. His connection with Osama bin Laden was confirmed by two detainees at the facility in Cuba at Guantanamo Bay. They confirmed that Kemal Kabigting had gone through training with them many years before, but they had not seen or heard anything about him since. Upon further investigation, the Headhunter agents were able to find a contact in Afghanistan who told them he had been close to Kabigting and that Kemal and bin Laden had had a falling out after bin Laden had been forced to flee to the mountains. Kabigting apparently had lost confidence in his friend and had gone out on his own, but none of the contacts could confirm just what that meant. They were not aware of any terrorist activity on the part of Kabigting.

Terry Crowley was at his wits end on the investigation. He turned to Henry Chin and said, "Henry, we need a break, a big break. So far we know that your friend trained with al-Qaida and had a relationship with bin Laden, but we cannot prove it. We know he had locations where we suspect the virus was developed and then shipped to and from, and yet we cannot prove that he had anything to do with it. His network is as tight as a drum. We cannot even find any monetary dealings that would indicate that he financed any operation connected to our investigation. The guy is very smart and very good at covering his tracks. The only way we are going to tie this down is to connect him to the late Mr. Sulanni; so far that is a dead end and that is not a pun, my friend."

Henry nodded in agreement and said, "Terry, you're right: we need a break. We need a miracle or we are never going to solve this case."

As both men started to get out of their chairs, the telephone rang. Henry answered it and said, "Yes, he is right here. Can I ask who is calling? Sure, here he is. Terry, it is your friend, Marty Harrington, from London."

"Hey, Marty! How the hell are you?"

"I am just fine, old chap, and I may have some good news for you."

"Boy, could I use some good news! Does it have anything to do with our investigation?"

"It certainly does, my friend. You know, our techie guys over here have developed a number of gadgets to help in our investigations. All that stuff you saw in the old James Bond movies was not just fiction, you know. Some of that stuff was actually developed and our agents have used some of this gadgetry. In addition, they have utilized computer software to redevelop old techniques and one of them has been in enhancement technology."

"What exactly do they 'enhance,' Marty?"

"For openers, how about the sketch that you sent us of our old, dead friend, Mr. Sulanni?"

"Okay, Marty. You have my attention. Go ahead." "Terry, I am about to fax you an enhanced version of the sketch that you sent us. You will find it quite interesting. Can you give me a secure fax line to send it on?"

"I certainly can, Marty."

Terry gave him the number and Marty said, "Give me about ten minutes and you should have the enhancement."

Twelve minutes later, the fax machine at the Intelligence Ministry came alive and the cover sheet was from British Intelligence in London. The next sheet that came through was the original sketch of Sulanni in the Bali Bar with another person. Terry and Henry both looked at the enhanced sketch in awe as they studied it and then looked at each other. Simultaneously they both said, "Holy shit!" Staring back at them was a very good resemblance of Kemal Kabigting. The badly needed break had finally arrived. *Thank God*, Terry thought. He turned to Henry and said, "Assemble the Operation Headhunter teams. We're going to plan our next step."

HEADHUNTER MISSION

"Team leaders," Terry announced, "we proceed at 22:00 hours this evening. The suspect is to be apprehended alive. Please keep that uppermost in your mind: alive. We do not want any screw-ups, because this guy has to be taken alive and put on trial. You have all been given his routine; ten o'clock in the evening is when he normally retires. Our surveillance team has been monitoring him for ten days now, and he never alters his routine. Once the lights go out in the mansion, we move in on him, completely surrounding the estate.

"Keep in mind that this guy is a terrorist; expect the unexpected. He is responsible for over one hundred million deaths across the globe, and over twenty million of them are Americans. As much as we would like to kill him, again, we must have him alive. The mansion has a security system that is very sophisticated, but we are not concerned with that. We will use flash bangs at every entrance and enter the mansion simultaneously. Does everyone understand me?"

All of the heads in the room nodded in agreement and most said, "Yes, sir."

It was five o'clock in the evening. "Okay, everyone. Have a light dinner and be ready to move at 21:00 hours. We converge on the mansion one hour later."

The teams began to filter out of the room and Terry looked over at Henry and said, "Well, friend, this is it. We're going to get this guy and let him know that it's payback time, baby."

At nine o'clock, all four teams were at the location and the forty agents began to surround the estate. They were all dressed in SWAT team gear: black with blackface, bulletproof vests, and carrying flash bangs to allow entrance to the mansion.

The lights in the mansion were all on, and the teams had to wait in the surrounding woods until the mansion was in darkness. There were no signs of activity anywhere on the grounds or in the mansion. Assuming that Kemal Kabigting was following his usual routine, he was either in his library or in his personal game room, where he spent hours. He had no family and only one servant who could be out for the evening.

At exactly ten minutes after the hour—22:10—the lights in the house began to go off one at a time, first the ground floor, and then the second floor. One light was left on for a few minutes longer, probably Kabigting's bedroom, but five minutes later, this went off as well. Terry Crowley picked up his radio and whispered, "Okay, teams, let's roll. Remember, we want him alive."

The teams approached the mansion from four different directions and as they crossed the manicured lawn surrounding the mansion, the garage door flew up and the black Mercedes came roaring down the driveway.

Terry Crowley yelled into his radio. "Teams A and B! Hit all entrances with the flash bangs! Teams C and D! Follow the Mercedes quickly!"

Terry and Henry ran down the drive to waiting Hummers, with teams C and D right behind them. One of the Hummers attempted to block the end of the driveway, but the Mercedes swerved around it and down into the ditch. It roared back up again and then out onto the main road. Terry was calling out orders at a rapid rate as he jumped into the Hummer, with Henry driving another right behind him. Four members of Team C followed Henry, and the Hummers sped down the road in pursuit of the Mercedes. Terry's radio crackled and he heard the Team Leader A say, "Agent Crowley, we have the mansion secure and there is no sign of the suspect."

Terry literally yelled into the radio, "That's probably because we are in pursuit of him right now at about ninety miles an hour! Maintain security at the mansion! Do not let anyone in or out and survey the grounds for anything or anyone that should not be there!"

The Hummers seemed to be making progress, slowly catching up to the Mercedes. Terry leaned over to the driver and said, "Just keep him in sight. We don't want him crashing that car and killing himself. Remember, we want him alive."

"Yes, sir, I understand. He is doing about ninety-five right now and this road narrows up ahead. He is dangerously close to getting himself killed."

The road did narrow, and the Mercedes approached a sharp curve, slowing down and then fishtailing until it was completely out of control. The Hummer was getting close when the Mercedes went completely out of control and slid into a culvert, then back up on the road, crossing to the other side, before slamming into a large oak tree.

Terry Crowley said, "Oh, shit! Let's hope he's still alive!" He grabbed his radio and said, "Approach very carefully, folks.

Remember, this man has killed millions. He won't think twice about killing you."

Once the Hummer came to a stop across the road from the mangled Mercedes, Terry and Henry jumped out of their vehicles, drew their guns, and carefully approached the car. As Terry neared the driver's side, he saw that the driver had the air bag in his face and appeared to be unconscious. He slowly opened the driver's door and reached in and felt the pulse. There was none.

"Shit!" He then grabbed the back of the driver's collar and pulled him back against the seat. This time, Terry exhaled, and less vocally said again, "Shit."

Henry yelled from the passenger side of the Mercedes. "What is it, Terry? Why do you keep saying, 'Shit'?" Terry straightened up and looked over the car's roof at Henry. "Henry, I'm saying 'Shit' because this is not our man! It isn't Kemal Kabigting! This guy is old enough to be his father, but he is not our terrorist."

THE KABIGTING ESTATE

As emergency crews were removing the body from the Mercedes, Terry and Henry climbed back into their Hummers and headed for the mansion. Terry radioed ahead to Team Leader A that they were on their way and would be there in about five minutes.

Team Leader A said, "Agent Crowley, we have been all through the mansion and there is something here that you need to see."

Terry answered, "Roger. Got that, but let's not discuss it on the radio frequency."

"Yes, sir. See you in five minutes."

The Hummer pulled into the driveway and continued on up the hill to the main entrance of Kemal Kabigting's mansion. Team Leader A met Terry and Henry and they exited their Hummers.

"Agent Crowley, wait until you see what is down in the game room of this mansion. It will certainly shed light on why our Mr. Kabigting was not driving that Mercedes." Terry and Henry were led into the main hall and to a winding staircase that descended to the game room. Waiting at the bottom of the stairs were the Team

A members. The lead member said, "Sir, right this way, over to the bar.

Terry approached the bar, as another team member popped his head up from behind the bar and said, "Sir, come this way. Just step around the bar."

As Terry and Henry reached the back of the bar, they saw how the team member had popped his head up from behind. He was actually standing at the top of a long stairway that descended under the bar. Terry and Henry stepped down the stairway, Terry counting as he did. By the time they reached the bottom, Terry had counted twenty-one steps. At the bottom of the stairway, they entered a tunnel that was wide enough to drive a vehicle through, even one as large as an SUV.

Terry looked down the darkened tunnel and saw that it was even paved. He turned to Team Leader A and said, "Any idea how long it is?"

"While we were waiting to hear from you, I sent a two-man reconnaissance team down the tunnel. That was about twenty minutes ago and they have not returned yet. They have radios and they called in just before you drove up. They said they were at the two mile mark and still had not reached the end."

Terry turned to Henry and said, "Damn this guy. I wonder what time he left the mansion and how far he's moved."

A radio crackled and the team called into their leader. "Sir, pardon the expression, but we can see light at the end of the tunnel. It looks to be at about the three mile mark and it definitely rises on an incline. Will report when we reach the end."

Team Leader A turned to Terry and said, "Sir, my guess would be that our suspect had an SUV and drove it down and out of this tunnel and across the terrain while we were sitting around the mansion waiting for him to go to bed." Terry Crowley frowned and nodded his head. "Yeah, I'm afraid that you are probably dead on right. We need to put out an all-points for this guy. Henry, call in and get a team to his headquarters suite in the Petronas Towers. Make sure that all major highways are being watched and double check on our security at the airport, train, and bus stations. We cannot let this guy get away."

The radio crackled again and the team reported that they were at the end of the tunnel and had found a Range Rover parked at the end. They exited the tunnel and saw nothing but miles of rough terrain. In the distance, to the south, they could slightly make out the light coming from the mansion. There was no one in sight, but they found tracks in the brush probably left by an SUV. The tunnel had doors that were open and when closed, the shrubbery covering the outside would never reveal that there was a tunnel below.

Terry turned to his team leader. "Have them bring the Range Rover back to our end so we can drive to the end and investigate."

A few minutes later, lights could be seen coming down the tunnel. The Range Rover came into view and stopped at the bottom of the stairway. Terry and Henry climbed aboard with Team Leader A and the driver made a U-turn and continued back down the tunnel. At the end, Terry and Henry got out of the vehicle and searched around the area for evidence of any kind. Their efforts were in vain, though, and after thirty minutes, they all climbed into the Range Rover and headed back to the mansion. It was going to be a long night for Operation Headhunter.

At daylight the following morning, a team was sent out across the terrain to follow the tracks left by the SUV the previous night. They drove for almost ten miles where they found a deserted airstrip. There weren't any planes at the field, but parked at the end of the runway was another Range Rover. Mr. Kabigting had apparently driven to a rendezvous with a private aircraft and had disappeared. The team sent to the suspect's Petronas Towers suite reported shortly before dawn that the entire suite was vacant: no furniture, no carpet, no computers, and nothing but a telephone sitting on the vacant floor in the main office. Everything was gone. The suite looked like it had been vacant for some time. Mr. Kabigting had followed his plan extremely well and had fooled not only the Malaysian Intelligence Service, but the FBI and CIA as well. There was not one clue to follow at this point.

The driver of the Mercedes was identified as the servant from the mansion, a Malay known as Mamood, Kabigting's private valet, butler, chef, and sometimes driver. He had no living relatives and would have been sixty-nine-years-old one day after his death.

*   *   *

The mood at the meeting of Operation Headhunter was one of absolute frustration and disappointment. The teams were told by Terry Crowley that they would continue their search for the terrorist. An all-points bulletin had been issued with a photo of Kemal Kabigting obtained from the Motor Vehicles Registration office. The photo was on the front page of every newspaper in Malaysia and had been posted on the CNN website. By noon, it would be on the front page of every newspaper around the world. Kemal Kabigting was described as the number one suspect in the distribution of the St. Gustaf flu, and responsible for the deaths of over one hundred million people worldwide.

Terry Crowley told his assembled teams, "Kemal Kabigting might get away from us, but he absolutely cannot hide. Every person in this world will know his face within the next twenty-four hours. We will apprehend this bastard."

SINGAPORE

The Learjet taxied to the private terminal at Singapore International Airport and was directed to the eastern side, where blocks were put against the wheels. The door to the jet opened and the stairway was lowered to the tarmac.

The first person to step out was Sonia Wong, followed by Kemal Kabigting, and then the pilot. Kemal turned to the pilot at the end of the stairway and said, "Michael, thank you for a smooth flight. I will not need your services for any return flight. I will be in contact when I need you." He handed the pilot a thick envelope and said, "Here is your bonus for getting me here so quickly." Michael smiled and said, "Thank you, sir. Call when you need me again. Ms. Wong, may I take you anywhere?" "No thank you, Michael. I plan to stay in Singapore for a few days and then maybe do some sailing."

"Okay then, I will be off again once I get this baby refueled. Nice doing business with you, Mr. Kabigting." "Thank you, Michael. We will be in touch."

Kemal and Sonia headed into the terminal with their bags and then out to the curb where a blue Mercedes was waiting for them. They were driven to the pier, a twenty minute drive from the airport. As the car approached the pier, Sonia pointed to the third yacht

355

docked at the moorings. "There she is, Kemal. Isn't she beautiful? I named her Lotus Flower."

Kemal was shocked when he saw the yacht to which she had referred. It had to have cost at least fifty million dollars. He turned to Sonia and said, "Beautiful lady, too many people, including myself, are paying you entirely too much money for your services. How did you ever afford this luxurious ship?"

"Kemal, I have saved a lot of money and I have also invested very wisely. You would be surprised what I am really worth. The best part is that I have kept my anonymity. There are only a few people in the world who really know what I do and what services I perform. I like to keep it that way. You are one of only a handful that really know me. That is why my yacht is the best place for you to be right now, since the entire world is looking for you. We will be able to hide for as long as you want, Kemal, and no one will find you."

"Sonia, how can I ever repay you for what you are doing?"

"Oh, I am sure I will find a way. Maybe not today, but sometime in the very near future. For now, let's go aboard and have a drink while the captain takes us out to sea."

They walked up the gangway and were greeted by the captain. He said, "Your cabins are ready, Ms. Wong. Once you drop off your bags, you will find your drinks chilling in the drawing room." With a short bow, the captain headed for the bridge and five minutes later, the enormous yacht was backing away from the pier and maneuvering into the channel to head out to sea.

Sonia was the first to arrive in the drawing room and when Kemal entered, she held out his cosmopolitan to him. "Here is to a wonderful cruise in the South China Sea. Any place in particular you would like to sail?"

"Sonia, it does not matter to me as long as I can stay on board and remain anonymous for at least a month or two. I need to do some planning and come up with a new look for Kemal Kabigting, since they have plastered my photo all over the world."

"Of course, darling. Then we will simply cruise and cruise, stopping only for supplies and fuel when needed. You will have all the time you need to decide your next step."

ONE MONTH LATER

After weeks of following up on hundreds of leads, all ending at dead ends, Terry Crowley was advised by Director Graham to shut down Operation Headhunter in Malaysia and come back home to Washington. The entire team was disheartened after being so close to capturing the terrorist that had wreaked havoc on the world, only to have him slip right through their hands. The leads had dried up and no one had a single clue as to Kemal Kabigting's whereabouts. It was as if he had vanished into thin air. Terry and Henry knew that somehow he had driven the SUV to a private airstrip and had probably boarded a private plane, but to where they did not have any information. It could have been to hundreds of places throughout Southeast Asia.

The country was gradually returning to normal. Every citizen in the United States had been vaccinated against the St. Gustaf flu, formerly the Spanish flu. There were no newly reported cases within the previous three weeks and patients were being discharged from hospitals every single day. Martial law had been lifted and communities were back to governing themselves. Popular opinion polls showed that President Sean Doyle had once again gained the confidence of the country. His overall approval rating regarding his handling of the crisis was at sixty-eight percent. The critics, of course, were still hitting him hard on every talk show, because he had not been able to capture the terrorist allegedly responsible for the pandemic that had taken place. The same criticism that had plagued President Bush for not capturing Osama bin Laden was now being played out against President Doyle for his inability to find Kemal Kabigting.

Terrorism had not been eradicated by any stretch of the imagination. Even though the St. Gustaf flu was no longer a threat, there were still terrorist attacks taking place around the world. There were still suicide bombings in Iraq and in Israel, and passenger trains were the target of choice for the terrorist bombers of late.

A special meeting was called by the President to critique Operation Headhunter. All of the parties involved were to be at the meeting and Agent Henry Chin was invited to represent the Malaysian Intelligence Service. The consensus was that the operation was a success to a point: the teams had determined who was at the head of the terrorist network and many cells had been eliminated as a result of work completed by Operation Headhunter. The downside, though, was that agents were unable to capture and bring to trial the sole person responsible for causing worldwide terror and the deaths of one hundred million people. The President was firm in his resolve to not allow this operation to simply close down. He directed the heads of the CIA and the FBI not to give up. They would have to downsize the operation; they would not have the manpower from Malaysia that they had enjoyed, but the investigation had to continue until agents were able to apprehend Mr. Kabigting.

Just as the meeting was about to end, the red phone on the conference table rang and the President picked it up. "Yes, Aggie, what is it?"

"Mr. President, I believe you are going to want to take this call. He said his name is Kemal and he has a message for you."

"Put him through, Aggie." The President put his finger to his lips to indicate silence and pushed the conference call button on the phone. "Mr. President, are you there?"

"This is President Doyle. Who is calling?"

"I think you know exactly who is calling, Mr. President. I cannot stay on long since you are already tracing this call, but I wanted to congratulate you on dealing with your pandemic as well as you did. Your son was lucky to survive the flu. Did he ever have chicken pox, Mr. President?"

"What the hell does that have to do with anything?" "Mr. President Doyle, Great Satan of the infidels, chicken pox is nothing compared to the scourge of smallpox. You will find out soon. Praise Allah."

Before Sean Doyle could respond, the line went dead. He leaned forward and said, "Director Graham, find out if we were able to trace that call."

Ted Graham made a quick phone call and when he hung up he said, "Mr. President, it appears the call came from a public phone; GPS pinpoints it coming from somewhere on the island of Bali. It could have been Kabigting himself or he could have had someone make the call for him. There is no way to tell if it was him or an underling. The pay phone is located in a busy marketplace where thousands of tourists visit while vacationing in Bali. Sorry, sir."

"Does anyone want to comment on that call?"

Bob Roche spoke first and said, "Mr. President, that sounded like a very valid threat against us in the form of another biological weapon."

Henry Volner agreed. "Mr. President, we have to find this guy, and soon, if we don't want another pandemic on our hands. I believe he's serious and we know he has the financial resources and followers who are willing to die for Allah."

The President looked around the table and said, "Folks, I want this bastard and I want him as soon as possible. I want a special team organized tomorrow morning. Director Graham, be sure to put Agent Terrence Crowley in charge. This operation will be top secret, and reportable to my office only. We are going to get this barbarian, no matter how long it takes. Thank you, and may God be with us all."

Printed in the United States
39633LVS00004B/247-333